Other works by M J Leaver

Love and Death

The Gifted (Gifted 1)

Fear to tread / Pinhead (Gifted 3)

Mourning Glory

The Culling

Aftermath

There was a stirring in the darkness. The chill, cold breeze that blew across the cracked flagstones of the floor and fluttered amongst the torn flags and banners, planted amongst the heaps of cracked and blackened bones that lay scattered in an arc around the central point of the land, where the throne lay, ceased momentarily.

There was a lull, a moment of stillness, and within that moment, sat inclined upon the throne where it leaned upon one arm of the chair, frozen into a position of relaxed indifference, eyes opened.

The wind renewed its motion amongst the ruins.

However, the direction of its chill course had changed. Where before it's travel had been perpetually to the west, it's travel was now northwards.

The fluttering banners changed direction, a few tearing from their mounting and being carried away on the winds chill course.

The figure upon the tarnished golden throne moved.

After centuries of still contemplation, the figures hand reached out to the staff that leaned by its side, then leaning its weight upon it it rose to its feet.

A faint shower of dust fell from its form as it rose and cracked lips opened.

"Interesting" it croaked with a voice both deep and solemn.

"I think this requires some investigation".

It raised the staff before it and swiped it at the dusty air.

A rent, a tear in the fabric of reality opened before it.

It could see the threads in their multitude, like a complex web, and it could see that there was a ripple that ran through some of these threads.

Not many, not yet, there were only currently a few that trembled at the touch of another.

This realm had been its alone, and to see it in motion again, and not at its hand but at the direction of another consciousness enthralled it.

It took a moment to gaze across the wasteland of corpses, ancient bones now, that surrounded it and it's once glorious throne.

"A pity" it murmured.

Then, it stepped forward into the breach in this universe, into the maelstrom of realities beyond, and the rent in The world closed behind it.

Two

Sophia awoke with a horrified start and threw herself sideways out of the bed and onto the deeply carpeted floor.

There she crouched on hands and knees, breathing deeply, gasping in lungfulls of air in a frenzy of panting. She began to retch in heaving spasms and her right hand beat at the floor, a monotonous, fruitless beat of desperation and fear.

John, his mind strangely wired for changes to his environment and connected to Sophia on a level he couldn't explain, had leapt from a deep seamless sleep and the bed in unison, the moment Sophia had hit the floor.

He crouched over her where she now lay curled into the foetal position on the floor, and his hand rubbed mindlessly at her back.

"Soph, what's the matter?" He found himself almost shouting.

He was more than alarmed. He'd never seen her like this before, and coming as it did, deep in the middle of the night and dragging him from his sleep, called somehow to his internal animal. To that long buried part of the brain that had lived with monsters in the dark. His fight or flight responses kicking in hard.

Moaning quietly and with ragged gasps, Sophia began to slowly uncurl, until she lay, star shaped, her limbs spreadeagled on the floor, staring Sightlessly at the ceiling above her.

"Its coming" she whispered in a croaking voice.

"Its found us. Oblivion".

Her body gave a shudder and then consciousness left her.

John shook her gently by the shoulder.

"Soph? Soph? Are you ok?"

There was no response from her still huddled body, curled on the floor and drooling slightly from the corner of her mouth.

Her long black hair lay draped across her face and in that moment John was struck by how fragile she looked.

Fear stroked it's cold hand across his spine. She was his girlfriend and he loved her to death. He would do anything to protect her, but at this moment, not knowing what was wrong, he didn't know what to do, he didn't know how to protect her.

He took her in his arms and lifted her from the thick carpeted floor. He headed for the door, throwing it open with his mind with an excess of force, shattering it from its hinges and hurtling it out into the hallway with a crash as the wood shattered against the opposing wall.

As he ran out into the hall, bearing her unconscious form in his arms, he shouted out in a desperate cry for help.

"Laz.!" He cried, " Laz, come quickly, Soph needs help"

He headed down the stairs in headlong flight, not quite sure where best to take her. He reached the dining room and his eyes fastened on the large oak dining table. That'll do, he decided, and he lay her there on the table top.

She looked so fragile he thought, laying there in the twilight lit dining room. Her limbs spread out as though crucified. The image disturbed him slightly, and without knowing why he pulled her hands together into her lap.

He continued to cry out into the darkness.

"Laz, where are you man, I need your help here".

He heard the thud of footsteps on the floor above, followed by the strangely indescribable wooshing noise as Lazarus slid down the balustrade for speeds sake.

" John? " he called "John, what's up, where are you boy?"

" dining room" John shouted in return "Its Sophia, there's something wrong with her".

Lazarus appeared in the doorway, naked bar the paisley boxer shorts he wore to bed, which looked strangely out of place on his muscular frame.

He jogged over to where John stood and looked down on Sophias still form where she lay on the tables highly polished surface.

"What happened?" He asked in a nasal growl.

 John briefly ran through the series of events. His abrupt awakening to find Sophia in such a state. Her gagging and gasping, the look of sheer terror in her eyes and on her face, and finally her words before her collapse into unconsciousness.

Lazarus frowned and ran his hands through his dark deadlocked hair.

"I think we're gonna need a little help on this one" he rumbled.

He quickly moved to the phone on the mahogany sideboard, lifted the handset to his ear and jabbed his finger at one of the numbers on the keypad.

Suddenly John found himself in one of those moments, one of those moments in your life when everything seems to be frozen in place, as though time itself has stopped. It felt like a pregnant pause in reality and for those seconds John wasn't even sure if he was breathing.

Lazarus was impatiently tapping his foot on the parquet flooring and scratching at the back of his head with his free hand.

Suddenly "Eleanor he barked, a seconds pause then "yes, I'm perfectly aware what bleeding time it is, but we need your help love. We've got a situation, n i think your our best call".

Another second passed, then "yes love, we're in the dining room. Now, shift ya arse hun".

He slammed the handset back into its cradle and turned back to John.

"Right" he growled "Eleanor's on her way. Let's see if she can't make some kinda sense outa this shit".

it seemed only a matter of moments had passed before Eleanor appeared, framed in the open doorway to the dining room. A feat, thought John, considering how far from here he knew her residence to be.

She was obviously hastily dressed in a pair of faded old tracksuit bottoms and a baggy old rolling stones t-shirt.

Her hair stuck up in a disarray of spikes and curls, and there was a tinge of grey apparent at her temples.

"So" she croaked, her voice quiet and bearing a hint of irritation to it.

"What's all the fuss about Lazarus? Why have you woken me up at this ungodly hour? What is it anyway?" She asked and she looked at the watch on her wrist, giving it a shake as she did so, as if to wake the thing up itself .

"Christ man, it's two in the bloody morning. I don't remain such a gem without my beauty sleep you old sod."

"Its Sophia" blurted John. "Something's happened to her, and now, now I can't wake her up"

Again he ran through the series of events. Telling her of the sudden wakening, the spasms and gagging. Her final words before unconsciousness.

Eleanor and Lazarus exchanged a glance. One that John thought carried some kind of hidden meaning or sense of alarm.

"Ok" grumbled Eleanor hoarsely "let's get to it shall we".

Lazarus took up a chair and placed it at the head of the table where Sophias head was positioned.

He held it back from the table for Eleanor to take her seat, at which point he pushed it forward to the tables edge and Sophias head.

He then stepped back into the rooms shadow and leaned back against the wall.

"go to it Eleanor" he growled "do your stuff".

Eleanor gave her head a shake and pushed her hair back from her brow. Then, with what appeared to be unusual tenderness, she placed her fingers against Sophias temples.

"Right chaps" she whispered "I want to go in nice and gently. We don't know what's going on in there, so if you don't mind I'd like you both to keep your mouths closed. I want silence for this so I can concentrate. Ok boys?"

"Sure, no problem" whispered John in return, whilst Lazarus simply nodded his head.

"Ok" Eleanor sighed, "here goes"

She closed her eyes and the room lay in darkness and silence whilst she probed into the mind of the young girl before her.

John felt the hairs Prickle up on the back of his neck, there was a sense of power, of something primeval teetering on the brink of some abyss. of strength retarded by sheer force of will, and at that moment his estimation of Eleanors abilities rose markedly.

That pregnant pause again. That waiting for something of consequence to occur.

The darkness began to feel oppressive, and the silence seemed to strain at his ears.

He felt the overpowering impulse to shout. To cry out his fears into the night. He held himself in check with difficulty, and glancing at Lazarus he thought he could see the same strain in the man's eyes.

Suddenly Eleanor gave a cry. An exclamation of shock, and she released Sophias head pushing herself back from the table with a start.

"No" she whispered to herself "how is that possible".

John had leapt forward at Eleanors sudden lurch back, and he grasped her by the shoulders and stared into her eyes.

"what is it" he cried, alarmed at the look of shock on her face "What's the matter with her, what can I do?"

She looked at him blank faced, her lips moved but no words emerged. She seemed unable to speak, at a loss of the words needed to explain her discovery.

9

Finally she managed to get a hold of herself and she stood up from the chair, pushing it aside and moving towards Lazarus with a lurch.

"I don't understand" she gasped "it shouldn't be possible"

"What is it?" John cried again " what's the matter with her? "

She turned to him and lay her hands on his cheeks. She shook her head and sighed "she's not there John. There's no one in there. She's an empty vessel. Sophias gone".

Three

John stared at her in dumb incomprehension, his mind frozen, his mouth agape.

"But, what, what are you talking about?"

He pointed to the table with a trembling hand.

"She's right bloody there for Christ's sake, what are you talking about woman? "

Eleanor placed a tender placating hand on his shoulder and stroked his cheek with the other.

"I'm sorry John" she sighed soothingly, "But her mind, her consciousness, it's not there John, it's gone, she's just an empty vessel now, there's no one at home".

John pulled back from her angrily, then shoved her away from him.

"No" he cried "she can't just simply have died. Look at her, she's breathing, you can see her chest moving".

"No John" Eleanor replied "she's not dead, it's just that her mind has vacated the premises. Her body's in perfect working order, she's just not inhabiting it right now is all".

John stared at her again, finding her attitude rather glib under the circumstances.

"So, tell me, what's happened, how come her, her person, consciousness, whatever you want to call it. How come it's gone? Why has it gone and where? "

Eleanor shook her head with a look of concerned dismay and sat herself back down into the recently vacated chair.

"I don't know John. I've never come across anything like this before. But I went in there very carefully and took my time to have a good look around. And what I can tell you is this, she didn't go willingly. There were signs of, how can I put it, signs of combat, signs of resistance on her part. She put up a fight, but someone, something, pulled her out of there. I've no idea who could be capable of something like that. Perhaps someone else in the foundation has a new recruit. I really don't know what else to tell you John. Even if there's a new member of we gifted out there I don't know why they'd want to do this to Sophia.

"Lazarus" she called. "Make a few calls eh? See what you can find out."

Lazarus nodded silently, then headed off to the lounge and the telephone there.

John now pulled out a chair for himself and sat quietly by Sophias head, taking her hand in his and staring intently at her closed eyes.

11

"So, so what do we do?" He asked in a muted subdued voice.

"if she's not in there then no matter how healthy she is right now, eventually she'll starve to death or something".

Eleanor clucked at him and patted him on the back.

"Don't worry about that son. I'm quite capable of stepping into her shoes. I'll simply inhabit her body for mealtimes, take my own later. I can keep her operational whilst we work out exactly what's happened and fix it."

"Oblivion" whispered John

"What?" Asked Eleanor, raising her eyebrows at him in enquiry " What's that your saying? "

"Those were her last words" he murmured quietly.

"She said it's found us, that it was coming. Then, Oblivion".

"Hhmmm" mumbled Eleanor "I wonder what that means".

"I don't know" John growled angrily "But I swear, I'm gonna find out. And then, when I find the bastard that's done this, I'm gonna make them pay".

Eleanor turned to face him and looked him squarely in the eyes.

"John, we'll all make them pay".

Four

The days passed in an atmosphere both tense and morose.

John found their mealtimes almost physically painful, as he sat opposite Eleanor, bearing the body of the beautiful Sophia and munching away at the Food before her with what appeared to his tainted eyes to be gleeful abandon.

"I swear" she said over the bowl of cornflakes before her one morning, "all this constant eating is beginning to drive me crazy. It feels like the only thing I do these days".

"What do you mean?" Asked John, his hackles beginning to raise. He covered his eyes with his hands and mentally began counting backwards from ten to calm his nerves. He had felt like a live wire these past days and he knew it wouldn't take a great deal to spark him off.

"Well" mumbled Eleanor through a mouthful of cereal "first i have to feed our darling Sophia, then lay her down, jump back into my own body, and feed myself. What with breakfast, lunch, and dinner, not forgetting the odd snack of course, it just seems to take up my whole day is all".

Feeling an irrational rage beginning to rise within his chest, John pushed himself back from the table and took to his feet.

"Not finishing your muffins John?" Asked Eleanor as he marched awkwardly from the room.

"No" he croaked in reply through gritted teeth, "help yourself, I'm full".

13

And he strode from the dining room.

He headed towards the library and as he grew nearer to it he felt his anger fade, replaced with a feeling of determination and hope.

Lazarus had not got anywhere with his calls to the other houses. There had been no new recruits and there were none within their groups possessing any kind of gift that could have inflicted this on them.

The library had been the only thing he could think of to do to try to help Sophia. There were lots of records there relating to the history of the gifted and he was searching though them in the hope of perhaps finding some precedent. Perhaps this had happened before, perhaps he could find a cure or whatever was needed to bring her back.

Kathryn, bless her, was an incredibly heavy sleeper and had slept through all of that nights events.

The following morning found her sitting opposite Sophia at the dining table for breakfast, and extolling on the faults and irritations of Eleanor. Of how she rarely helped in the tidying of the mansion and how she left all of the washing up and picking up around the place to the rest of them.

Eleanor, in Sophias body for feeding purposes, fell into gales of laughter at Kathryns ignorance of the situation. This rapidly degenerated into a fit of choking as she inhaled a bit of the muffin she had been eating.

Kathryn was across the table in a bound and began to pound Sophias body on the back, until with a disgusted gasp Eleanor spat a wad of half chewed muffin onto her plate, at which point she raised her hand to put a halt to Kathryns efforts

"Are you ok sophia my dear?" Asked Kathryn in a voice of concern .

Eleanor gave out a long drawn out sigh as Kathryn returned to her seat.

"Kathryn my love, there's something I need to tell you".

Eleanor began, with some difficulty, to explain the events of the previous night, and the current situation of her inhabiting Sophias body to keep her sustained and alive.

Kathryn gave a moan of concern and alarm.

"How's John taking it? " she asked in agitation.

"Not great" replied Eleanor, picking absent mindedly at Sophias teeth with the point of a steak knife.

"Its as though he holds himself responsible. As though he should have been able to protect her somehow. Which, of course, he couldn't. We have no idea what the hells really happened here.

This whole scenario is a big bloody mystery. Lazarus hasn't had any joy calling on the others. They're as much in the dark in this as we are.

So, anyway, John's decided to throw himself into research. See if he can't find any clue to all this crap".

Kathryn rose from the table haltingly, as though unsure of what to do with herself.

"Right" she grumbled "John" and she strode from the room, having decided on a mission of consolation..

As expected, following Eleanors words, she found him in the library. Pulling ancient volumes from shelves and more contemporary books

15

that peaked his interest, and tossing them into a pile in the centre of the room, where he then sat on the floor and began to flip through pages at random, not knowing what he was looking for, but believing somewhere deep within himself, that he would know it when he found it.

Kathryn hovered within the arch of the doorway, unsure how best to approach him in this, his moment of despair.

"John" she called quietly.

He looked up at her from his nest of books and papers and she could see that his eyes were red rimmed with the shedding of tears.

"What?" He replied gruffly .

There was anger there, she could see. Rage at what had happened and rage at his own powerlessness.

"I" she stuttered, unsure what to say under the circumstances "I'm sorry about Sophia John. Eleanors just told me. If there's anything I can do to help you, please, just let me know, ok?"

John gave his head a jerking nod "sure. Thanks Kat, But right now, I don't really have a clue what to do".

Kathryn watched him in silence for a moment as he dived back into the mound of paperwork surrounding him.

Slowly, she shook her head, telling herself that he'd come to her if he needed anything, she was sure. Right now, she was as much in the dark as everyone else.

She retreated, and headed off to find Lazarus. Perhaps he might have some idea of what to do.

Now, as John once more raided the library, to begin once more his quest for some kind of useful information, he found himself growling quietly under his breath.

The tension of the past few days. Constantly seeing Sophia at mealtimes and in the gym, where Eleanor took her to keep her in shape and her muscles toned.

The constant boi!ing rage he felt inside at the injustice of it all.

All of this was beginning to tell on him, and his nerves were constantly on edge.

He found himself snapping at everyone. Losing his temper and falling into irrational rage at the most inconsequential of annoyances.

He knew, somewhere inside of himself, that he would have to find something soon. For his own sanity, let alone that of his friends around him.

He turned from the pile before him and headed for the spiral staircase in the centre of the room. These actually descended rather than the ascent most people would anticipate. They led to what he called the sub library. A place where the older tombs were kept. Perhaps he'd have more luck there. At the bottom of the steps he opened the library doors and flicked at the light switch to his side.

The library was positioned within the centre of the mansion, this part down at basement level and with no external walls.

This had been a security measure from back in the early days of the groups inhabiting the place.

There were highly valuable and perhaps incriminating works within the library's confines, and keeping these documents safe and secure was of great importance.

Hence the use of the basement. Here there were no windows and no external illumination of any sort, and the library relied on the powerful daylight bulbs fastened within the chandeliers hanging high above.

The click of the switch produced no effect, and the library remained shrouded in darkness.

"Shit" cursed John, and he flicked the switch up and down in rapid succession, growling under his breath and feeling the heat of the familiar rage rise within his chest.

"Aaarrrggghhh, God dammit" he shouted into the persistent darkness. His efforts at the switch having produced no effect.

"Now now my dear Ivan" came a familiar voice from the blackness of the room before him.

"fruitless anger is hurtful to the heart my boy. To the digestion too I imagine". And there was a deep throaty chuckle from the gloom.

"Alexei? " asked John is a stupified crackling voice.

"Is that you?"

He could picture the burly old Russian in his mind, the large fur hat on his head and his grizzled dark beard.

The Russians gift was a power over darkness. He could travel within the shadows in a form of teleportation and he could manipulate the darkness itself, clouding the eyes of his enemy's as he manouvered throughout the night.

He hadn't had any contact with the man for some time. Not since their attack on the facility that had been pursuing them, and his bloody revenge on their security team.

Alexei had made an appearance then, and hinted that he admired John's deadly skills and that he might call on him in the future.

Since then, John had tried hard to push those memories to the back of his mind. He didn't think of himself as a killer, nor did he find any relish in the number of lives he'd taken.

And yet, here was Alexei, bringing all of those memories back to the forefront of his mind, and a chill ran its icy finger down his spine.

"Come, my boy" came Alexei's voice from the void. "Come sit with me. I believe we can make an accord between us to our mutual satisfaction".

Before him the darkness faded slightly, forming a pathway of gloom. Pure blackness lay to either side, but a narrow path, still dark but brighter than its surrounds, led John into the room and at its end, to the reading couches at the rear of the room.

There, Alexei reclined back into the cushions of a large comfy armchair, his feet raised up onto the low reading table between the seats.

He was puffing slowly at possibly the largest cigar that John had ever seen, and there was a sly smile playing across his lips, as he beckoned John forward and to an opposing armchair.

"So, my dear Ivan" he growled quietly, "we meet again at last".

John threw himself down onto the proffered seat, and in an almost adolescent, childish act of defiance, threw his own feet up onto the same tabletop.

"What are you doing here Alexei?" John asked, his face screwed up into a look of confusion and mild annoyance. " and what's all this 'Accord' crap? "

"Ahh, my boy. I see you find my interruption to your researches a touch more than a mild inconvenience. I understand your feelings boy. Lazarus had informed me of your situation, has kept me updated of things, as it were.

He told me you were searching for a previous instance of such a thing, for anything that might have a bearing on things as they stand.

Hearing this, I inconvenienced a few of my staff, and I put them to a similar task within the labyrinth of our library, which, incidentally, is placed deep within a mountain in our land, and in a most inhospitable environment.

I really don't know why antiquity felt it necessary to provide such protection to a bunch of old tombs and papers, but that they did.

My people really haven't appreciated my demand, but they have obeyed me, and I believe they might have been successful ".

"What!" the word exploded from John in a burst of sudden emotional fire.

In a flash his feet had disappeared from the table top and he was leaning forward in his chair, his body literally vibrating with barely suppressed excitement and energy.

"What have you found" he gasped, his body now rocking back and forth on the chairs edge.

"Now now, Ivan my dear, let us not get ahead of ourselves here. Yes, I have something which I believe may be of interest to you. Though from the brief look at it I've allowed myself, I'm not too sure it's for the good. However, regardless" gruffed the old russian, shifting himself slightly amongst the cushions on which he lay.

"I regret to sound mercenary in my dealings with you my boy, but I require the use of your particular skills. That, I'm afraid, will be the price of this particular transaction".

John ceased his incessant rocking and leaned back once more into the lush upholstery of his chair, suddenly overcome with a creeping wariness and suspicion.

He knew enough about this man to know his hands to be thoroughly dirty and that he was a big, if not the biggest figure in the underworld of his nation.

That, and the knowledge that the Russian considered his particular skill set to be one of murder.

"So" he sighed, a feeling of inevitability washing over him. "You want me to kill someone I take it?"

"oh no my dear Ivan" a broad grin breaking across his face "I'm sure you will need to kill a number of people".

Five

The corridor was stone, walls, floor and ceiling. Old looking stonework as of the type one might picture lining the inside of an ancient castle.

It was also incredibly bright. Bright white light glaring the length of the hallway from the spotlights set up at either end.

Within the hallway stood four men, obviously guards from the way they stood, immobile, almost at attention, and bearing the ubiquitous Kalashnikov in their hands, and clutched to their chests.

Even the guns themselves had led torches strapped to their barrels, their own light drowned out by the painfully bright spotlights.

One wouldn't have thought that there could have been the slightest hint of shadow under the circumstances so arranged. However, in a small cramped space behind the spotlight at one end of the hallway, the very shadow cast by the equipment itself, allowed a small area of shadow and darkness.

And it was within this small area that John now found himself, wrapped in the burly arms of Alexei, who had brought them to this place as soon as John had agreed to his terms.

There had been very little preamble, very little explanation of what was expected of him. Upon his begrudging assent the Russian had risen from his seat, enveloped him in his arms, and blackness had descended upon him.

And suddenly, in the briefest of moments, he had found himself here.

"It is lucky your not a larger boy" muttered Alexei quietly in his ear "or we might not have been able to do this".

John, feeling uncomfortable still engulfed in the man's arms, whispered back to him.

"So, what is it I'm supposed to do old man!"

Suddenly he found some kind of blanket or something shoved rudely into his hands.

"You will need to take this boy" he grumbled "and you will need to get past all those men".

He nodded to the hallway where John saw the four men standing immobile and alert. "At the end of the hall, you will find a door. Locked.

You enter the room". Here he paused a moment, as though unsure of the right words.

"you enter the room, and then you turn out the light. I will do the rest from there".

John turned his head awkwardly to look the man in the face. He couldn't be sure of what expression he found there. It seemed to be a mixture of eager anticipation of something, but there was also a tinge of fear.

Fear? He wondered to himself. He looked back at the guards in the hallway. This man knew what he was capable of, what was there to fear.

He regretted that he didn't have his knives with him. What he classed as his 'combat' wear. The Russian hadn't given him time to go and fetch himself any kit, but still, this shouldn't pose any problem at all.

"Ok" he whispered hoarsely "here goes then".

He rose from his crouched position behind the glaring spotlight, slung the blanket or whatever it was over his shoulder, and began to walk forward.

As he did so he raised his hands before him, palms outwards as though in supplication.

Immediately, a guard, startled at his sudden appearance, began to raise his rifle.

John clenched his right hand into a fist and with the power of his mind he crushed the man's heart, and the man spasmed where he stood, his eyes rolling back into his head and he fell to the floor.

The other guards suddenly sprung into motion, almost as though they had been expecting something of this nature and felt themselves prepared.

All now raised their weapons and began to open fire.

John swiped at the air with his left hand and the guards rifles were torn from their grasp and hurtled to the far end of the hallway, the bullets they had been able to fire before being disarmed ricocheted harmlessly from the invisible shield he had raised around himself and John continued to walk forward, unperturbed.

He suddenly clapped his hands together, and two of the guards were smashed together with enormous force. He could hear the crushing sound of their bones and skulls being shattered in the collision.

The one remaining guard drew an enormous dagger from a sheath at his belt and ran at him, screaming in defiance and fear.

For a second, John simply stared at the man as he ran at him. He felt a sudden pity for this man, faced as he was by an opponent he couldn't possibly resist.

He quickly shook the feeling off. This was no time for second thoughts, no time for weakness. Sophia needed him, and nothing was going to stand in his way.

And so, in order to end this, he simply clicked his fingers, simultaneously disintegrating the man's brain. There was no spasm, no scream of pain, not even a grimace on the man's face. He simply collapsed to the floor, sliding across it due to his speed and finally coming to rest at John's feet.

He hadn't suffered, he'd simply died, instantly.

He continued forward until he reached the door at the end of the hallway and behind the spotlight. It was a large oaken door with polished brass fittings and a large curved handle that looked to him mildly oriental looking.

He didn't reach for the handle, but felt around its frame with his mind, gently and tentatively, and yes, as he'd suspected, there was, hidden within the mantle above the door, some kind of trigger mechanism.

He stepped back from the door, and mentally he triggered the mechanism as intended.

Suddenly, with a metallic screech, two scythe like blades whirled down from the ceiling, swinging past each other in a whirl of sharpened metal, sparks showering the hallway as they ground against each other in their downward swing.

Each of the blades finally came to a halt as they embedded themselves into the walls to either side.

That done, the way was clear, and with a quick twist of the mind John unlocked the door and pushed it open with his foot.

The door swung wide on well oiled hinges, and the first thing that struck John was the incredible brightness of the place. There was an amazingly bright white light emanating from what appeared to be some kind of large four poster bed at the back of the room. He couldn't quite see the cause of this intense emanation however, due to the huge, muscular and stocky man, that stood facing him before the bed, a wide grin plastered across his face as he cracked his knuckles and crouched slightly into a position of impending attack.

"Oh for Christ's sake" muttered John quietly under his breath.

He'd hoped that the casualties in the hall would be the last of his victims and that he was done with the killing.

Yet here was one last more, so he would dispose of him as quickly and efficiently as possible.

He grasped the man's trachea with his mental fist, and squeezed it tightly.

Nothing. The man's throat didn't contract under the pressure at all and so he increased the strength of his grip, up to a level that should have bent steel, and yet the only reaction he obtained was that the man gave a slight cough, as though he had a slight tickle at the back of his throat.

"Oh, shit" John groaned. And the man charged at him.

John threw himself to one side as the man swung at him with a huge sweeping roundhouse blow.

He missed John but connected with the wall behind him, and John saw the brickwork shatter and collapse beneath the blow. Showering the floor with debris and crumbled stone.

Again John took a mental swipe at the man. He aimed a heavy concussive blow at the man's brain. This should have obliterated it and dropped him like a stone. But John found his attack deflected somehow, as though this man was indestructible, made of tungsten or some other practically indestructible element. From the damage he'd inflicted on the wall it was apparent that he had incredible strength too.

John realised that he'd found himself in a bit of a predicament here. Finally he was facing an enemy that could perhaps defeat him. His neck was on the line here.

He wondered if Alexei had known about this danger, then discarded the thought. He had too much to worry about right here and now to start thinking down that route.

He'd hold those thoughts for later, if he could get his arse out of this mess.

The big man, shirtless, the better to display his impressive muscular torso, was quick on his feet, and he spun to renew his attack as John continued to weave around the room in his efforts to evade his grasp.

Again and again he cast mental blows at this man's vitals, and at each attempt he was defeated, the attacks simply being deflected or resisted with indifference.

He was at a loss. Even if he'd come prepared with his array of knives, he realised he'd be no better off. Nothing he threw at this man seemed to have any effect.

He was obviously one of the gifted and his ability appeared to be indestructability or something similar.

John could feel his heart beating rapidly in his chest. It had been a long time since he'd last felt himself to be in any kind of real danger, and yet now, here he seemed to be faced with true peril, and it wasn't a sensation that he was enjoying in the slightest.

He continued his random dodging around the brightly lit room in his efforts to evade this man's clutches and the man continued to dart at him, fists swinging wildly as he attempted to smash John into a pulp.

John was at a loss as to what to do. He couldn't just continue to run around like this, it was becoming ridiculous.

So, he made a decision to stand his ground, and raising his protective shield around himself he turned towards his adversary and threw a powerful cannonball of force at his head.

He saw the man rock back slightly on his heels, his head turning to one side as though he'd received a punch in the face. He took one step backwards, but that was it, that was the full extent of John's efforts. A blast of invisible energy that to all intents and purposes should have removed this man's head from his shoulders in a spray of gore.

John was astonished and momentarily took his eye off the ball.

His enemy rushed forward, but instead of his usual attempts to punch at John, he wrapped his arms around him in a vast bearhug. Squeezing hard at John in an effort to break him in half.

John's invisible shield held to some extent, but even that began to yield to this man's enormous strength. John began to feel his ribs flexing under the pressure and realised in astonishment that his own power wasn't sufficient against this assault.

Momentarily he could picture his death at this man's hands. What was he to do?

Nothing he had tried so far seemed to have the slightest effect against this guy. He was simply shrugging off blows that would have pulverized anyone else. This gifted individual had been left here as the ultimate guard. It had been an incredibly good choice.

John was looking death in the face and he couldn't see any way out of his predicament.

As his adversary continued to try to squeeze the life out of him, John put as much energy as he could into his shielding, yet still it was yielding to this incredible pressure.

Suddenly John was struck with an idea, and taking a portion of energy, energy that he could barely spare, John wrapped a shield of force around the man's face and head, cutting off all oxygen to the man's lungs.

And so they stood. Two men wrapped in an embrace of death.

As John began to feel his ribs flex and crack under the enormous pressure, he saw the man begin to gasp and pant, his face slowly becoming purple then blue.

The squeezing tightness slowly began to relax and John felt huge relief as the pain in his chest lessened.

Finally the man released John altogether, staggered backwards clutching at his face as it turned more and more blue. His eyes bulged and he slowly collapsed to his knees. Finally he collapsed altogether and lay motionless upon the floor.

John leaned back against a wall and wiped at his brow with the back of his hand. He was panting slightly himself as the man's squeezing of his chest had begun to restrict his own breathing by the end.

He left the mask of energy over the man's face.

He had been surprised by this guys power and he didn't want to take any chances.

He vastly preferred the idea of this man being dead.

Finally, he could return to his task. He walked over to the large four poster bed from where the extraordinary bright light seemed to be emanating.

There, spreadeagled on the divan, lay an attractive young girl of about twelve or thirteen or so. Her ankles had been chained to the bed and judging from her continued unconsciousness after the recent battle around her he judged that she had probably been drugged.

She was like a living spotlight. Pure unadulterated bright white light poured from her flesh, lighting the whole room with its intensity.

So, this had been his mission it seemed. To rescue this girl from her captors, who, judging from all of the efforts taken to light the hallway, were well aware of Alexei's abilities.

He cast his eyes over the floor, hunting for the blanket or whatever it had been that Alexei had stuffed into his hands earlier.

Finally he found it, lying at the foot of the bed where it had fallen during his recent adventures.

He examined it as he picked it up from the floor.

It appeared to be some kind of sleeping bag kind of thing, but with a zip that drew completely round at either end, leaving no room for a head to poke out of it.

He suddenly understood what Alexei had meant by 'turn out the light's ' and he gave a wry smile.

Glancing at the chains that bound her feet to the bed, he swiftly snapped the chains with a flex of his mind. He then gathered the girls limbs from their spreadeagled position and lay her straight, with her hands gathered in her lap.

He then slipped the blanket under and over her body, the room growing dimmer and dimmer as she became enclosed within its confines.

She gave a slight moan and her head rolled to one side, but she remained unconscious throughout.

Finally, with only her head remaining exposed and the room grown dim and dark, he heard a cough from a dark corner of the room.

"Thank you my boy" Alexei whispered huskily from the shadows.

"Daughter?" Asked John, with a flash of intuition.

"yes my son. Adopted of course. But yes. I have enemy's and my protection men proved inadequate".

"Well" chuckled John "if that guy" he gestured to the asphyxiated man on the floor, "if he was involved, I can see why".

"finish the job boy, I will be gone only a moment, then I shall return to take you home. And to give you your gift.".

John nodded silently, then completed zipping the bag closed, plunging the room into complete darkness.

He felt her lifted from his hands, then knew he was alone.

A minute or two passed and John sat himself down upon the bed to wait.

He knew Alexei wouldn't leave him stranded.

Within a short while he felt a sudden change to the air and Alexei lay his hand upon his shoulder.

"Well my child. Shall we go home now?"

Six

John found himself back in the familiar environment of the library. As he took in his surroundings, the light's above him flickered briefly then came on, illuminating the place, and revealing the mess of papers and books scattered everywhere, evidence of his frantic search for answers these past days.

Alexei was revealed, once more reclining upon the soft cushioned upholstery of the armchair, his feet again resting on the reading table before them, and a broad grin spread across his face.

Much like the cat that's got the cream thought John wryly

He slowly lowered himself into the other chair. Wincing slightly as he did so, and clutching at his ribs, his own face a mask of pain and discomfort.

"Are you not well Ivan my boy?" Asked Alexei, and John was surprised to find genuine notes of concern to his voice.

"Aahhh" John sighed, throwing Alexei a mocking grin as he rubbed at his sides and grimaced.

"That last guy was a surprise old man. He came close to bloody killing me. Did you know they had such a powerful guard sitting over her? You could have warned me". At this he frowned and cast Alexei an angry look.

Alexei shook his head slowly "No no my boy, I didn't know he was there. I knew there were gifted figures involved in this little dance of ours of course. Reports from my protection unit made that incredibly clear. But I didn't know he would be in the room with her. My only intelligence was the layout of that hall and the efforts they'd made to prevent my arrival on the scene. My thoughts had been that you would simply negate the guards and shroud my girl so I could bring her home. No more my boy, I swear".

At this he waved his hand before him, casting the figure of a cross in the air.

John was surprised. He'd certainly not cast Alexei as a religious person. Shouldn't judge the book, he thought to himself.

"Well" John stuttered mutely, as though to himself "that bastard practically killed me. If I hadn't thought of a way outa things, I'd be a gonner, let me tell you. That guy had power. He was stronger than anyone I've come across before and quite frankly I hope to hell there aren't any more like him out there"

Alexei frowned at this. Then shook his head, as though to stop himself from uttering a stray thought.

"We prevaricate boy". He reached into a pocket deep within the confines of his black fur coat, then withdrew what appeared to be a moderately small package, carefully wrapped in white tissue like paper, and he tossed it onto the reading table before John.

"is it my birthday? " John asked jokingly

"Our covenant child, our contract. You gave me your assistance. Now it is my turn to lend you mine".

John stared down at the small package where it lay on the table. He felt himself awash with conflicting emotions. After all his fruitless and frantic research, here it was, being handed to him on a plate. The thing just sat there, like an unexploded bomb. He had no idea what that tissue paper contained, but he knew, judging from the waves of anticipation radiating from Alexei, that he at least thought it was key to his endeavors. He felt almost frightened to touch the thing. As though all his hopes might explode in his face and leave him desolate and helpless.

He gave himself a shake, attempting to rid himself of this strange malaise that had come over him, then he reached out his hand and lifted the small package from the tabletop delicately, as though there was indeed some chance of if exploding in his face.

He held it momentarily, then looked up at Alexei, to find that the old man was now leaning forward in his chair, his face radiating eager anticipation.

"you've seen this already you said" John murmured under his breath.

"Oh yes Ivan my boy. I investigated it as soon as it was brought to my attention. I do believe it's what your looking for, but I really don't know where it's going to take you. To be honest with you child, I found it rather disconcerting. Possibly even a touch alarming".

Again, looking hard at the man's face he could see the truth of his words.

Then Alexei stood. "Actually boy, if you don't mind, I'll leave you to your discovery. I have a child of my own that needs my attention right now, and she has to be my priority. I have your understanding, yes?"

John felt momentarily taken aback. He'd anticipated sharing this discovery with the old man for some reason, but the truth dawned on him, that he'd just rescued the man's drugged and chained daughter from his enemies. Of course the man had other things to be focussing on right now.

"Oh, no, sorry Alexei. You head off, she'll be needing her father right now, I'm sure".

He also stood and held out his hand.

Alexei gripped it tightly then gave it a brisk shake.

"I'm sure we'll be seeing each other again soon Ivan my boy. You try to take care of yourself, you hear me".

At that moment, the light's above them suddenly dimmed then went out completely for a second, before flickering back to life.

And the old man was gone.

Seven

Alone in the library, John came to the realisation that he didn't want to do this alone. He didn't want to be isolated and without support when he opened this thing, and so he left the library and headed towards the lounge area in the hope of finding someone to share this with.

When he arrived there he found himself to be in luck, for both Kathryn and Lazarus were sat before the tv, supping at their respective teas and coffees as they watched the news together. Catching up on world events with an eye for the unusual or suspect happenings, hidden within the usual hodge podge of current affairs.

"Heads up guys" he called as he entered the room, to grab their attention away from the tv.

"What's up?" Responded Lazarus as he swigged at his coffee. "your looking rather flushed lad, and actually, now I come to mention it, your looking a touch beat up. You come from the gym or something? "

"I've had a visitor" answered John, taking for himself a seat opposite Lazarus, and he reached for a mug and filled it with coffee from the thermos on the table.

"Really?" Asked Lazarus " anybody we know? "

"Oh yes" John chuckled "it was our old friend Alexei, and he brought me a gift"

At this he gently placed the tissue wrapped parcel upon the coffee table before them all.

For a moment there was silence between them, and Kathryn looked back and forth between the two men expectantly.

Finally, Kathryn blurted "Well, what is it John?"

John shook his head slowly, as Lazarus leaned forward in his chair and hesitantly reached for the package on the table.

"Its unlike Alexei to just give gifts John, there's usually some kind of reciprocal arrangement in place somewhere."

John gave a quiet laugh, "oh, don't worry about that Laz. That's already taken care of"

With his hand hovering tentatively over the parcel Lazarus gave John a questioning look, but he didn't ask anything further. If John wanted to tell him he would.

"Do we know what it is John?" He asked quietly.

"No" answered John "other than that he thought it might be helpful with our Sophia situation".

Lazarus nodded at this "makes sense" he rumbled "I'd told him everything we knew about the situation and that you were trying to research into things. So, it looks like he put his lads into a similar search and, possibly, they found something".

"Yep" answered John "that's what he told me. He said they'd found something relevant, but he also gave me a kind of, how shall I put it, a kind of provisional warning with it. He seemed to think that it might be both helpful, and dangerous".

Lazarus's hand still hovered above it.

"so John, you haven't looked at it yet? "

"No" replied John "for some reason, I kinda felt the need for witnesses, and maybe the need for, oh, I don't know. Backup?"

Lazarus nodded at this. "A gift from Alexei should always be approached with caution my child." He paused a moment, then, taking a deep breath "you want I should take a look boy? "

John rubbed painfully at his ribs, leaned back, pushing himself into the lush upholstery of the chair and gave his head a couple of jerking nods

"Yeah Laz, I'd appreciate it if you did it. I'm feeling strangely anxious about the thing. It's like, he's offered me some kind of hope, and I'm scared of being disappointed".

"don't worry yourself son" growled Lazarus in that deep gruff voice of his. "Lets take a look shall we"

As he picked the package up from the table top, he paused, looking over John's shoulder, and a smile broke onto his stern features.

"Ahh," he cried happily " the whole bands here, excellent".

John glanced over his shoulder and was unsurprised to find Sophia in the doorway.

No longer his Sophia. He was mildly annoyed to find that she had put on weight. The familiar sharp high cheekbones had become puffy under a layer of fat that she wouldn't usually carry.

Although it was necessary that Eleanor keep her fed and exercised whilst she was this empty vessel, John felt that she had perhaps become a little too focussed on the feeding and the ability to eat multiple meals a day had become for her some kind of challenge maybe.

To be honest, he didn't know what was going on, but it was evident to his jaundiced eye that she was eating too bloody much for his liking.

"Hiya Eleanor" he mumbled under his breath "welcome to the party".

"Ooh, are we having a party" Eleanor exclaimed joyously, "and where was my invite?" .

"Come" rumbled Lazarus "Come sit my dear. John here has received a gift from our old friend Alexei. It's reported to be of significance to our ongoing Sophia problem. We were about to take a look. It's probably for the best that we're all here for this. We've as yet no idea of what it is".

Eleanor took a seat amongst them and John remarked to himself how they were now all sitting in an expectant circle around the mystery object.

It tickled him for some reason and he found himself chuckling quietly to himself for no reason.

It must be the nerves, he thought. I'm brimming over with anxiety right now and I need some kind of release.

He looked to Lazarus, where he sat impassive and immobile, the object still held in his hand.

Lazarus, in his turn, looked from one face to the other until he was sure everyone was paying attention.

"right then, we all ready? " he called to the group.

"Aye aye captain" replied Eleanor, overcome with a sense of jollity and excitement at the prospect before them.

"Yeah, sure" replied Kathryn, looking anxiously at the parcel in Lazarus's hands.

John nodded briskly. Just keen to get this whole fiasco over with as soon as possible.

"Get on with it old man" he almost growled.

"Right then" Lazarus grumbled, as though to himself, as he began to unwrap the parcel from its tissue paper protective covering.

The layers came off and were tossed onto the table top absent mindedly.

Until, finally, laying spread upon Lazarus's open palm, lay a small, dark brown, ancient looking leather booklet.

It's edges where scuffed and torn and the patina of the leather was faded. This thing had obviously seen a few years.

"Well?" Barked John, surprised by the sound of his own voice in the lull that had fallen over the rest of the table in expectation.

"What is it?" He cried.

"well John" replied an infuriatingly calm Lazarus.

"I'd say at a glance that it's some kind of notebook or something".

"Oh for Christ's sake man, we can all see that. But what's it about, what's it say?"

"hold your horses boy" came Lazarus's measured response, as he pulled a pair of glasses from his breast pocket and positioned them on his nose.

He didn't need glasses, reading or otherwise. The nature of his ability meant that he was always in the peak of health. His body literally couldn't degenerate like that of others, and much to John's chagrin, his true age was still unknown.

No, these glasses he simply used for magnification, when something was either too small or too faint to see with a normal healthy pair of eyes.

"Its old John, and the print on the cover is heavily faded. Just give me a second and I'll tell you what it says".

He paused momentarily, then "Ex Oblivione" he almost sighed.

"What?" Cried Eleanor in mock dissapointment.

"What does that mean?" Asked Kathryn quietly.

"it means" Lazarus said loudly "From Oblivion"

"Huh?" John's ears had perked up at this "Oblivion?. That's the last thing Sophia said. This must be the clue we were after. Here" he gestured to the book in Lazarus's hand "Toss it over here: and let me see".

Expressionless, Lazarus passed the notebook over to John gently. "Be careful with it lad. It's very old and only a short step away from becoming dust".

John opened the book at random and stared at a page. nonsense.

He flicked to another, and again found nothing but seeming gibberish.

Angry now, he tossed it back to lazarus, who caught it with care, before slipping it into his jacket pocket.

"What's all this crap" John cried "none of it makes any sense man".

"that dear boy" answered Lazarus calmly "is because it's written in Latin".

"Oh, great" John cursed "so now we'll have to get ourselves a Latin English dictionary or something and toil away at trying to translate the damn thing. Yet more time wasted".

"No John, we wont" came Lazarus's muted response "for some of us can read Latin boy".

John looked at him in muted astonishment.

"Just how old are you Laz? " he asked quietly.

Lazarus ignored the question but instead stepped away from the table and headed off to his rooms.

"I'll have you a translation for breakfast tomorrow" he called over his shoulder as he left.

The remaining three were left sitting in silence for a while. Each looking the one to the other in astonishment at the turn of events.

Finally, Eleanor cried "well, I think it's time I fed the real me. I'll put our little lass here to bed n go grab myself some lunch".

At this she jumped to her feet and wandered off into the mansion and John and Sophias bedroom.

Kathryn remained in her seat and looked at John pensively ."How are you feeling John?" She asked, the concern clear in her voice.

John realised that he was rocking backwards and forwards on his seat in a state of heightened nervous tension.

He forced himself to stop but the tension was still there. They were on the brink of something here he felt sure, but still he found himself in a powerless position with nothing he could do to speed things along or help in any way. Now it was in the lap of Lazarus.

Tomorrow wasn't far away he knew, but he wasn't feeling rational right now.

He knew what he had to do, he had to hit the gym. His gym, the one he'd personalized for his own use and his own gift. He needed to release this tension, and he knew the best way to do that was to mock killing a few things.

"I'll be fine love" he murmured to Kathryn as he rose to his feet. "Just need to burn off a bit of this anxiety I'm feeling right now".

Kathryn nodded "Just be sure you look after yourself John. Sophia needs us right now, but she needs you more than anyone".

John squeezed her shoulder as he passed. "Thanks Kat, I'll keep it in mind".

And he headed off to his gym.

Eight

John flicked on the light's as he entered the large room he'd set aside for his training and exercising purposes.

The room itself was a vast space within the manors compound. The walls had all been painted a Matt black and the floor area was littered with humps and bumps and fractured areas of wall like constructions, all in an effort to mimic broken ground and desolate buildings.

The far end of the room was hidden in shadow, and it was there that they had installed various mechanisms to challenge him.

on a wooden frame by the entrance hung his 'Combat wear' as he referred to it to himself.

It was an array of military style body webbing, festooned with an array of skull headed black stiletto knives. There was also a glossy looking black blank faced mask or helmet. When wearing the headwear with the facemask down he could see clearly in the darkest of conditions. An ability very useful in some situations.

John went through the motions of putting on his webbing array. Tightening the various straps and buckles until he felt comfortable with all the gear arranged around his body.

Content with that at last, he finally donned his helmet, visor up.

He looked across the large exercise area and a feeling of calmness descended over him at last.

This was something he enjoyed. Something he was good at. At least, he considered himself good at it.

He reached across to the control panel on the wall and set the difficulty level to high. He switched off the lights, plunging the room into pitch blackness, then slid the visor down on his helmet.

Suddenly, to him, the room became a twilight scene, an almost Amber grey lit arena, awaiting developments.

Finally, he reached again for the control Panel and flicked the dark red switch marked 'On'.

There came a dull humming sound from the dark end of the hall, then silence once more.

Upon the far wall, a target, in the shape of a large red handprint, slowly illuminated.

That was his target then in this scenario, randomly selected by the computer that operated this training routine.

He had to place his hand on this target, and the room itself would be doing its damndest to stop him.

Right, he thought. Time for action.

He approached the first fragment of wall at a running crouch.

Immediately there was the roar of gunfire.

Gesturing with his hand he threw up a protective shield, deflecting the approaching bullets until he reached the shelter of the wall.

Once there he crouched down and mulled over his next move.

Action, he thought, and in a swift motion, raising his shield once more, he threw himself upwards into the air, flying up until he could rise no higher.

As he did this he threw bolt after bolt of cannonball sized balls of pure force at the opposing gun emplacement.

There was an enormous crashing sound from that darkened end of the hall and the rain of bullets ceased.

He came down to land again further into the room, shielding himself this time behind a rise in the terrain. His head ducked down and on his hands and knees he peeked around the edge of the rise.

Immediately, a humanoid figure popped up and fired at him from the waist.

He pulled back, then thrust himself forwards once more. A hand pointing forward at the firing figure and projecting pulses of kinetic force. Blowing the figure in half.

He rapidly pulled back his head as a flurry of blade edged disks flew towards him, some embedding themselves into the mound behind which he currently hid.

He steeled himself for a moment, then in an acrobatic leap he threw himself over the rise, raised a shield before him and threw deflecting blasts of force to repel each of the flying disks of death as they flew towards him and he ran forwards.

He came to a broken fragment of wall, now close to his target.

This time his 'opponent' for want of a better word, projected a blazing torrent of fire towards his position.

He cursed inwardly to himself, as fire wasn't something he could simply dodge around and raising a body shield felt like cheating. He thought for a moment, then with a decisive nod to himself, he stood, raising before himself a force field into a dividing blade of sorts. Much like the blade of a snowplough. This done he was able to stride forward, the fire being deflected to his left and right, finally placing his palm onto the target area.

There was an audible click, then a whirring noise, and the system shut down. The room returning to its dormant state.

Lazarus had questioned John's creation of this arena, as with his ability he could simply shield himself from start to finish and simply walk from one end of the room to the other without any danger from all of the weapons trained against him.

John had tried to explain that he didn't want to just rely on his powers, that he wanted some kind of challenge. He felt he was in danger of relying too much on his gift. Becoming unfit and lethargic and unready should any real danger threaten them.

Lazarus had laughed it off and told him he was being unnecessarily pessimistic.

But still, John had persevered. There had been something inside him that persisted in anticipating some kind of danger that he couldn't see. And now of course, the danger had come, and Sophia was gone. And he'd been completely unprepared for it and unable to save her.

He marched back to the doorway and flicked the light's back on.

The room looked much the same as before, barring the blades embedded in walls and the smoking fragment of wall.

He shook his head. Today's training had felt like a failure to him. His shielding of himself to escape the fire had felt like cheating.

it was like the old comic books. Once they'd created superman, an indestructible character, everything felt like a cheat.

At least the other superheroes had weaknesses, flaws that their enemies could capitalize on.

But superman?

A cheat.!

And if he used his gifts to their full extent he felt like bloody superman, and he hated that.

He left the gym, still wearing his webbing of blades, which he hadn't used at all during his training, and headed for the garden.

He felt that, perhaps a bit of fresh air and sunlight might improve his mood.

Meanwhile, in the dim light of his study, Lazarus pored over the small booklet Alexei had left them and as he read he transcribed onto a notebook with his free hand.

He had thought that his latin skills might have been a bit rusty, not having used them for what felt like a millennia. However everything had come back to him in a rush and it felt to him as simple as if he were reading plain english.

This translation shouldn't take him any time at all, and it was an interesting and disturbing read to be sure.

He leaned back into his chair, and reached for his coffee.

He took a sip and grimaced. It was stone cold, he'd been too engrossed in his work and had forgotten about it.

He cursed mildly and made his way to the kitchen to make himself a fresh brew.

As he stood by the sink waiting for the kettle to boil he looked out of the window.

There he saw John, angrily tossing his blades at the trees then calling them back to his hand to toss yet again.

He was worried about the boy.

This Sophia business was beginning to grind him down he could see. They would have to come up with something soon, otherwise the lad might go off the deep end.

He wasn't a doctor, but he'd been around a long time and he recognised the signs of depression when he saw it.

He gave his coffee a stir then returned to his study and his translation.

Tonight he'd have this finished and together they could see if it would help them out of this hole they'd found themselves in.

From what he'd read so far he thought they would have some options. It would depend on Eleanor he thought and his suspicion of her abilities.

Only time would tell.

Nine

Evening came and found the four of them gathered around the dining table.

John sat leaning forward onto the table top with his head in his hands. He was still wearing his webbing of blades, not having changed all day.

He was rocking slightly backwards and forwards in his seat and it was evident to all there that he was extremely on edge.

Both Eleanor and Kathryn sat together opposite John, and meaningful glances flew backwards and forwards between them as they silently watched John and looked to Lazarus for some kind of hope.

Lazarus himself sat at the head of the table, the ancient notebook and his own modern notebook laid out before him.

"Right guys" he growled in his distinctive deep voice. "I've gone through Alexei's little gift and I've managed to translate it all. We needn't wait till breakfast, I can run us through it now. If that's what you want of course".

"Yes Laz, do it now." Growled John.

"Do you want me to read it out verbatim, or do you want me to just give you the outline and the salient points we can use? "

John's head rose quickly from his arms and he fixed Lazarus with a steely stare.

"Just give us the highlights Laz" he sighed, his voice sounding already defeated and morose.

"Good answer" grumbled Lazarus. "This old notebook is in itself an oddity. It dates back to ancient Greece, n back in those days most of their writing was done on rolls of parchment. So, for someone to have created an actual codex like this is most unusual.

Anyway, as you no doubt realize, as ancient as it is and the style of writing back in the day, there are a lot of asides and the like at the beginning and a lot of praises raised for those in positions of power and whatnot.

So, cutting all that out and streaming it back to the salient points, I'll take you all through it."

"Now" he said quietly, his deep rumbling voice reverberating across the table.

"Firstly, you have to bear in mind that even as long ago as this was written, there where even then, groups associated with we gifted. They had their artefacts hidden and they would empower the occasional person, more for the purposes of carrying on their organisation and traditions.

We're talking now of times of constant war. The constant striving of one tribe against the other in the search for land, elements, wealth and power.

The group of gifted at that time considered themselves to be philosophers, mainly epicurean in nature, and they tried their best to stay away from the conflicts and to live their lives in a state of simplicity and mutual support.

They did pretty well for themselves all things considered. They lived simple lives on a simple diet, and withdrew from areas of conflict.

Being gifted, they could if they wished have made a big splash on the times. But they followed a theology of sorts that required them to withdraw from the world. And so, there they were, hidden amongst a time of constant battles and an age of heroes and kings. They tried occasionally to steer the state into one of democracy. Well, as democratic as could be achieved in an age where the majority of the inhabitants were slaves, who obviously had no political voice. Neither of course did women. But women being women, they had plenty of hidden power with their influence over their menfolk.

Ahh, I'm straying off of my path aren't I?

Anyway, according to this little tomb, there came a time when one of their number broke the mould.

They gave this guy the name 'Oblivion'. "

Johns head rose sharply from the table and they all heard the grinding of the feet of his chair as he pulled it forward and pulled himself up, all attention now.

"Now, I know that sounds really melodramatic doesn't it. 'Oblivion' sounds to us really scary and ominous, but you gotta remember that this was his name in Latin, and in Latin it doesn't have the same connotations that we give it these days.

Although we're in ancient Greece here, this is after the Roman invasion. The street talk of the times was all Greek, but written works had become by this time something that had to be in Latin.

Latin had become the universal language of literature, and it was recognised everywhere as the universal tongue.

Consequently, the gifted of the times named each other using the Latin tongue in their communications.

Also, they usually named each other in relation to their gifts or powers. for example, if your ability was great physical strength they might call you fortis. If you could produce light they might call you Lux or Lumen. If you could produce fire then you might be called incendere. So, you get the gist yeah? "

The others at the table nodded mutely, John rocking backwards and forwards on his seat in a state of agitation. He was obviously teetering on the brink thought Lazarus and so he hurried on with the task at hand. "Oblivion means 'forgetfulness' or in his case, the ability to wipe the memory of others. This guy could cause anyone to forget whatever he desired. He could, should he wish, cause a man to forget his own name.

It appears that this guy started to abuse his gift. He could blatantly steal from someone and cause them to forget that they had ever even owned what was stolen. The group disbarred him from their society, but of course, he would simply cause them to forget his banishment and return to the fold. He could commit crimes then cause all to forget that the crime ever even took place.

Finally, he decided to extend his powers.

Firstly, he decided to spend another night with their artefact, to add to his power so he thought.

However, we ourselves know from bitter experience the effect such a second exposure can have.

He managed to extract somehow the hidden whereabouts of the other artefacts. All hidden throughout the world. The locations of the artefacts today weren't where they've always been. They've passed through different hands over the years and they've moved around the globe accordingly.

Also, his plan was flawed, in that they did not as they thought, know the location of 'All' of the artefacts.

At this period of course, they had no idea of the new world, the Americas and Canada to be.

Neither were they aware of the antipodes, and so some of the artefacts would remain out of his reach, and his plan would never be achieved.

During this period they were aware of only four artefacts spread across their idea of the globe.

He came to the decision that he would visit all of these artefacts, and bathe in the power of each. He thought he could become a true power over the globe.

He was, due to his abusing of his gift, enormously wealthy, and he raised a small army and began to travel the World.

He found the first of the artefacts in china.

His army slew many of the inhabitants of the area, but the gifted there managed to repel him and keep his men at bay, using their gifts in their defence.

Consequently, he fell to subterfuge.

He approached their defences in the guise of a lowly peasant, fell into conversation with their guards, then passed on into their dwellings, their having forgotten he was even there.

He used this ruse throughout his search of the place, until he found what he was looking for.

Then, whilst the residents of the place sat on guard against attack, and had their meetings and discussions amongst themselves over their defences and how to repel the enemy, he locked himself away with the artefact in their room of power, and spent there the night, as one seeking the change.

It had occurred to him that a different artefact might provide him with more power, a different ability to add to his armoury. If this could be true, then gathering the artefacts themselves together could be dismissed as a project, He would simply gain power after power, until he could become indomitable and overwhelmingly powerful.

And so, that night he spent within the proximity and influence of this other artefact, not knowing if there would be further change or not.

If not, he would simply steal the artefacts and continue his army's march, with the goal being to gather them all together.

Legend among the gifted has always been that should all of the elements be brought together, there would be an apocalypse. An end to the world we know and a descent into a world of madness, death and destruction.

He, he felt quite content with that prospect. He felt that this world had cast him aside, that he had, as with his power appropriately, been forgotten. Armageddon would be a comfort to a man if he was in charge of it. If the artefacts were all under his control, then whatever destruction they wrought would be by his hands and under his control.

Regretfully, by this time, and after his double exposure to his home artefact he was quite mad. That, and beginning to mutate.

When he awoke the following morning, he could feel within himself a new gift, a new ability.

He emerged from these hidden Chinese caves with yet another mental gift.

In addition to his power over the memories of others, he discovered the ability to steal another's complete consciousness. He could leave a man an empty shell, whilst he would now possess all of their memories, all of their knowledge and all of their abilities and talents."

At this John's head jerked up and his eyes flashed at what he'd just heard. This was what had happened to Sophia. This man, this Oblivion, her final words. This was what they needed. An explanation. A cause that made, at least, some kind of sense.

From this point on Lazarus had all of his attention. He wasn't going to miss a word.

"Needless to say", continued Lazarus, "it was yet another gift that he rapidly abused.

Once returned to his army he continued their march onwards, towards the next enemy and the next artefact.

They assailed the headquarters of the Russians, and yet again were repulsed by their defenders.

The Russians outnumbered his forces enormously, and so once again, he withdrew from the attack, and once again assumed the disguise of a mere peasant, and approached the guards at the gate.

The same routine was achieved and once again he found himself in the presence of yet another artefact.

Another night spent hidden within the room of change. And another change achieved.

He exited the Russian confines to find himself nigh on indestructible. That and now bearing enormous strength."

John thought back to that guy he'd ended up fighting for Alexei, and tried his best to muffle a groan.

"He could bend a thick bar of iron with his bare hands, and missiles and arrows would simply deflect from his flesh, leaving him completely unharmed.

His men, his troops, began to worship him as a god, and from this point onwards he led his men from the front. Cutting swathes through his enemies with ease.

Through the use of his stealing of minds he now possessed great martial skills. He was the ultimate general and his men followed his every word as the word of god.

They came to the final, as far as they were aware, the final artefact.

They were now in France, amongst the gauls and angles of the times. His men seized a town and ravaged it. He allowed his men all licence and there was much massacre, rapine and theft.

This town was near to the hidden caves of the local gifted, and this time he disdained the military approach completely.

He left his men to their leisure and once more disguised himself and using the same familiar technique, he intrigued his way into the hidden depths of their facility and found their treasure. The final artefact, so he thought.

And once again a night spent, hidden within their room of change.

The following morning he emerged transformed, but as yet he knew not how.

He returned to his encampment and ensconced himself within the local mansion house of the town's governor.

He bid his men to leave him and to take their positions around the perimeter of the town, to repel strangers or enemy forces and to leave him for the moment in isolation, whilst he tried to discover the nature of this new gift and to familiarise himself with its abilities.

And it was at this point that he discovered the power of the 'world walker'.

This was a gift of legend. Something that hadn't been seen for generations. And here he was, in possession of probably the most powerful gift ever recorded.

He was enraptured and overcome by this sudden power.

He fell into a stupor of deep thoughts.

With this gift, he could leave this paltry world where he had been undervalued, dismissed and cast aside to the betterment of others.

With this gift he could seek out another world, a world of his own, of which he would be master.

He gathered his forces into formation upon the fields surrounding the town and he lauded them their successes and their bravery.

He extolled their virtues then told them that, as their very god, he was going to take them to their elysian fields, their world of wonder and peace.

He then opened a vast gateway in reality, the men saw stars and threads of light cascading before them, and he marched his men, mounted at their lead, through this tear in the world, and then reality crashed closed behind them.

That then is the legend of oblivion. And that should have been the end of his story. He was gone, he had left our world and so no longer offered a danger to us.

However, two men, two of his vanguard who had walked through the gateway with him, their God at their lead.

These two men returned.

The men were haggard filthy wrecks. Neither of them retained much of their sanity.

They had both undergone some kind of incredibly tormenting experience, and both felt themselves very lucky to be alive at all.

They were brought into the presence of the two consuls, and they were both questioned as to what had happened to them. Where was their army that had caused such devastation in its travels? Where was this 'godlike ' leader of theirs?

Both men, broken as they were, tried their best to explain what had happened to them, but they made very little sense to anyone.

From what they said their master had lead them through a window in the world. Initially it had seemed as though they were simply in a dense forest of threads of light. Their leader had reached out and had seemed to pull on one of these threads. Suddenly they had found themselves in another world. A world where the sky was a bright green and the clouds a dark brown, clustered in masses and projecting great blasts of coloured lightening in a deafening roar.

Their leader had shaken his head decisively, then they were suddenly again amongst the threads and another was chosen.

This time, the world to which they arrived looked much like our own, although two large moons hung in the daylight sky, and the air smelled faintly of jasmine.

There where herds of goat like animals prolific among the grasslands that surrounded them, and his men had raced to trap some of these beasts so that they might cook themselves up a great feast in celebration of their success.

The first of the men to reach a beast was given a very brief moment of horrified shock as the beast turned on him and literally pounced. Opening huge jaws to reveal enormous fangs and it literally bit his bleeding head off.

Having spread out to catch these beasts many of the men didn't see this happen, and so were caught in their turn by these unexpectedly ferocious creatures.

Oddly, their God of a leader had found this all vastly amusing, and had fallen into gales of laughter. Clutching at his sides in his mirth.

"Yes" he had shouted to the heavens. "This shall be our home. A world to keep my men strong. To keep them sharp and aware. In this world we shall breed a race of heroes".

By this time the men had become aware of the danger and had retreated from the beasts. Taking them down instead with the aid of their slingers and archers. They would still have their feast.

An encampment was built and sentry's set in place.

The men brought out the booze and the flesh was roasted on the spits. They fell to the feast and there was much revelry and drinking. Don't forget that every army has its hangers on too. Those that follow in its wake in the hope of capturing booty for themselves. Then there were the whores. Every army had quite a following of prostitutes, their reason for being there an obvious one. They could make a lot of money during any military campaign. And so, they threw themselves into a frenzy of debauchery. Their god of a leader lording it over his men and drinking his full with them all.

They all fell to their cups and the night was one long party.

The dawn light was an amazingly luminescent blue, which had his men staring in silent awe at its magnificence.

The Lord himself sat in silent contemplation and the camp functioned as camps do in a strange silence, as his men finally came to realise that they were in a different world, and that all that they had known before was gone.

He summoned his generals to his tent and they sat there together, mute for a while and lost for words.

Now, you remember what happened to mark after his double dose as it where, of the artefacts power?

You remember how he started to mutate?

Well. As he sat there in rumination with his generals, the discussion falling to the building of a city and the beginning of their evolving into the next master race, the generals noticed that he had small horns budding from his temples. That his skin had begun to darken and thicken and crack. That his finger tips now ended in claws and that his eyes had begun to redden.

None of these generals were brave enough to raise this with him, but word soon began to spread throughout the camp that their commander wasn't a god after all, but a demon from the depths of hell.

For some of his men this wasn't a problem in the least. God or devil, their supreme leader wasn't of this world and could bring the power of magic to their efforts.

For some of the men however this posed a problem.

These were God fearing men who had concern for their souls after this life, and working for an entity from the underworld might not look good on their cv come judgement day.

Dissent began to whisper throughout the encampment.

Meanwhile, Oblivion had planted his staff into the soil at his feet as he stood in the centre of the plain and announced that this would be his capital. Men were sent to scour the environment for resources. Marble and granite. Iron, copper and tin. Even gold was found in vast quantities in the mountainsides.

His men were put busy to work on the building.

His works would be made of marble from their very beginning. Mine's were established and the smelting of ore was begun in earnest.

Quarry's were begun and the marble of his city was transported in huge quantities and in slabs of vast size.

There was much talent amongst his men and several became artists. Rendering the wilds of the country in ink and oils.

During all of this activity, their God had receded into the background. Confining himself to his quickly erected temporary accommodation and issuing orders through his generals. Hooded and enshrined in darkness, his windows blacked out and his throne ensconced in the darkest corner.

He had become aware, partially at least, of his ongoing transformation and mutation. And he didn't want to alarm his men or for rumours to spread throughout his army.

However, the city near completion, and the necessities of the men's workload diminishing accordingly, a man came along talented with hammer and chisel and a sculpture of their overlord was commissioned as a vast marble edifice, to stand behind the man's stone throne where it stood in the middle of the central atrium of the city.

The man Was afraid, and begged to be given some other task. Certainly he could carve for them whatever they wanted, but to carve a statue of their master? No, he didn't want to do that.

Regardless of his fears, it was insisted upon. He would carve a statue of their master.

And so he began.

Slabs of dark or black marble were sourced for him and he fell to his work.

Throughout, he kept himself and his work in isolation. Nobody would see the statue until it's unveiling upon completion.

The longer the man spent upon his work, the longer he spent sitting with their Lord in order to create an accurate representation, the more he visibly deteriorated. He lost an enormous amount of weight, once being a stout man, he became a thin stick of a figure. His face seemed to have rapidly aged and become haggard and full of anxiety.

The day of the great reveal finally came, and the masses of his men gathered within the grand concourse at the city's centre.

The master sat, hooded as always, upon his great stone throne and the covered statue stood behind him in its enormity.

Banners and flags had been hung everywhere around the concourse, and a number of musicians had gathered to trumpet his eminence.

Finally came the great drumroll, and the now wizened, trembling wreck of a sculptor stepped forward and pulled the heavy drapes from where they hung covering the edifice.

The statue stood there for all to see. It was a work of true art, the sculptor having managed to transmit the true image of his subject into the cold stone.

Now, don't forget, back in those ancient days the statuary was all painted, in order to present a more truthful representation.

We imagine their statuary to be bare marble as that's all that we have ever seen of their work, but that's simply because all the paintwork has worn or weathered away over the generations.

So, this gargantuan statue, finely worked and representative of it's model, looked very much like a large double of their lord.

Aside from the fine blue trimmed, red cloak which the statue bore, the long clawed fingers were clear to see. The twisted horns that grew from the temples. The long fangs that protruded over the bottom lip. The gnarled grey green flesh of the face and arms. And finally the large, oval and red eyes. Slitted like those of a snake.

The statue was in a posture of a half crouched position, and looked as though it was about to leap forward into the crowd.

For a moment there was simply silence.

The musicians had lowered their instruments and the drummers had dropped their sticks, or whatever you call them.

The masses simply stood there and gaped at the monstrosity before them.

For the majority of these men hadn't seen their leader since the day of their initial transport to this world. They were now seeing for the first time the monster he had become. And the men suddenly realised they had been building a city under the orders of a demon, not a god.

The moment of silence passed and suddenly all hell was let loose.

Some of the men fled to the hills.

Some of the men fell to rioting, and fires were set within the city and men began to tear down what a moment before they had been building.

Some men fell to their arms and attacked their once god as he sat, looking bemused upon his throne.

He didn't even rise to meet them, but simply struck them with his great staff and swept them aside in a swathe of blood and broken bones.

He looked to his sculptor, who unmoving, still stood, shaking, beside his great work, the corner of its drapes still clutched in his hands.

"You did this" he hissed, anger blazing in his eyes.

The sculptor, who had always known that something like this would happen when the men saw the true nature of their leader. The sculptor, simply stepped before the throne and fell to one knee before his lord. Prostrate in his worship and resigned to his fate.

"Yes" he croaked "that I did my lord".

At this, the monster once man, raised his staff high, then brought it crashing down onto the sculptors head. Killing him instantly .

The man had always known that this would be his fate, and so had resigned himself to his end already.

And so, the city fell, at its very moment of triumph.

There was raging and rioting in the streets and others ran from the scene of devastation and fled to the wilds to hide within the forests and such.

Two men came forward, trembling in fear and dread. Their hands were raised in supplication and their heads were bowed in their awe and worship.

They pleaded with their lord, their voices choked with fear and dread at what his response might be.

They begged for the chance to return home. To see once more the loved ones they had left behind and the soil of their once beloved homelands.

There was a silence at this. The creature once known as Oblivion sat before them on his stone throne and looked down upon these two trembling and shaking men as they prostrated themselves before him and poured handfuls of dust over their heads and wiped away at their tears.

Finally, he deigned to speak, and in a deep throated grumble he bed then to rise.

Then, looking each man in the eye, he sighed "You have been good workers my children. You have fought valiantly in my battles and stood by my side against my enemies. And now, you beg to leave my employ ".

Again there was a period of silence, and a deep throated hum emanated from him as he thought on the matter. Then "Very well my sons. I shall return you home. You would do well to praise my deeds amongst your kindred, and to pass on the word of Oblivion. Tell them all that I shall one day return. Tell them that my power shall bring them all to their knees one day.

For now I shall spend some time in thought.

Now, begone, the pair of you, and remember me well".

At this he raised his staff idly and waved it in their general direction.

Suddenly the two men found themselves engulfed in a veritable web of strings of light.

They were turned around and around in a spin of confusion and disorientation.

And then.... There they were, lying, alone and shivering in a winter field, somewhere in the lands of Greece."

At this, Lazarus leaned back into his chair and wiped a hand over his brow.

He shuffled the papers before him into a neat pile, then pushed them all away from him with a long drawn out sigh.

There was a silence across the table and it seemed to drag on for quite a while before finally Lazarus broke it once again.

"And there you have it folks. That's what we know about our man Oblivion. That's ya lot".

There was a crash as John leapt up from his seat, the chair being thrown back to the floor behind him.

He began to pace rapidly back and forth the length of the table. His hands tore at his short blonde hair and his eyes streamed with tears. His face was a mask of conflicting emotions. There was fear, desperation and despair there. A confusion of conflict raged within him and he angrily cried at Lazarus.

"Well what the hell use is any of that to us old man? This was millennia ago. This Oblivion guy will have died a hell of a long time ago. We need to find out what's happening now for Christ's sake. Sophia's in trouble now. What bloody use to us is a bloody history lesson?"

Lazarus remained unmoved. Relaxed in his chair, though his hands were now rubbing absently at his temples.

"Your forgetting something son" he rumbled.

John turned to him and stared at him angrily.

"And what the hells that then you old fool". he almost shouted.

Eleanor and Kathryn were grasping each others hands anxiously, and frightened glances flew back and forth between them.

"You forget boy. This guy was a worldwalker".

"Yeah? And what the hell of it? "

"Well, if you think back boy to your exploits with sophia. You'll remember that she had the ability to travel through time. It came in rather handy on a few occasions if I recall correctly".

John stopped his pacing. Frozen for a moment in recollection and realization.

" So.... What are you saying Laz? "

Lazarus dropped his hands from his temples and lay them, spread, palm down on the glossy surface of the old oak tabletop.

His eyes became unfocussed, as he withdrew into his thoughts.

"What I'm saying boy, is that if he has the power of a worldwalker, and he can utilise time, he could be doing this from his throne in ancient Greece. Or he could have travelled here and be acting from somewhere here in our own time. He could be anywhere in the multiverse, and still be hosting our Sophia".

John silently picked up the fallen chair from the floor and sat once more at the table.

He sat silently for a moment, then "what are you saying Laz. What are we supposed to do? "

Again, the room was silent for a moment.

Kathryn broke the silence. "Do you have any kind of plan Lazarus? I can't see what we can do. This man could be anywhere, hell, anywhen for heavens sake"

Finally Lazarus's head rose and he stared from one face to another.

"Ok" he murmured "here's my thinking. Sophia herself might be gone, but we still have her here physically. Now, we haven't tried this yet, but my thinking, my hope, is that Eleanor might have access to her powers.

Now, obviously we'll have to try this out, but if she does, then perhaps we can go after the guy. Maybe go back to his ancient Greece or something. If she can access the power, we have options. We can go on the offensive. Find this bastard and get our Sophia back.

What bothers me is that I don't understand why he took her in the first place. What use is she to him".

John shook his head silently. His eyes far away, as was his mind. Deep in thought.

Finally, the silence of the room having become uncomfortable, Eleanor burst out into fits of sobbing.

70

"I never thought about her power. It never occurred to me that I could use her powers. I, I'll have to try. We have to save her. Shall I try now?

Should I see if I can do it now? "

Lazarus quickly raised his hand in admonishment "hush love. No, not here, not in the bloody dining room. As with all gift trials, we'll use the gym. Firstly we don't yet know if it's possible. Secondly, if you can, you'll not have Sophia's control over it.

There could be issues shall we say. Do you remember Sophia's first attempt?

There might be dangers, we have to be prepared."

John was back on his feet and pacing once again in an air of fevered excitement.

"Right. Let's do it then. What are you waiting for? Let's get down the gym and give it a go."

Again, Lazarus raised his hand in calm rebuke. "No John. Not yet. We have to be prepared for this. We're all tired, it's the end of the day. We all need to have a nights rest and then prepare ourselves. Gather what equipment we might need. We'll begin our... Experiment?...in the morning. Refreshed and prepared".

There was a momentary flash of anger in John's eyes. But then, he shook himself and regained his composure. "No, your right. If we're going to do this, we have to do it right".

He walked towards the doorway, and raised his hand in farewell. "Right. I'm off to bed then."

He gave them all a wink and a sly smile. "I need my beauty sleep too don't I?"

He left them then, and the remaining three suddenly felt like conspirators in some kind of outlandish plot.

Eleanor broke the silence first.

"I don't know about this Lazarus old boy. I don't know if I've got access to her powers, I've never, well, looked if you take my meaning. And if I can, well, I'll certainly not have her skill, her prowess as it where. I'll be going in blind. I'm not gonna know what to do. Honestly Laz, I'm gonna be lost with it".

She was still grasping Kathryns hand tightly, rather uncomfortably tightly for Kathryns taste, but she could feel the waves of anxiety pouring off of her, and so persevered with her moral support as much as she could.

Lazarus still sat there, completely calm and unperturbed. He almost shone with an aura of self assurance. Complacent in his calmness.

"Don't worry Eleanor my dear. Everything will be fine. I understand your concern completely. But we'll all be there together. We'll all have your back, and we'll be there for you every step of the way. Whatever happens, we'll be able to cope with it. You haven't tried to use the power yet, it might not be as bad as your anticipating. Ok love? You able to keep yourself calm and collected for this hun? ".

Eleanor looked back and forth between the concerned face of Kathryn and the infuriatingly calm face of Lazarus. Then, she leaned back into her chair, casting her face to the ceiling and closed her eyes. There was a moment of silence and Lazarus and Kathryn exchanged glances of curiosity and slight concern.

Suddenly Eleanor snapped back to herself, a look of determination on her face.

"Right. I've got it now guys. I'm fine. It'll all be fine ".

At that she rose, slightly unsteadily from the table.

"Right. John's got the right idea. I'm off to bed. Goodnight chaps".

And she strode from the room on slightly wobbly legs, heading to her bedroom.

Kathryn rose to follow her.

"I'll just make sure she's OK Lazarus. You know how emotional she can get. And she's certainly not used to having others depending on her. Our Eleanors always been one for looking after herself. The needs of others have never really been on her radar. She's gonna be a ship lost at sea with all this business".

Kathryn nodded at Lazarus in lieu of a shrug, and made her way off into the mansions darkness and Eleanors room.

Lazarus was left alone in the darkness of the dining room. He flicked randomly through the bunch of papers before him. Then, tossing them aside in a rare show of anger, he threw himself back again into the upholstery of his chair and rubbed vigorously at his eyes.

"Shit" he sighed to himself "I've a feeling this is all gonna go to hell".

And finally, with a lurch to his feet, he made his own way to bed. And, he felt sure, a world of uncomfortable dreams would follow.

Ten

Sophia awoke to darkness. She was enshrined in an eternal Vista of blank nothingness. Also, as she hung, powerless and terror ridden, she realised that she was indeed hanging. She could feel no surfaces beneath her flesh and in reality had no idea at this moment which way was up.

She was completely disoriented and the fear, primeval and all encompassing, flew through her in waves, each one cresting and submerging the last.

Where the hell was she?

One moment she'd been lying comfortably in their bed, spooning with John and starting to caress his chest, fruity feelings beginning to arise within her.

Then suddenly there was a vague memory of pain, of struggle, and finally the sensation of tearing. A ripping feeling that seemed to come from deep within herself. Then nothing.

Till now.

Well, there was still nothing, admittedly. However, she was awake again now. She was aware of herself and her surroundings

And her surroundings seemed to consist of nothing but a blank black void. No up, no down. Simply a dark nothingness.

She was bloody terrified.

Was she dead?

Time passed, but with no sensory input of any kind she couldn't tell how long. It might be moments or an eternity.

Finally, with a suddenness that startled her, there was a growth of light before her. The illumination of a scene, a marble columned atrium, festooned with greenery, vines hanging from portico and a large fire burning at the centre..

A circle of benches surrounded the area and upon one of them sat a short dark haired man, who was beckoning to her with a broad grin adorning his sly looking face.

Abruptly, she found a surface beneath her feet. She could see nothing there, just a continuation of the void, but the sensation of a solid surface she could feel distinctly through her soles.

She peered forward at the distant beckoning man with a strange feeling of mingled fear and distaste, yet seeing no other option, she walked towards him. Relieved to have some control once more over her motions and finally an idea of which way was up.

As she neared the man he seemed to grow in stature and there was the expansion of his musculature. Golden rings appeared on his fingers and armbands graced his biceps.

It was as though he was trying to impress her in some way. Adorning himself and attempting to improve his appearance.

However, she still thought his face looked incredibly sly and there was an evil looking edge to his eyes.

"Come, come sit Sophia my dear" he cried as she closed the distance between them.

Her feet finally resting upon the marble tiled floor of the atrium and the ornate mosaic laid within it, she hesitantly walked towards the benches across the other side of the area from this strange individual. This way she could face him whilst simultaneously being as far from him as possible.

"Do we know each other ?" She asked, her voice cracking with the barely suppressed sense of fear that pervaded her whole self.

"Oh" cried the man with a mirthful smile "I think I know a little of you Sophia my dear.

Once wealthy, reduced to penury by your fathers imprisonment, always feeling like an outsider, trust me I can empathize. Suddenly finding yourself drawn into the world of powers, escaping from your insane mother, discovering that you possess an extraordinary gift, and finding true love".

Sophia gazed at him in stupified wonder. realisation dawned on her. This information he seemed to have on her was something that might be drawn from a simple wiping of the surface of her mind. These were simple extracts, highpoints as it where, of her life to date. There was no depth here, no detail or rationale to it all.

He knew a little, that was for sure, but he didn't know the ins and outs of her life. She knew, somewhere deep within herself, that she'd struggled somehow, that she'd been able to resist him, at least partially. He'd not engulfed her as he'd sought to, as he would have an ordinary mortal. She too was one of the gifted, and that fact had somehow lent her some level of resistance.

So, now he was trying something new.

An interview of sorts, a discussion. Now he would be searching her out for points of weakness. For cracks within her armour, something he could get his proverbial fingertips under and lever her apart.

"Ahh, Sophia" sighed the strange man, smiling deviously and stroking at a non existent beard.

"The very personification of wisdom. Are you wise Sophia my love? Do you think you possess the ability to survive life's trials? "

She found herself lost for words at this, at what she perceived as a vaguely veiled threat.

"I, I think I can hold my own mister, ...mister?"

Her question hung in the air momentarily and a look of deep thought passed across the man's face, as though he was trying to think of a name for himself.

"Er, you can call me Pancras, Sophia my dear".

Sophia briefly wished she knew more about baby names and the like. She knew that this would have some meaning, much as she had always known that Sophia was ancient Greek for wisdom, she believed that this man had picked himself a meaningful name, and knowing it might have given her a slight edge, an insight to how he perceived himself.

She quickly shook this thought off though. She'd have to make do with what she had, which she conceived as sod all but her wits.

And so, her wits would have to do.

"Right. Ok Pancras old chap. What the hell am I doing here, and where is here exactly. One minute I'm happily tucked up in bed, next thing I know I'm hanging in this dark void of yours"

"Well, as I said before" answered the figure calling himself Pancras. "You are a walker of worlds. A very rare thing indeed. However, it so happens that I share this gift. I too can travel the dimensions, and until now I thought I was the only one capable of such a thing.

Due to some unfortunate developments, I have been, how can I describe it, rather detached, er, switched off as it were for rather a time. With the aid of our gift I essentially froze myself in time and place, alone with my broodings.

Then, suddenly, I detected something in the ether.

Disturbances and fluctuations amongst the web of worlds, and I felt that only someone with my very gift could be responsible.

And so, I awoke and sought the source.

This, eventually, led me to you.

Now, I possess other gifts in addition to my walking of worlds, amongst them the ability to seize the consciousness of others. To essentially seize their minds and hold them within myself, for the purposes of... Er... Discussion, shall we say.

I had finally found you. You blazed like a beacon within your dimension and I was able to watch you through the curtain of the void without stepping through it.

I saw you lying there besides your love and the decision was made before I even realized it.

I reached through the rift with my mind, sought and captured yours, and essentially stole it from your body.

You now exist as an independent consciousness deep within my mind, and your here to assist me with my endeavours in this new world of yours.

You will tell me what I need to know, and I will rise once more to my place of power and authority over this world."

"Your bloody crazy if you think I'm gonna go along with this" hissed Sophia

"You've abducted me and you think I'm gonna simply comply with this nonsense. There's no way I'm gonna help you in any way. I insist you put me back in my body and just leave me the hell alone.

There's no history between you and I. We have no grievance. You've no right to do this to me"

"No, perhaps not" purred the man softly "but comply you will. There are things I need to know, and you will supply me with the information I require".

Again, Sophia felt that chill rise within her spine and cold fingertips graze her mind.

She fought it. From somewhere within herself, something instinctive kicked in and her consciousness raised barriers against this intrusion. She attempted to raise shields and to withdraw her thoughts from the surface of her mind.

"Hmm" sighed the man before her.

"I see that our relationship is going to be an interesting one. However my dear, you cannot conceal everything from me. Some of your thoughts are far too strong, far too important to you for you to hide them from me. They blaze from your mind quite clearly.

Hmm, John eh..?

Seems an interesting, though troubled boy. Your love of this person is too intense for you to hide. Though some details are concealed, there are details you consider unimportant and therefore you've left clearly visible. These will aid me, and trust me my dear, you will comply".

He stroked again at his non existent beard and ran a hand through his dark hair.

"Well Sophia, needless to say, I have various important tasks before me, so I will leave you for now.

Please, make yourself at home, and I will return to you soon. "

With this, Sophia felt the floor moving beneath her feet and saw her surroundings blur and shift.

It was a dizzying sensation and for the briefest of moments she felt herself all turned around and confused as to her location.

Suddenly, as if with an audible click, her surroundings settled into position. Locked in place it seemed.

It was her bedroom.

There before her lay their large kingsize bed, neatly made up, the crisp sheets folded with precision.

There was the dressing table, her hairbrush and cosmetics.

The armchair lay in the corner as always and staring out of the window she could see the grounds of the manor. The greenery of the trees and hedgerows.

"What? How?" She blurted, and she swung back to the dark man.

But he was gone.

Eleven

before heading to bed, John grabbed up his mobile and made a call to his dad.

If he was heading off into a precarious situation, he felt he owed it to his father to make some kind of contact, in case it turned into a goodbye.

The phone only rang very briefly before it was snatched up at the other end.

"Hello?" Came his dad's voice, sounding strangely anxious over the airwaves.

"Hi dad, it's me" replied John, "how's tricks?" .

"Ahh, hi son. Good to hear ya voice boy. Things are much the same as usual here. How's ya studies getting along? ".

Of course, his parents thought he was away studying at a university. The ruse used to have brought them here originally, before the more fantastical side of things had been revealed.

"Oh, good, good. Can't complain. Actually, that's one of the reasons I called really. Just to let you know that we're off on a kinda skiing break, something to lift the old spirits you know, so I'll be out of touch for a while."

"Skiing?" responded his dad with a chuckle "you've never ski'd in your life son. So, shall I expect to see you next with a broken leg or something?"

John laughed, "maybe dad, maybe. So, how's mum?"

"aahh, yeah" his father's voice faltered "I'm sorry to say we've still seen hide nor hair of her son. Nobody knows where she is.

As you know, I reported her missing to the police. That's all I can do really.

I'm sure she's fine. Just run off for a while with one of her new blokes. She'll turn up eventually ".

"Oh" John sighed. The disappearance of his mum disturbed him significantly. He knew her well enough to know to have expected a call from her or something. To have simply disappeared off of the face of the earth was most unusual.

He continued a brief and pointless conversation with his father a short while before hanging up.

Where the hell had his mother sloped off to?

Ahh well. There were more important things to worry about right now.

He headed off to his room to find Eleanor waiting outside his door.

In the evening that followed the group began to find themselves puzzled at Eleanors behaviour.

She insisted on visiting each of them in their rooms, and spending several hours with each of them in silence as they tried, usually without success, to get to sleep.

However, she never gave any explanation, but simply left them at the end of the time, wishing them goodnight on her way out.

Her final visit was to lazarus, and in his case she was with him for the whole night.

Whatever she was up to was seeming to take a long time in his case. And in the end it was he who woke her come morning. Shaking her gently awake from the squat position she'd taken up at the head of his bed.

She'd then looked mildly panicked, until, after a brief moment within which she'd appeared to think intently. Finally, with a look of mild relief, she took herself in hand and headed off to her own room. There was always the chance that she might grab a little bit of sleep before Lazarus went round and woke everyone up.

Twelve

John was up n out of bed at the crack of dawn. He was filled with a rising excitement at the prospect of seeking out this Oblivion Bastard and kicking his arse.

This was however coupled with an increasing anxiety that Eleanor wouldn't be able to utilise sophia's gift, that her power, her ability, might have gone the way of her consciousness.

But regardless of what was to happen, he wanted firstly to make sure the gym was prepared for Eleanors attempt, then he'd go wake the rest of the lazy buggers up and they could get cracking.

'and find out either way' he thought, his stomach giving a lurch at the possibility of failure.

He jogged his way to the gym, stretching out the kinks in his spine and the heaviness of his limbs.

Once there, he looked at the gym area and the clutter of gym equipment that filled the space.

'right then' he thought, and he made his way to the centre of the room.

Positioning himself there at the centre, he closed his eyes and raised his arms up to either side.

There was the squealing sound of metal on the laminate flooring as the heavy weights, the rowing machine, and the treadmill, along with other pieces of equipment were forced away from him. Finally coming to rest with a thud up against the far walls.

His eyes sprung open and he looked with satisfaction at the large clear space surrounding him.

"Job done" he whispered to himself, "now, let's go wake those lazy sods up shall we?"

He carried on with the jogging and made the room of Lazarus his first port of call.

He pulled himself to a halt outside the door to Lazarus's room, and gave it a sharp rapid knock.

"Come in lad" came the familiar baritone voice, and John opened the door and poked his head through the gap.

He'd expected to find the man sitting up in bed or something, but instead he saw that he was sitting, fully dressed, at his desk, and perusing through a handful of papers with a look of, what? 'concern?' on his face.

Looking at the papers in his hands he thought they looked suspiciously like the ones he'd had before him at the dining table during last night's talk.

"I thought I'd be seeing you early this morning son" growled the bear of a man as he swung round in his seat to face his visitor.

"Well, yeah" choked John, finding his voice almost failing him in his growing impatience.

"We've gotta get things rolling old man. We've got to get the girls up and get cracking. We don't even know yet if Eleanor's gonna be able to do this thing. Sophia's out there somewhere, and we've gotta save her somehow. We can't be wasting time with this, surely? "

Lazarus gazed at him, his face a mask, inscrutable. Finally, he leaned forward in his seat, his elbows on his knees and rubbed at his eyes.

And John wondered to himself if the man had been to bed at all since last night's talk.

Lazarus looked back up again at John, and nodded at the webbing of knives he wore, tightly strapped to his body, the blades all capped with their skull pommels.

He'd never liked those blades and had always felt there was something slightly 'Evil' about them in some way he couldn't put his finger on.

"Well, I see your all prepared boy.

Now, I'm really sorry about this son, but your just gonna have to slow yaself down a little."

"What?" John blurted angrily "What the hell...?"

"now hold ya horses boy, we're still going ahead with this thing. However, I've made a judgement Call on this, and I think we're undermanned. I don't know how well we'll do up against this Oblivion character, so I've made a few calls".

John sort of stumbled further into the room, finally taking a seat on the neatly folded blankets of Lazarus's bed.

"So, what are you saying then Laz? I don't understand".

"We've a couple of extra hands on their way to join the team boy. Alexie's agreed to lend a hand with transport, so we shouldn't have to wait long boy. So, don't get too disheartened. We'll be on our way soon enough lad. We'll wake the ladies from their beauty sleep n grab ourselves a breakfast. They should be getting here about 9am, so we've plenty of time n we'll still have an early start".

"Who....who's coming" John stuttered from his place on the bed.

Lazarus rose to his feet and held a hand out to John.

"Come on boy. Let's go wake the ladies n I can tell you all about it over breakfast, ok?"

Feeling slightly numb, John took the proffered hand and followed Lazarus out of the room and down the hall to the bedroom of Kathryn.

Lazarus gave the door a slow knock then opened the door wide and walked into the room.

Kathryn lay, spreadeagled on her bed, arms and legs akimbo, her eyes covered with a black sleep mask and snoring quietly.

Lazarus walked to her bed, then suddenly and unexpectedly, gave the side of the bed a heavy kick, and growled "wake up woman. We've business to be getting on with".

Kathryn raised a hand and lifted one side of her sleep mask. Peering blearily at Lazarus with the one eye.

"Well" she slurred slightly as though still half asleep "Thanks very much for the wake up call you old sod." She turned her head and took in the sight of John, standing in the doorway and covered in his arsenal of blades.

"right then" she continued, pulling herself up onto her elbow and pulling the mask from her face.

"You two can bugger off. Give me a minute and I'll be down as soon as I'm ready. Ok?"

Lazarus turned back to John at the door.

"Right son. That's one down. Let's wake our other beauty now shall we?"

The two of them headed up a further floor to the room Eleanor was currently using whilst they were undergoing their Sophia problem.

She actually had a small cottage of her own on the outskirts of the mansions estate and nearer to town. But under their current circumstances she'd taken a guest bedroom on the upper floor.

They reached her door, and Lazarus was just about to give it a knock, when it suddenly swung open before him, and Eleanor in the guise of Sophia stood there before them. Hands on hips provocatively and wearing a black jumpsuit and a brown leather jacket.

Thigh high boots adorned her feet and a sword was slung on a leather thong over her shoulder.

She was ready and prepared that was for sure.

"I could hear you two coming a mile away. You didn't think I'd go back to bed did you Laz?" she barked. "I'm sure Kathryn appreciated your wake up call didn't she?"

Lazarus chuckled.

"You never cease to amaze me woman. How long have you been waiting for us two to turn up at ya door huh?"

"Long enough you old bugger. Now, right, let's get this thing going shall we.

Breakfast everyone?"

The three walked down into the dining room to find Kathryn there already, laying out plates on the table for everyone. She gave them a nod as they walked in.

"Morning chaps. The bacons on already. Full English for everyone yeah? "

"Oh yes" crowed Eleanor "I think we need all the sustenance we can get for this enterprise, don't you guys?"

The men hummed their assent and took their places at the table.

It was only a short time before they were all tucking in to bacon, sausage, eggs and hash browns. The table remained silent whilst they ate, but there were meaningful glances exchanged between them all throughout.

They all knew they had a job to do and that they didn't know what they would be facing.

The tension was palpable.

Finally, their meal finished and their plates pushed away, they knew it was time to get down to business.

Lazarus began "I've told John here already, I've made a few calls and I've called in some aid. Were gonna have a couple of new recruits to our group, to kinda toughen up our team a little.

This Oblivion guy is gonna be a tough guy to handle, so anything we can do to boost our resources is for the best.

So, for starters I've had a chat with our lovely Valerie , you remember her don't you John?"

"The Canadian lady? " asked John, struggling to remember their brief conversation so long ago now.

"Yeah, that's right son. Well remembered. So, anyway, I gave her a call, we go back a long way me n her. So, I explained our situation, as best I could, and asked if she would have anyone available who might volunteer to help us out. She asked around for me, she would have come herself, but apparently they've got a bit of a crisis of their own going on at the moment with the locals, so she was kinda tied up.

Anyway, I'm getting sidetracked aren't I?

Anyway, like I said, she asked around n came back with a volunteer. Apparently he's a bit of an unusual guy, but great to have around you in a fight".

"what's his gift? " asked Eleanor, as she examined her teeth on the side of a butter knife.

"No bloody idea love. Guess we'll find that out when he gets here won't we.

I also obviously spoke to Alexei, n he was more than keen to lend me one of his chaps.

He seems to have taken a shine to you boy" he said with a withering look at John.

"You'll want to watch that. Alexei 's a great ally to have around you, but he can get you entangled in unsavoury affairs at times. Often without you even realising it."

"do we know this chaps gift? " asked Eleanor again, the knife now safely laid down onto the table top as she leaned forward on her elbows with an anticipatory look in her eyes.

"Oh yes" Lazarus sighed, leaning back into his chair and looking around quickly to see if there was anywhere to rest his feet.

He spotted a low stool nearby and grabbed it up, resting his legs on it and sagging further into his seat.

"There are four things in life son that you should always grab at every opportunity. And that's the chance to eat, drink, pee and rest".

"Lazarus" grumbled Eleanor, "his gift?" .

"Oh, yeah, sorry love. Monster raising I guess you'd call it.

He has the ability, using whatever materials are available, such as the rock of a wall or the earth at your feet, to create large golem type of creatures. He can control their actions at will. Or, apparently, one of his tricks is to create one around himself, like a suit of armour. All very strange I admit, but I'm sure he'll be an asset.

So, I think you'll agree. He might come in very handy, yes? "

Eleanor nodded mutely and there was an appreciative hum from Kathryn.

John sat nodding quietly. "Yeah, that might come in handy I'm sure" he murmured.

That anxiety was rising in him again and he looked over at Eleanor.

"Are you sure you can do this Ells?" He asked, and he could feel a tremble in his voice .

She gave him a compassionate look and there was a moment's silence.

"I'm gonna give it a damn good try John, I promise you that".

Lazarus glanced at the ancient looking watch on his wrist and rose from his chair.

"Right then. They shouldn't be too long" and he began to draw the curtains together.

John, realising what Lazarus was up to, leapt to his feet himself and began to assist, the room being large and having an excess of windows.

There was a little shower of dust from the enormous high pelmet above the dark satin of the curtains, since they were drawn together so rarely.

The room darkened accordingly and dark shadows stretched their length across the floor.

Lazarus and John both returned to their seats and there was an uncomfortable, anticipatory silence, that Eleanor felt obliged to fill.

"So, Laz old boy, what preparations do we need to make for this thing? Is there anything we need to do, anything we need to get together before we try to do this? "

Lazarus frowned momentari!y, then his face brightened.

"Uh, yeah, I guess so. We'll need to choose our clothing carefully, we don't want to stick out like a sore thumb as soon as we get there, wherever there is.

I've got us a bag of currency for us to share."

"Huh?" blurted John "how can we have currency? We don't even know what bloody world we'll be going to?"

 Lazarus gave him a condescending smile.

"Just disks of gold and silver son. They'll be unembossed with any insignia obviously, but gold and silver tend to be the currency of pretty much everywhere, and the lack of any motif shouldn't cause any issue".

"Ahh, cool" John said with a smile "that's good thinking Laz".

"thanks son" Lazarus replied with a chuckle.

"Right, well we'll also have to think about armaments.

Swords, knives, axes, whatever fits in with the place. But it might also be wise to have some heavier weaponry, concealed obviously, for any serious conflict we might encounter.

So, I'm thinking some guns would be wise.

anything any of you can think of to bring along.

You know the score guys. We want to look like we fit in, but he prepared for anything".

John nodded decisively. He'd just had a couple of ideas of his own.

"right then" John blurted "We've got clothes, cash and arms. Anything else?"

Everyone looked back and forth between each other.

"Er, supplies, food and stuff?" Suggested Kathryn meekly, as though she was going to be dismissed as a fool.

"No, good thinking girl" barked Lazarus. "We'll obviously need to eat. And we can't rely that we'll find food in our environment".

"Right then" cried John, leaping once more to his feet. "Lets get this show on the road".

The group dispersed throughout the mansion to gather their bits and pieces. However, Lazarus remained sitting in the dining room.

He had apparently arranged with Alexei for this to be the drop off point for their new recruits, and so he awaited their delivery there, whilst the others suited themselves in their appropriate garb and gathered their weapons. Kathryn spent some time in the kitchen gathering together their supplies for the trip that lay ahead.

A journey they still as yet didn't know if Eleanor would manage to pull off. As confident as she appeared in the moment, John could see the anxiety there in her eyes. Hiding there in the background. Suppressed and avoided.

Finally, the group were prepared and they made their way to the gym, whilst John went back to the dining room.

He arrived there to find four people seated at the table. Lazarus sat opposite Alexei, the two of them deep in conversation.

However, they were both speaking in Russian, so John couldn't understand what they were talking about. Whatever it was, they both appeared intent on some serious subject, and Alexei gestured furiously to punctuate his points.

To either side of the Russian sat two unknown individuals. Obviously their new volunteers on the enterprise at hand.

One, a dark haired youth sporting a soul patch beard on his chin and with gel spiked hair, watched the two men at their argument with a wry smile on his lips. Obviously enjoying the whole affair.

To Alexei's other side however sat a mysterious figure. Wearing a dark cloak and heavily hooded, his face was hidden from view and there was an air of mystery about him.

John lay a hand on Lazarus's shoulder "you want to make some introductions old man?" he announced loudly.

Lazarus jumped with a start, obviously surprised by John's sudden appearance. Unusual for him, thought John. He was usually well aware of his surroundings. He must have been distracted by his conversation with Alexei, he decided.

"Huh? Oh, hi son. Sorry, allow me to introduce our new recruits. On the left here" he gestured to the youth with the gelled hair, "this is Vladimir. He's the chap with the gift of, er, monster creation kind of thing I was talking about earlier". The youth gave John a casual wave of the hand.

"I call it morphing. I'm sure there's a better name for it, but I just can't bloody think of it. You can call me Vlad" he said, in what John thought was a surprisingly girlish voice. Quite high pitch and unexpectedly feminine.

"And you are?" Continued Vlad.

"ahh shit, sorry" blurted John , suddenly feeling terribly rude and foolish for not having introduced himself. "My names John. Er, you can call me... John".

They both chuckled together, and John thought to himself that this was a good start. Building a bit of rapport between them.

He glanced over at the darkly hooded figure to Alexeis right, as Lazarus gestured towards him.

"And this is Isaac"

The dark figure also gave a small wave, and John thought he saw.that he was wearing greenish looking gloves of some kind.

"Now" continued Lazarus "Isaac said he'd give us a demonstration of his gift in the gym before we, hopefully, embark".

"Ok, cool" replied John , he gave Isaac a thumbs up " I look forward to it man ".

"Also" continued Lazarus, "I'm sorry for all the Russian talk. I find it easier to get my points across to Alexei in his native tongue.

We were having a little disagreement about our trip. He seems to think that this Oblivion character might be more than we can handle.

Whereas, I of course, disagree. "

John turned to Alexei, where he sat with a frown on his face.

"Alexei" John cried, his voice full of enthusiasm, in the hope of breaking through the man's apparent despondency.

"It was you that gave me the book man, it was you who led us down this path. What did you expect us to do? Abandon Sophia?

You knew we'd never do that. And surely, you must have read the book yourself before you gave it to me. You knew what it contained. Why hand it over and then kick off that we're following up on it?"

Alexei simply sat up straight and prim in his chair and gave John a wry grin.

"I simply believe Ivan my dear boy, that this Oblivion will have grown in power over the centuries. I believe he would have been a handful for you back in his early days. But now, now I think he might pose for you great danger".

At this he pushed himself and his chair back from the table and rose to his feet.

"But I see, as always, that my advice is to be ignored. And so I leave you now. Good luck Vladimir my boy. Enjoy the battle".

Alexei then walked to the end of the dining room where the shadows lay, and quickly he was gone.

Following Alexei's sudden departure, the room had abruptly seemed to become a place of awkwardness and discomfort, and so, with an almost alarming intensity, Lazarus leapt to his feet and declared "right, let's to the gym then lads".

They arrived at the gym to find the ladies sitting on a bench by the wall and in animated conversation. Eleanor was obviously now bearing sophias form, wearing the black catsuit, leather jacket and sword slung over her shoulder.

Kathryn was wearing a velveteen dress in a dark scarlet and bore two swords of her own, crossed at her back. There was also a large dagger sheathed across her belly, and at a glance the two women looked quite formidable.

"right guys" cried Isaac, his voice quite a deep murmur from within his hood. "I guess now's the time I give you all a demo huh?"

"if you'd be so kind" replied Lazarus with a chuckle. "It'll be nice to see what Canada's had hidden up its sleeve for so long."

At that, the figure of Isaac bowed, then tore the long robe off over his head.

And there, for a moment, he stood. Revealed to all in his magnificence.

John was surprised to see that his gloves hadn't been green, but that that was his actual skintone.

His entire body, now unclothed bar a pair of combat shorts, was a dark emerald green.

His chest and abdomen was vastly muscular, his arms and legs bulged with muscle, and from behind, rising snakelike over his shoulder, was a tail. The edges of which appeared bladelike and it ended in a vicious looking spike.

His hands, which he now extended out before him, suddenly extended razor blade like talons, about three inches in length.

"Right" he snarled, his front canines having now extended out and over his lower lip.

"You'll have to set me up a few targets if you want to see any action guys".

Lazarus, Vlad, and John spread out and gathered together a number of the benches that lay against the walls. These they then stood on end in random areas of the gym. Some spread out, some gathered in close format, in an attempt to simulate a human grouping.

They then returned to stand by Isaac, and waited in expectation.

"Ready guys?" Isaac asked.

 they nodded their accent.

"Right" he snarled, and suddenly he was off.

He moved like lightening. He first hit a small grouping which was instantly shattered to pieces in a flurry of claws and bladed tail.

Blades had now extended the length of his forearms and shins, extending to points at the elbow and knees.

He vaulted and spun in the air, his tail slicing through bench after bench.

At one point it seemed as though he'd run up a wall, shedding bench after bench as he ran across the ceiling, finally, after a flashing green blur of a spin, he dropped to the floor besides the others, ostensibly his starting point.

The others gazed back and forth between him and the destruction he'd wrought.

Some benches, seemingly untouched at first glance, were seen to slowly slide into component parts.

Not a single bench remained in one piece and the whole exercise had lasted less than two seconds.

"Now that" croaked Vlad, "that was bloody impressive man".

"I can see why they kept you quiet boy" rumbled Lazarus.

Isaac, meanwhile, was shrugging himself back into his voluminous robe. The blade like tail tucked up over one shoulder. His talons withdrawn.

For now he kept the hood down, and John had the opportunity to examine his face.

It was a fairly normal face, he thought, if you excluded the fact it was green, the short hair a deep black.

The eyebrows were sharply arched over brightly, almost backlit purple eyes.

Those eyes were almost hypnotic. John just couldn't stop himself from gazing at them.

It was obvious that he was having an issue as Isaac suddenly asked "You having trouble with the eyes man eh?"

And he pulled some shades from somewhere within the confines of his cloak, and popped them on his face.

"Don't worry about it man. I get it a lot ya know, yeah?"

the eyes now covered with the black lenses, John snapped back to himself and finally found his voice.

"that demonstration man was something incredible to watch. Your a bloody killing machine I swear. I've gotta thank you for joining our little war party Isaac. I think your gonna be a bloody handy man to have around.

By the way. What made you volunteer for this. It's gonna be bloody dangerous and we really don't know where we're gonna end up"

Isaac shrugged, then pointed to his green face.

"John. As you can imagine, I really don't get to go out much, ya know. So, how shall I put it, er, being in constant confinement gets to be a bit of a bloody drag. So, I thought, the opportunity to get out, have a little adventure and rescue a girl. I just had to snap it up mate".

John turned to Vlad, a grin beginning to spread across his face. Things were actually happening now. They were taking action.

"how about you Vlad? Why'd you join the team? "

Vladimir smiled back at John. "I come from Russia John. We are hard men there. We like to fight. And I wanted to find a challenge for myself.

So, essentially John, I'm here for the fight.

Oh, and to rescue a beautiful woman of course.

I like the idea of rescuing the trapped princess from her enemy.

I can be the avenging knight, rescuing a Maids honour. "

"Excellent" cried John, clapping both men on the shoulder. "Now we just have to see if we can get there".

"I tell ya what" said John" make sure you've got all ya stuff together,n then we'll give Eleanor a kick up the arse n see if we can't get going"

He and the others each ran to their individual packs, each containing some of the supplies from the kitchen by Kathryn.

John gave himself the once over.

Yep, he was wearing black leather boots, black cotton pants and a black leather waistcoat type affair. Over this was his webbing of blades, Upon which he'd tied some small black draw string bags, scattered amongst the blades themselves.

This has been his token no to the suggestion by Lazarus that they might consider bringing along some more contemporary weaponry. In this case, each of his black draw string bags contained a grenade. The idea had seemed to make sense, as with his gift he could put them exactly where he wanted, to do the most damage.

Finally,he looked around, then gathered up his large black cotton hooded coat, under which he could conceal his armaments, which he shrugged on,slinging his pack over his shoulder.

He looked over to see that both Vlad and Isaac were similarly prepared, then "Right lads, let's get to it then shall we?"

They walked over to where the girls still sat on the bench by the wall.

" Eleanor? " asked John "Are you ready for this then? "

Before Eleanor could respond, Lazarus jogged over to the group of them. He held in his hands a bundle of small square black objects, which he then began to hand out to everyone.

"Walkie talkies guys. Small and concealable. I thought it'd be a good idea if we could keep in contact should we get split up."

"good thinking man" barked Isaac.

"No need for that really Laz old boy" Piped up a voice from the bench.

It was Eleanor, who, brushing her hair from her face, finally stood up to join them.

"When we get there. Or before if you like. I can put us all on a mind link. we'd be able to communicate telepathically".

"What?" cried Vladimir in a concerned tone "You mean you'll all be able to hear all my thoughts?"

Eleanor chuckled quietly "No no dear boy. You'll have to think to yourself that your speaking to the others as it where. Then you will be. Your everyday, passing thoughts n stuff will just stay there in that thick head of yours. To communicate, you'll have to think 'Communicate' to get through to anybody".

"Oh, wow. You can really do that? " cried Isaac. "Would you communicate to everyone or can you just talk to one individual or something?"

Kathryn pursed her lips, then smiled broadly "oh, you can talk to individuals or the group if you want. You simply have to think of yourself as speaking to that one individual etcetera and you will be. But your normal, background thoughts and stuff will remain private my lad. You've no need to worry about that. "

"Sheesh" breathed Isaac, and he went to hand the walkie talkie back to Lazarus, but Lazarus held up a hand in denial "No son" he said "keep a hold of it. If anything happens to Eleanor we'll lose our connection. Best we have a backup I reckon".

John grunted affirmation and jammed the device into a pocket.

"right then guys. Are we all kitted out now? "

There was a general mumbling of accent amongst them, and John turned towards Eleanor where she had regained her seat with Kathryn on the bench.

"Okay, okay" she trilled, "I'm on it guys. Just give me a second, ok?"

She seemed to give herself a shake and Kathryn placed a reassuring hand on her shoulder.

"You can do it love" she whispered in her ear "go show em how".

at this Eleanor lurched up from the bench and strode decisively to the centre of the room.

She raised her hands before her in a simulation of prayer. Then, frowning, she shook her head slightly, tossing her hair over one shoulder.

Then, she spread her feet a touch, as though bracing herself a little, and took a long deep breath.

Finally, in an extended exhale she breathed the word 'Tractus', and she parted her hands to either side.

What first began as a vertical line of light in the air before her, widened as her hands parted, until at last there was a ragged tear in the fabric of reality. A gateway opening onto a realm of threads of light.

"Bloody yay" cried Isaac. "Well done that Girl" .

"I can feel her" breathed Eleanor, a look of startled surprise on her face.

"What?" Shouted John , leaping forward towards her, only stopping at the extended arm of Lazarus.

"hold fast son. Let her finish".

Eleanor glanced over her shoulder at the group, a wide grin on her face.

"I can feel her out there" she trilled "honestly. I can't tell exactly from where unfortunately. It's as though she's moved around out there a little. What do you want me to do John? Go for the first place I sense her or hunt around a bit more?"

"go for the first place Ells. If she's not there we can try again yeah?"

"Ok John" Eleanor sighed, and it was as though she plucked at one of the threads that hung there, glowing in the ether.

Suddenly the threads were gone, and in their place was a forest clearing at night. Moonlit and strangely beautiful.

"Right then guys. Let's get going" cried John. And the group moved forward into the green clearing. Finally, Eleanor followed the rest of the group, and she closed the gate behind them.

"So, where are we Ells? " asked John, as he stared upwards at the night sky and wished he knew his constellations.

"How the hell should I know" replied Eleanor.

"So" continued John "we could be in another world, or just another time yeah?"

"guess so John" she sighed. "Don't forget boy, I'm all new to this worldwalking business"

"It's another world boy" grumbled Lazarus, and John saw he was staring up at the stars the same way he had been.

It seemed that Lazarus did know his constellations.

"Right" Lazarus continued " keep it tight boys. John, you wanna do a quick look see? "

John gave a curt nod, then launched himself upwards into the sky.

At about five hundred feet, he stopped, hovering unsupported, pinned to the heavens, and had a good look around.

Mostly, all he could see was more and more forest. It seemed to go on as far as the eye could see. But no, there, just there, about ten miles away or so, there he saw the forest was broken by a village or town of some sort.

It appeared to be walled, but there didn't appear to be a citadel or castle of any kind within it's boundaries.

He looked down at the forest below him and saw movement.

There, sliding through the shadows of the undergrowth at speed. He couldn't quite make out what they were, but they certainly weren't human.

He dropped, landing lightly amongst the group.

"Firstly" he said calmly "We've incoming. Look like some kind of predators, I couldn't really get a good look, but they're coming in fast. Twelve and nine O clock Laz".

He glanced round at the others and saw that both Isaac and Vlad were looking confused. Vlad was actually looking at his watch for heavens sake. A digital at that.

"Boys" he called "I mean straight ahead and to your left. Speed they were moving I'd say they must be nearly on top of us by now."

"Right then" shouted Isaac, suddenly overcome with bravado. He stepped forward to face whatever threat lay ahead of them and shrugged off his robe, revealing his muscular frame and his bladed tail.

He extended his claws and his fangs descended as he fell into a crouched, waiting position.

John and Lazarus turned to their left. Lazarus undoing the axe from his shoulder and John pulled open his hooded coat to reveal his blades.

Meanwhile, the others retreated into the middle of the clearing.

Kathryn took Eleanor by the hand, and suddenly they both disappeared.

Firstly came the sound of them. A deep gutteral growling that sounded strangely like some kind of speech, but without words.

They listened, attentively, attempting to pinpoint they're exact location, before, suddenly, they burst from the greenery and threw themselves upon their adversaries.

The combat didn't last for more than a few seconds.

As the creature emerged before Isaac, he threw himself into a whirl of flashing talons and razorlike tail. Immediately eviscerating the beast and tearing out its throat.

The animal that burst out before John and Lazarus was immediately caught, immobile, in the grip of John's mind as he reached for a blade.

However, before that could come into use, Lazarus had stepped forward and swung down his axe, cleanly cutting the creature into two halves.

John continued to hold it in place as it raged and slathered and tore powerlessly at the air.

Slowly, it's motions reduced in ferocity and power, until finally it was still, and he released it to drop to the earth.

Isaac, claws and fangs withdrawn, picked up his robe and shrugged it back on to his body.

He was wearing a broad grin on his face. "Now, that was fun" he chuckled.

Lazarus was kneeling down beside his own victim and examining the body.

They appeared to be almost monkey like in their layout, although they'd attacked on all fours.

Their faces were twisted into horrible, monstrous like masks of dread. Large fangs protruded from their jaws and their feet and hands bore terrible long claws.I

John gave the body a kick

"Nasty" he hissed in a long sigh.

Lazarus was busy doing something with a knife in his hand. He now rose to his feet. His face an inscrutable mask, still managed to look somewhat disturbed.

"Even nastier John" he growled deeply.

He held up what he'd been cutting from the creature for everyone to see.

It was a long Clawed finger bearing a ring of gold around its base.

Looks like this one was married.

Thirteen

The group had started a fire and set up their camp around it. It had started to darken and they had decided to leave the ten mile trek to the town until the morning.

Now was their opportunity to discuss their options and to make some kind of plan.

John asked Eleanor if she could still feel Sophia's presence, but Eleanor shook her head.

"No John. Nothing. I feel as though she's been through here, yes. But I think she's moved on".

"then why don't we do the same then" John asked in irritation. "Move on ourselves, see if we can't track her down".

Lazarus stepped in at this point, wagging the dismembered finger before him as he spoke.

"we will John, don't worry about that. But first I want to see what our man Oblivion has been up to here. This thing here proves something straight away that disturbs me somewhat. Those things that attacked us earlier. They used to be human."

There was a rumble of incomprehension throughout the group. A murmur of anxious repulsion at the very thought that those things could ever have been men.

"So, firstly I'd like us to find out what the hells going on there. Maybe it's a natural occurrence in this world, but strangely I don't feel that's the case. The village John saw was walled, n I'm betting that for him to have seen that over ten miles means that they're pretty high walls.

Now we know what they're keeping out.

So, I suggest that we hit the town at first light tomorrow and make our enquiries.

Everyone agreed?"

Again there was a murmur throughout the group, then Eleanor spoke up.

"Yes Laz, I agree."

Kathryn, Vlad and Isaac all nodded their assent.

Only a surly and sulking John remained. Lazarus lay a comforting hand on his shoulder. "We're getting there boy. The more info we can get on our man before a confrontation, the better armed we'll be, yeah?"

John looked him in the eye, then seemed to deflate. "Sure Laz" he sighed "I guess your right old man".

Now, obviously a night spent out in these woods would require some precautions. These strange aggressive creatures where out there, and they could be attacked at any minute.

So, conversation fell to who would be taking what watch throughout the night.

However, the conversation was cut short when John announced that he'd take the whole watch alone.

"It'll be easier for me to do it guys. I can just throw a protective dome over the camp. That'll keep out any intruders.

If any of the rest of you stood watch you'd be limited to what direction you could face, and we've already seen them attack from two directions at once.

So, best I do it. It'll be easiest.

If any of the rest of you want to take watches with me during the night, I'd appreciate the company.

Give me someone to chat to. Oh, n help me stay awake too eh".

There was a chuckle from the others and a general agreement. So, now they set themselves to arranging who'd keep John company and when.

When the others had gathered together their bedding and were beginning to settle for the night, Eleanor made her way to Isaac and sat at the head of his bed. "Don't mind me" she said to him "You just go to sleep and ignore me. I won't be here long".

Isaac gave her a questioning glance, then, shrugging his shoulders, pulled the blanket over his head and lay down.

Eleanor gave Vlad a wink across the clearing. "Your turn later my son" she chuckled to him.

Vlad looked somewhat nonplussed at the prospect and looked around as though for help.

John had taken up a position at the encampments centre. Pulling his camping gear together into a pile as something to lean back against.

Vlad came over to him with his own rucksack in hand and sat down besides him. Leaning back and using his pack as a pillow.

"You pick the short straw?" Asked John amiably, grinning at his new companion for the next few hours

"Ahh, don't do yourself down mate" chuckled Vlad in response. "All this adversary hunting business is kinda exciting don't you think? You guys have done this kinda thing before. Fighting some dreadful foe and all that business. Words got round back home about you ya know. I'm a fan, you can tell me all about it all".

John looked across at Vlad with raised eyebrows.

"Seriously?" He asked in surprise. "your telling me I've got some kind of fan club or something? "

"Well, you've certainly caught Alexei's eye I can tell you that."

John shook his head "sheesh" he sighed.

There was a moment of silence, then John asked Vlad "so, what exactly brought you along on this trip then? Heading into unknown dangers and stuff. I take it you volunteered? Alexei didn't drag you into it unwilling like did he?"

Vlad laughed "Oh no, no. There was no compulsion on me. The thing is, where I come from, there's a lot of, how can I put it? Er, there's a kind of hierarchy based on your exploits, your contribution to the good of the tribe as it where. In order to get anywhere within the system you need to prove your worth. You need to show that you've triumphed over adversity and that you've faced down your fears. It's all a lot of macho bullshit, I know that, but that's Russia for you friend".

"Jeez. You have my sympathies mate".

There was a lengthy silence as they both stared into the forbidding forest that surrounded them.

The thought of those strange monstrous creatures out there was disturbing. They knew they were safely shielded by John, but the mental image of a number of these creatures turning up and battering and clawing at the invisible shield was rather disconcerting.

Then... "So John, this lady of yours we're here to save, she a looker?"

"Huh? Wha? " spluttered John "oh, er, well if you take a look over there at Eleanor you'll see for yourself. That's her body, Eleanors just wearing it for now".

"What? I don't understand mate. If she's here, who are we rescuing?
"

"We're rescuing Sophia mate. It's her mind that's been stolen, her consciousness. We've been left with an empty shell. That's how Eleanor can inhabit her as it were. So, our mission is to track down this Oblivion bastard that's stolen her and get her back. And if I have my way we'll leave the bugger dead when we've finished with him."

"Oh wow man" breathed Vlad " this is a lot more bloody interesting a mission than I thought it was".

John chuckled quietly.

"Yeah man, interesting, That's certainly one word for it old chap".

"Yeah. I'd just thought we had to find your lady and pull her out. But no, we've got your lady, what we're looking for is her mind for God's sake. That puts a completely different kind of spin on things".

"That it does Vlad my man. I take it then that Alexei didn't brief you on this trip very much?"

"Uh, no, not really" Vlad replied, chuckling himself now. "He simply made an announcement that there was a mission up for grabs assisting you UK brothers of ours. My hand had shot up before he'd got any further than that to be honest.

113

He picked me out. Guess it was finally my turn. Then, he simply brought me here. There weren't any words exchanged between us really. Oh, other than he mumbled 'don't show us up' to me before he left. Maybe he was leaving the prep talk and mission description to you guys."

"Ahh" sighed John "guess we should have asked the both of you if you knew what you were getting yourselves into before we left shouldn't we. Sorry man".

"Nah, don't worry about it buddy. I like a surprise me".

Now, the both of them fell into a fit of giggles.

Their conversation fell into the realm of basic chit chat and time passed as it is so won't to do.

There was a muted beeping from Vlads Digital watch and he glanced at it in surprise.

"Huh, that was quick. Sorry friend, shift change it seems. I'll go give Isaac a kick if he's not awake already"

He rose from his squat position and patted John gently on the shoulder.

"See ya in the morning yeah?"

"Sure" murmured John quietly.

Alone at last, John found himself staring up at the stars and an unknown constellation.

He was overwhelmed with a feeling of sadness.

The love of his life was lost to him. The fact of Eleanor inhabiting her body felt like an atrocity to him and he hated seeing her and knowing Sophia wasn't there.

He felt so powerless and the frustration was killing him.

Gradually, his sadness morphed into rage.

He brimmed with an almost uncontrollable anger at the unfairness of it all, and he swore to himself that when he got his hands on this Oblivion guy he was gonna tear him to pieces.

Suddenly, he heard the shuffling of feet off to his left and glanced up to see a very tired looking Isaac stumbling towards him.

One hand covering his mouth as he tried to stifle a yawn and the other rubbing at his red rimmed eyes.

John dismissed his anger as Isaac approached.

It was pointless letting himself stew like this. Besides, Isaac looked quite comical as he almost tripped over the root of aæe tree and had to grasp it's trunk to support himself. You'd have thought he was drunk rather than simply abruptly awoken.

"Hi Issac" called John as he approached.

"God's man" mumbled Isaac in reply "I knew I should have gone for first watch. Second watch just gives you enough time to finally get to sleep, then some gits kicking you in the ribs and bawling at you to get up. I feel completely wasted now I tell ya".

John chuckled sympathetically.

"yeah man. You soon learn on a gig like this to always opt for first watch. It's the only way you get to feel you've had any sleep.

Trust me. I've not really been on many missions yet to be honest. But travelling with Lazarus on board, you soon pick up his tricks.

He's been around a long time old Laz, n he knows em all."

Isaac crumpled down to the earth by Johns side and imitated the using of his pack as a pillow.

He groaned as he moved and John carried on chuckling.

"I feel like I've had a good kicking man" cursed Isaac. "Everything aches".

Johns chuckling stopped abruptly and a dark serious expression appeared on his face.

"Ahh, don't moan about that just yet Isaac my man. I have a suspicion that we'll all be getting a damn good kicking later on in this mission.

The guy we're up against is a tough Bastard and I have a suspicion we haven't got any idea of his true powers.

Being a worldwalker, what's to have stopped him visiting yet more artefacts. Acquiring yet more gifts".

 "Shiiiiit" Breathed Isaac. "N we're here to kick his arse huh?"

"that's right old chap" yawned John, again rubbing at his reddening eyes.

"It's our job to take the bugger out and probably save the bloody universe whilst we're at it. "

"Jeez man, you look tired brother" said Isaac.

"Why don't you give yourself a little nap eh?

I'm here now n I can keep the watch, no bother."

John gave a subdued, muted chuckle.

"Oh, I'd love to take you up on that man, but I've got to stay awake to keep us shielded.

Take a close look over yonder" and he pointed a finger to the hedging at their right.

Isaac peered closely, then took a deep breath of surprise. There, hiding amongst the hedging were at least five of those strange creatures that had attacked them earlier. They appeared to be pawing at thin air, their claws scraping at nothingness.

"bloody hell John" cried Isaac, pulling himself to his feet.

"And that's not all" replied John, and he swept his hand around to their left, and then jabbed a thumb over his shoulder.

Issac, looking at where John pointed, saw yet more of the creatures. There were hoards of them. Clawing and scrabbling at the thin air before them.

"They've got us completely surrounded if you look close enough. They try to conceal themselves in the shrubbery and stuff, but they're not very good at it".

Isaac stood gape mouthed at the number of creatures that stood in such a multitude and so close to their encampment.

"God's John. What do we do?"

"Oh, nothing for now old boy. We ,or rather you chaps should try and rest up. My hope is that come dawn they'll disperse with the sunlight.

I'm thinking that they're predominantly nocturnal creatures. Think back, it was twilight when they attacked us before.

Anyway. That's why I have to stay awake and keep the shield in place.

I can feel them you know.

The shield is like my skin, my flesh, it's part of who I am. And I can feel their breath on me, their perpetually scraping claws, It grates on your nerves after a while don't ya know."

"Does, does it hurt?" Stuttered Isaac.

"Huh? Oh, oh no. There's no pain involved. Just sensations, ya know? It's like being continually prodded and poked. All very irritating really".

At this he gave a forlorn laugh.

Isaac frowned down at John and shook his head.

"I don't know how you can stand it man. Something like that would drive me absolutely crazy"

"It's for Sophia Isaac, and she's my better half. For her I'd endure anything."

There was an uncomfortable silence between them, broken by a sudden laugh from John.

"Sit down man, your making me uncomfortable".

Isaac sat, pulling his backpack back into pillow position.

"So, anyway Isaac. To try to distract you from that rather unnerving image out there, let's have a chat eh?"

"Oh, er, sure man" spluttered Isaac, his eyes inexorably drawn to the host of beasts surrounding them.

"Just look away man and try to think of something else. We're shielded, so you've nothing to worry about. Unless they're still here come morning of course. Then we'll have to have a cleanup."

"Jeez" sighed Isaac. "You kids today eh? I really don't know how you manage to cope with all this crap".

John cocked an eyebrow at Isaac." kids?

Sure, I guess I am at that, I'm only nineteen. But how old are you then? I don't mean to be rude" at this he gestured vaguely at Isaacs appearance. "but I must admit, I kinda find it hard to tell".

"Yeah" chuckled Isaac " it's not easy being green" he sung quietly to himself.

"Now, where's that come from? Kermit the frog wasn't it?"

"Hell, I don't know man" laughed John in return "before my time I think".

"Well, to tell ya the truth John, I'm only in my late twenties. So, we're not all that far apart to be honest".

The two fell to idle chatter and waited for the approach of dawn.

Fourteen

When it came, it began as a dull red glow on the horizon. John suddenly discerned the occasional chirping noise from the woodlands surrounding him. Then, it was as though a switch had been flicked, and that horizon abruptly exploded in a roaring blaze of light and colour. It felt to him as though some kind of enormous bomb had gone off. The transition from its initial subtle hues to this superfluity, this cascade of light, was unlike anything he had experienced before. It's likeness to a bomb was added to by the noise.

At that moment of transition, from that dull red to this hugely intense vibrancy, there was an explosion of sorts, from the treetops.

The forest seemed to literally burst with airborne life. Birds of every possible size, and colour suddenly launched themselves into the air in a multitude of raucous cries and shrieks.

And it was loud too.

John saw both Lazarus and Vlad leap to their feet from where they'd lain on the ground wrapped in their blankets or sleeping bags.

Vlad was in fact still in his bag. He stood there in the bag staring up at the teeming sky, still zipped up to his chim.

Lazarus on the other hand had leapt straight for his arms and now stood staring up with his huge axe clutched tightly in his hands.

John meanwhile hadn't moved an inch. Even though Isaac besides him had immediately leapt to his feet and was now busy crying out in wonder and gesticulating madly.

No, John still lay unmoved. For some reason he couldn't have explained he'd kind of expected dawn to bring some form of excitement.

As he lay there, staring up into the bird filled sky, there was a wry smile playing over his lips.

This had turned out to be a rather pleasant surprise to arise to. He didn't know what he'd expected, simply that there would be 'something'.

Looking around the periphery of their camp he could see that the creatures of the night had disappeared too. So, all was well with the world... For now anyway.

He rolled over and pulled himself to his knees with the audible creaking and cracking of his joints. 'Gods, he ached' he thought to himself.

Climbing painfully to his feet with a sheer effort of will, he rubbed at the small of his back and groaned loudly.

"Morning John me lad" cried Lazarus in an incredibly irritating jolly voice.

John eyed him gloomily, then addressing the group as a whole, he said "right everyone, arm yaselves up n get ready for action. I'm switching off".

At that he mentally dropped his shielding and with a deep sigh drew his hand down over his eyes.

It was only now that he realised that holding that large shield in place for such a long period of time had drained him a great deal and he felt a strange kind of mental tiredness.

"sorry John" cried Lazarus, "that all nighters done you in I bet"

"Your not bloody wrong old man" replied John. "I wouldn't rely on me too much first thing today I'm afraid. My brain feels like mush and I'm sure my reaction times shot to hell".

"Aye" Lazarus exclaimed "I'm sure using and holding that gift of yours in place all night will wear a man down. Don't you worry yourself too much this morning son. We'll handle everything for now while you pull yourself back together. I just hope your back on form by the time we reach this village of yours".

The group fell to gathering together their equipment and packing their sleeping bags and blankets.

John simply slung his pack to his shoulder and he was done. He now simply walked the circumference of the camp, watching the others busying themselves over their paraphernalia and checking the boundary for sign of the nights intruders.

He could see claw marks on the bark of trees and tears in the surface of the earth. At one point he could see where a creature had attempted to tunnel under the boundary.

'Smart' he thought to himself. It wouldn't have worked but it was a logical idea. Perhaps these . creatures were a little less feral than he'd thought.

"right then chaps" came the gruff loud voice of Lazarus. "We all ready?" .

He turned to see the group all gathered together in the centre of the clearing. Their bags all appeared packed and the ground seemed clear of debris. 'right' he thought 'guess we're off then'.

"Ok Laz" he cried "the town was thataway" and he pointed in the direction of their goal. "ten miles or so at most".

"Right then" Lazarus growled "I'll take lead, followed by Isaac and Vlad. Then you John. We'll keep you in the centre since your so fagged out. Then Sophia, sorry, Eleanor, and Kathryn for our rear. You ok with that girls?"

"Sure" piped up Kathryn with a laugh. "Leave the ladies till last as always eh? Bloody typical ya bloody misogynist."

Meanwhile, John didn't have the energy to talk, and so simply nodded at lazarus's suggestion.

And so the group moved. They fell into their designated positions and followed Lazarus into the brooding forest.

Both Isaac and Vlad seemed very jumpy. Both of them scanning to the left and right as they moved forward and their hands gripping their weapons tightly.

Isaac was bearing a curved short sword, very much of the Spartan variety. Whereas Vlad had gone for a form of spiked mace. It looked rather heavy and imposing, but Vlads muscular arms seemed to wield it with ease.

Ahead of them Lazarus walked steadily forward, brushing aside interposing foliage with his huge axe. His feet moved steadily, as if to an unheard beat, and their progress through the forest seemed swift and unstoppable.

Suddenly, it seemed to John, they found themselves at the forests border, where lay a large clearing of a hundred yards or so to the bordering walls of the small village.

"So guys" asked Lazarus "how do you want to do this? You want to go over the walls and assess this place in a covert way or just go knock at the door?"

"I say we sneak in and have a look about" suggested Isaac.

"Don't be so bloody daft" coughed John despairingly. "In a town as small as this everyone is gonna know everyone. They'll all be deeply into each other's business, and a strange face will set off fireworks . No, we do the sensible thing and go knock at the door. Show ourselves to be innocent travellers and then try to pick up on the gossip".

Lazarus looked around at the faces of the group assessing their thoughts at a glance. Then "OK John. We go in the front door like civilized people and announce ourselves. I can't see where we could go wrong with that. I'm sure these are enlightened folk and that they'll be civil eh?

If it turns out to the contrary we're more than able to scrap our way out of things I reckon."

At this he began to walk out of the cluster of trees under which they lurked and strode towards the gateway to the town, beckoning the others to follow after.

The rest of them fell into a straggling line at his rear, bearing none of his enthusiastic energy.

There's was more of a lurch and a shuffle than a stride, but they tried to make up for that in their bearing. Attempting to look confident and natural.

As they reached the gateway they could see that it was a large oaken structure, definitely created to take a beating with its iron banding and studding. The hinges were concealed and as they looked closer they could see that it had the facility to drop a portcullis of some kind to further defend the structure.

To either side of this forbidding entranceway there lay a doorway to a closed off room and at its entrance stood a heavily armoured man bearing a long pike and with a Longsword and dagger at his hip.

Both men were stern of countenance and eyed them with obvious suspicion as they approached.

In a hale and hearty voice Lazarus hailed them both as he walked towards them.

"Well met my brothers" he cried "will you allow entrance to your good city to a pitiful band of travellers. We've just spent a night in that rather forbidding forest of yours, and needless to say, little sleep was gained whilst we endeavoured to keep ourselves safe from those awful creatures within.

Please, have pity on a fellow traveller through this life and give us the chance to break bread and find some lodging, within which we can finally find some rest"

All this was said in a rather breathy voice and John was sure he could detect the touch of a West country accent, which made him smile to himself. Lazarus was putting on a great performance and he wondered to himself how often he'd done this kind of thing before.

The guard to the right stepped forward with his pike held defensively across his chest.

There was a strange look of perplexity on his face, as though he couldn't believe what he was seeing. Was it they're survival of the forest that astonished him John wondered.

"But, but where have you come from" stuttered the guard, plainly shocked at their presence.

"Are you, are you denizens of HIM ?"

At the mention of HIM the guard seemed to genuflect, although it wasn't a cross he drew in the air before him. John thought it was a circle, but he couldn't be sure as the motion had been too swift.

"Er, no son. We've nought to do with 'HIM'. " replied Lazarus. Making quotation marks in the air with his fingers as he said the word 'HIM'.

"We're simply travellers in your land, seeking sanctuary, and we were hoping to find perhaps some food and briefly some lodging in your fine town".

The face of the guard was pale and he seemed visibly distressed at Lazarus's mocking like behaviour towards 'HIM'.

"But" he spluttered "if your not from 'HIM' then where in Zeus's name are you from. We're the only people on this world. That we know. So where have you all come from stranger?"

His hands had tightened on his pike and he had taken a backwards step, bringing the weapon between them.

Lazarus likewise took a backwards step and raised his hands, a perpetual smile on his lips, not of mockery or condescension but one of appeasement attempting to sooth and pacify the obviously shaken guard.

So, according to this guy, there weren't any other people on this world but them. That kinda screwed their passing travellers explanation then. Time for plan B he guessed.

"Right. Well, OK then son. To be totally honest we have amongst us a worldwalker. We're not from this world of yours but we're seeking someone. An enemy.

We know he's been here but is here no longer. So, we're on his trail and any information you can provide us will be a great help."

Coming clean. It was the only way to go he thought, and he had a fairly good idea already who this 'HE' was.

Trembling, the guard began to lower his weapon, staring at Lazarus with wide eyes.

"You. You have a worldwalker? "

He turned to his colleague at the opposing doorway, who had up until this moment merely stood his ground, unmoving and with his pike raised before him.

His countenance was a mixture of shock and disbelief and the two men exchanged wide eyed glances.

"I'll, I'll go get the tribune" stuttered the man in the doorway. And he retreated into his room behind him.

Obviously there was some form of alternative entrance to this town other than the huge ironbound doorway before them.

The wait, thankfully, was a short one.

The unearthly silence between them all during his absence was uncomfortable. They all just stood there exchanging glances between the remaining guard and each other. No one seemed to know what to do with themselves, whilst the guard just stood there staring at each of them in turn. His hands still grasping his pike tightly as he appeared to be trying to identify which one of them was the worldwalker by sight alone.

Finally, his colleague returned accompanied by three other men and a rather attractive, thought both Isaac and Vlad, young woman. One of the men bore with him a small bunch of twigs or sticks, hidden within the midst of which was something metallic.

John couldn't see what it was, but he had a good idea.

As soon as the man had mentioned 'getting the tribune' he'd thought "Roman".

That being the case, the patrician class carried, or would have carried for them, a bunch of sticks within the midst of which was a small axe.

He couldn't remember why or what the significance of it was, but it was a detail he remembered from his reading up on ancient history. It was just something that signified their stature somehow.

The conflicting detail that bothered him slightly was that nobody was wearing a toga anywhere.

The closest thing was the simple white dress worn by the woman. Everyone else was wearing breeches and shirtsleeves, or padded jacket in the case of the guards.

"what is this? " barked the woman in a surprisingly husky voice.

John thought that from her appearance he'd expected a voice far more feminine and light. Not this angry sounding growl.

The guard who had leapt to attention at her appearance, now stepped tremblingly forward, bowing his head in supplication as he approached her.

"My lady. Strangers, from the forest. They have said...they say that one of them is a worldwalker".

The woman's eyes flashed and her head spun to face them where they stood, huddled together like bashful children.

Lazarus stepped forward, taking the ladies hand and bowing his lips to it.

She snatched her hand back violently.

"who are you people?" she almost snarled "and what have you here?"

Lazarus took a step backwards a look of bemused astonishment on his face. He nodded his apologies and when he spoke it was in a tone of servility tinged with humour.

"My apologies my lady" he said "we are merely travellers in search of something, and we wondered if we might intrude on your hospitality for rest, refreshment and perhaps information".

The woman took a few steps forward, forcing Lazarus to step backwards once more.

"So" she growled "am I to take you to be the leader of this band of yours" and her hand swept across the area where they stood.

"What? Oh, oh no m'lady. My apologies for any confusion. The position of leader is held by our man John here".

At this he leant across and gave John a hearty and painful smack on the back, forcing him to stagger a few steps forward towards the woman in white.

"You bastard" snarled John under his breath to Lazarus.

"Well it's true John." He whispered back. "It's you we're all here for boy" .

The woman spun on her heel and faced John.

The frown on her brow deepened and he vaguely heard her murmur to herself "So young?"

She surprised him by gently laying a hand upon his shoulder.

"Why...are...you...here...child? " she asked slowly and brokenly.

John felt the familiar rage rise within himself and found it hard not to violently brush her hand away. He groaned and she could see his inner turmoil as he groped for words.

"We" he stuttered "We're searching for someone. Someone's been taken from us, and we intend to get her back".

The woman stared at him in mute silence.

Her eyes seemed to devour him, taking in the plethora of knives that adorned his body, and if asked he could have sworn they sparkled.

"Come" she barked "we won't talk of this here".

She then turned and gestured to a nervous looking guard, who immediately fell to banging on the main gate and bawling out a command that it be opened.

They could hear the heavy sound of braces being lifted and tossed aside. Then the metallic sound of bolts being withdrawn.

Throughout, the woman stood impassively and in silence. Her face was giving nothing away.

Finally, the huge wooden doors began to swing wide, and she turned to her two companions.

She mumbled something to the three, and the men suddenly sprung forward, darting through the opening ahead of them.

She turned back to them and turned to face John.

130

She held a pale hand out to him. "Come" she breathed.

John took the proffered hand in his and allowed himself to be drawn imperceptibly forward towards the open gateway to the town.

The others followed mutely, glancing back and forth between themselves as though to confirm that they were doing the right thing.

Passing through the arch of the gateway they found themselves led into an open courtyard.

It appeared much like your usual town. People ambling aimlessly around. Some people running market stalls. Fruit and veg mostly from what could be seen. There were people drawing wagons loaded with various produce and drawn by cow like beasts, the like of which none of them had seen before, and obviously native to this strange world.

The woman led them across the courtyard towards a tower like building that appeared to be roughly at the town's centre. The opening to the structure were two ornately carved wooden doors over which hung a sign.

'Court of justice' read the sign, in what John thought looked like Latin script, but which Eleanor, or rather Sophias ability allowed them to understand.

As they approached, the doors swung wide and they entered an immaculate looking reception area. There was a large wooden desk behind which stood a man dressed in a resplendent uniform of strange design. He was obviously an official of some sort and he leapt to attention at the appearance of the woman.

"Relax Ajax" sighed the woman casting him a relaxed wave of the hand. "We're heading to the boardroom. Please arrange for some refreshments to be brought up to us won't you"

She then led them to a large broad stairway. The steps appeared to be made of something marblelike in nature. Everything just appeared so polished and artful that John wondered to himself how often this place was used. Everything just seemed so new and untarnished in any way.

Perhaps they just had fantastic housekeepers.

She led them up the stairs, some way, passing closed doors en route, the stairway circling back around on itself as they ascended.

Finally the steps ended at a landing, leading to a large engraved door. Through this they passed, finding themselves finally in a large room, sparsely decorated and containing at its centre a huge oak like table surrounded by heavily upholstered chairs, each one looking like a throne unto itself.

"Please. Take a seat" spoke the woman, turning to face their entire group and seating herself at the tables head. Her hand finally releasing Johns, with what almost felt like a caress.

John exchanged a glance with Lazarus, then nodding he sat himself at the other end of the table, facing the woman, since he seemed to have been elected the group's leader.

The others took seats at random around him and everyone settled comfortably into the upholstered chairs with an audible sigh of contentment.

"Right" breathed the woman in white, leaning back into her chair luxuriously. "I believe we should begin with introductions. My name is Amelia, and I believe you would say that I am in charge of this little town of ours."

One by one the group gave their names, each of them at their most polite and respectful, coming to an end with John, as their mutually presumed leader.

"And I believe you would say that we are on a hunting expedition. Something has been stolen from us and we are in pursuit of the culprit" said John slowly in a low growl and passing his hands through his short blonde hair, before clenching them into fists on the table top.

She smiled slightly at this "Memories perhaps? Was it memories that were stolen?"

"No" growled John coldly "in this instance it was a person's whole consciousness. Her soul you might say. And we're here to track the Bastard down and get it back".

"Ahh" she breathed, leaning forwards towards John with a slight frown on her forehead.

And suddenly it was one of those moments.

As their eyes met across the table, it was as though the world paused for breath. The moment seemed frozen and encased in a purposeful aura.

Something indefinable seemed to pass between them. An unspoken urgency and sense of dread.

She now leaned back into her chair, her eyebrows raised. "So, she is your love? This one who's been taken?"

Another pregnant pause from John, then "yes. She is my love. And I want her back".

"yet another victim of ' HIM' then. You have my sincere sympathies. I've not heard of 'HIM' stealing a soul before, it's always been memories to my recollection.

Well, before anything else, please bare with me as I explain our own presence here on this world. Once again the result of 'HIS' actions.

It was, in retrospect, a very simple ruse. He simply gained himself control of Apollo's temple outside the city of Pompei.

Apollo is a very popular God and many people would visit his temple to give offerings or sacrifice on a daily basis. Within a handful of days he'd had a few hundred visitors. My own visit was out of, er, investigation shall we say.

I had become slowly aware that those that entered the temple never seemed to reappear.

Word was spreading that people were missing and confusion abounded.

So, I took myself to the temple, not knowing what to expect and so armed. I had bound a centurions gladius at my back beneath my robe. As the only girl born amongst a family of eight boys I considered my ability to fight well honed.

So, I entered the temple.

I had a little difficulty seeing at first due to the darkness of the temples interior. It took my eyes a while to adjust.

Finally I could make out the altar ahead of me. But things were wrong. There were no fires in the braziers, fires which were to be kept permanently lit. There appeared no attendant of any kind and my hackles rose. I turned to leave, to gather others, to draw some official attention to this issue. However, when I turned I found my way blocked. It was terrifying, and I don't scare easily. There, blocking my exit, stood a huge demon. Large horns, fangs, claws and eyes of fire. Demon is the natural conclusion I think.

I grabbed for my sword and gave a shrill scream.

The demon simply laughed at me and raised a staff before 'HIM'.

I struck 'HIM' a mighty blow with the gladius, a blow that should have severed his arm then plunged it point first into his chest.

The blow to his bare arm literally raised sparks as though I was striking flint, and had as much effect. The stab to his chest simply stopped. It was like stabbing a rock.

I heard 'HIM' say, "ahh, a feisty one. Good". Then I suddenly found myself momentarily lost amongst a forest of threads of light, before finally finding myself sprawled on verdant grassland with no habitation or any sign of man to be seen anywhere.

"build me a town" the creatue said, and then, 'HE' opened the universe, stepped through and was gone.

It took me but a short while to gather my wits, then to track down some of the others that he had kidnapped. They had camped out near the forest, some of them fashioning bows for the purpose of hunting to feed themselves. Some of the women had already begun to fashion themselves small gardens in an attempt to grow edible plants. There were a few disparate groups, separated from each other by their perceived hierarchy. Slaves in one group, merchants and the like in another, and yet another conceived of the elite. You understand my meaning.

Anyway, I can be quite belligerent when I put my mind to it and I forced them all to cast aside this foolishness and drew them together into a single group. Then it was the case of identifying those with skills, carpenters, metalurgists, builders and the like. Much to the fury of the previously elite. They had no skills, nothing to offer the group, and so were given the more menial tasks.

It was not long before we had created a new society. Eventually building this town you see now, after a few years had passed.

Elections were made for positions within our budding peoples, again much upsetting the previously elite. They were always worth watching and it took a few internments and eventually executions before they were completely integrated.

Remarkably, due to the great influence I'd had in drawing us all together and the instigation of various laws and the like, they elected me their representative, their leader through whatever troubles awaited us.

For we all felt sure that our abduction by a monstrous demon couldn't bode well for the future.

Anyway, by the time 'HE' made his reappearance, our town was roughly how you see it now. Minus the high walls.

One day, 'HE' simply appeared in the centre of town. There was no forbidding elemental precursor. No thunder or lightening to announce him. He simply appeared.

In a way that made the whole incident even more appalling. Even more terrifying.

'HIS' sudden, silent appearance. No warning at all.

Suddenly 'HE' was just there.

'HE' cried out for all to attend him as 'HE' had instructions for us.

Two young and impetuous warriors attacked him with swords in a savage and brutal strike from either side. And yet, again he simply shrugged off their blows with a blood curdling laugh and swept them both aside with a lazy sweep of his staff.

One of the men died instantly, the other is now crippled by his injuries and survives by begging in the street.

They were good men. Young and strong. Simply swatted away like flies.

Well, by now the majority of the townsfolk had gathered in the square, those that weren't quite sensibly in hiding that is.

Firstly, 'HE' gave us all an order.

"Build me a throne" 'HE' said, 'HIS' voice a deep baritone. "Yes. An iron throne. As ornate and decorative as you can make it, but no precious metals or jewels. Simply iron. I want it ready for when I next return."

His scarlet eyes flamed as he stared , across the hoard of upturned faces before him.

"Right, well I was only passing. I've acquired a new gift and I thought I'd give it an experimental try. Now, who amongst you considered yourselves the elite, the important, wealthy, powerful? "

"A few trembling hands were raised"

"No, I know there were more of you than that. I was there at your departure don't forget, and I can distinctly remember the promises of money or position if I spared your miserable lives. Now, once again please".

" now more hands were raised and some people began to wonder if the new gift of 'HIS' might be beneficial to them, and began to shoulder themselves forward."

"Ahh, that's more like it" 'HE' purred. "Now go and stand over there". He waved his staff towards the town's gate.

Around forty or so people did as instructed and gathered together in a huddled trembling group by the gate.

"right then" muttered this demon creature "as I said before, this is a new acquisition this gift, and I've not tried it out before. I have a vague idea what it'll achieve and I'm looking forward to the show, but bare with me a moment".

The creature appeared to frown as though deep in thought. Then, suddenly it's eyes cleared.

It took both its taloned hands and rubbed the palms together. Then, with a wide fang ridden grin it blew across its outstretched hands towards the grouped elite where they cowered together in fear.

It was like a cloud of dark powder. It was blown fiercely over the group, settling upon them like a settling of dust.

'HE' now stood with his hands upon his hips and watched them closely. We all did.

What was going to happen? we all were wondering.

We didn't have long to wait to find out.

Suddenly they began to twitch. They all seemed to bend at the waist as though bowed over in pain. Their hands were clenching and unclenching spasmodically. Abruptly a face would raise itself to the sky in a silent scream and we could see how their features had become deformed. Fangs now protruded from their mouths and some had grown horns. Their eyes were of a jet black, their eyebrows grown large and joined on a heavy forehead. Ears now pointed and neck scrawny and corded. Their fingers sprouted claws and these strange deformed monsters, faces raised to the heavens, howled in unison.

We had all retreated together in horror and fright and the creatures seemed to stare at us and visibly took long sniffs of the air. Drooling.

And then, with a bound, some on all fours, they ran for the forest and the cover of the trees.

"Ahh, how remarkable" 'HE' growled mirthfully.

"I regret to inform you that if you become bitten by one of my children and survive, you will in turn transform into one of them and join their pack.

However, they are nocturnal," ' He' gazed up at the sun. It still lay to the east as it was early in the day "so, you have some time yet to construct some defences".

And at this, he simply opened one of his tears in the fabric of the world, and turning back to us briefly before he left, said "don't forget my throne". And then he was gone.

Fifteen

Sofia lay the length of the sofa in the lounge and stared at the clouds in the bright sky beyond.

They were frozen in place these clouds. She had been staring at them for a long time now and no movement had been perceived at all.

It was all a sham she knew. Not just the clouds, oh no, but this entire manor. Every room and piece of furniture around her had simply been lifted from her mind, her memories.

Even she. This body with which she traversed the halls and the rooms. This too wasn't real.

This was all just a fabrication designed to lull her into cooperation, to relax her and to take her off her guard.

This bastard calling himself Pancras had somehow sequestered her consciousness, had ambushed her mind and stolen it away.

Initially she had felt some concern over her body. The flesh and blood Sophia. What would happen to it in her absence? Would it die?

But then she'd thought of John and the others.

They'd have come up with something she was sure. There's no way those guys would let her die, even if she was just a shell.

No. She'd taken account of her situation now and her early alarm had passed. Now she was thinking, thinking hard.

She knew that in those first early moments of her enslavement he had been able to wrest a great clutch of her memories from her. How much exactly she didn't know. Perhaps if she was lucky it was just surface stuff. But still, she did not know, and that bothered her.

Now. Now she was prepared, and if he tried to take any more memories from her she was determined to put up a fight.

She closed her eyes and flexed her mind once again. But no, she had no access to her power, her gift. It appeared that it required the presence of her flesh. Most frustrating, and kind of surprising in a way. It had always felt to her that it was a mental thing. The flexing of her mind had been such an intrinsic part of the process.

Well, apparently not.

Now, without her power to hand, she felt strangely naked and vulnerable.

She wondered how best to defend her memories in case HE returned for more. How do you put up a psychic shield she pondered.

She decided in the end that she would just try to blank her mind as much as possible. Then perhaps she could concentrate on some kind of story or plot. Fixate on something like a book or movie or something. She didn't know how effective a defender it might be, but it had to be worth a try.

She just wanted to go home. To her real home, her real body. She just wanted John.

"greetings my wise child" came that petulant sounding deep voice.

Her eyes came back into focus from their thousand yard stare through the large window at the frozen clouds and settled on the armchair opposite, where sat the figure of the one calling himself Pancras.

There'd been that foolish jest at her name again she thought. She had a suspicion that he wouldn't tire of that soon enough for her liking.

"Greetings Pancras" she answered, all the while she was busy singing Bohemian Rhapsody in her mind. She'd not been prepared and it was the first thing she could think of.

"Well, to business" he continued " there are a few things I wish to know Sophia my dear. The whereabouts of your artefact for one, and if you happen to know the whereabouts of any others? "

Sophia 's lips were sealed and Freddie Mercury did his magic somewhere at the back of her mind.

A slight puzzled expression crossed his face and an eyebrow rose. "Who's Beelzebub?" He asked in a tone of confusion.

'Yes!' Thought Sophia 'it's working', and she gave herself a little mental fistbump.

"I see we're going to have some difficulties today aren't we. If you think you can block me out my dear, rest assured, it's not going to be that easy".

She gave a wide smile and lay back in the assurance that she'd found the trick of it. She'd just keep her mind buzzing with songs and nonsense and she'd be able to block this son of a bitch.

"John" murmured Pancras, almost stealthily.

Immediately thoughts of her man engulfed her.

His father, his missing mother, his finding of his webbing of blades, his killings, his perpetual regretfulness and air of sadness at the lives he'd taken, his hiding of the artefact beneath the odd looking tree.

'ahh, dammit' she cursed to herself. The bastard had tricked her, and all it had taken was one word too.

"Ah hah" cried Pancras "that's what we're after. Thank you. But, what world was this?. It wasn't yours was it?"

But now Freddie Mercury was back and busting a gut belting out those lyrics. She was damned if she'd give him any more.

"Hmm, your walls are back I see. Let's try something else... Artifact".

Nothing. She was giving him nothing. And she was pleased to see the look of anger in his eyes.

"right then. If I can't get the location from you, then I'll have to look elsewhere won't I.

Your John was there wasn't he? In fact I believe it was he who actually hid the thing. I do believe I'm going to have to find your John. Ask him directly as it were.

Keep looking out of the window my dear, and you'll see what I see".

And then he was gone.

A brief visit today it seemed, and it wasn't like he'd given her a particularly harsh interrogation.

She kicked herself at her slip up at the mention of John. It had been so unexpected and he'd managed to get a large amount of info on her man.

Dammit.!

She shifted her gaze back to the large leaded window now, and saw that although it was still a sunny day out there, the view had changed.

Now everything was in motion, it was as though she herself were moving, like Riding in a car. But in this instance the forward motion consisted of lurches, alternately left then right. Also she could see the manor she lay in in the near distance, and she was approaching it at a steady pace.

She realized that she was looking through his eyes now, and that he was making his way to the manor.

In search of John.

Sixteen

The eyes of Pancras took a moment to adjust after stepping through the rift and into this bright place.

He now found himself standing on a luscious green lawn. Well mowed and surrounded by mature trees and scatterings of flowers.

Ahead of him he could see a large rectangular looking building of some sort of red stone or brickwork.

This must be the place they called the manor, he thought to himself. A fairly sizeable residence for sure, considering her groups small number. Still, he'd seen bigger.

He approached it blatantly. There was no caution needed here, he was nigh on indestructible these days, no one could oppose him.

As he reached the front entrance to the building he admired its heavy oak construction, banded and studded with steel and bronze. Yes, a very nice piece of work and should keep practically anybody out.

Suddenly he gave it an almighty kick, tearing out it's lock and ripping it from its hinges. The door was hurtled inside, coming to rest at the base of a large wide staircase.

He walked into the hallway then stood silently for a moment. Listening.

If there had been anybody nearby they'd have heard his entrance. And so he waited for someone to come running.

Nothing.

Well, this was a large structure. They might be in a relatively distant part and have not heard all the noise. He was going to have to search the place.

How damned irritating.

And so, he began to walk from room to room until he'd covered the whole of the ground floor.

He'd been quite impressed with their gym, although it had given him the strangest of sensations. He couldn't put his finger on what it was but there was some kind of familiarity to it. He was also somewhat perplexed by John's training room, not having known to turn it on to activate it.

He'd come across the almost concealed narrow winding stairway which had led to their room of change. However their artefact wasn't there, so he left that room plagued with a sense of having been cheated and nursing a feeling of inadequacy and anger. Regardless of the fact that he'd already known that they'd hidden it somewhere.

So, the ground floor was, it seemed, a washout.

Next step, up a floor and continue the search there.

He was beginning to become a little anxious that the place was empty. That everyone was out.

But surely, he thought. With their Sophia in such an empty state, they'd be busy looking after her shell. Not just going out. Oh, but perhaps they've taken her to some sort of medical facilities where they could keep her empty body alive. None of these fools would have any idea what was going on with her. That amused him somewhat, and he smiled to himself at the thought of their ignorance.

Still, if they were looking after her themselves then they'd probably be utilising a bedroom, and from what he'd seen, most people of this era seemed to locate their sleeping quarters upstairs. So, let's give that a try.

He marched, quite loudly, up the luxurious stairway to the first floor. Noticing for the first time as he reached the landing that there was yet another floor after this one.

At this he cursed.

Ahh well, let's get to it.

He searched the floor in its entirety. Stomping grumpily from room to room, swinging open each door and ducking his horned head under the lintel for a quick glance around before moving on.

Nothing....again.

He was beginning to become convinced that this manor was empty, and he very nearly gave it up and moved on there and then.

However, he was then struck by the thought, 'you've come this far', and decided to finish the damn job and search the final floor.

Consequently he stomped loudly and Ill temperedly up the final flight of steps.

He came to the first door, opened it, ducked and looked then slammed it closed again, splintering the frame and tearing out the hinges, and moved on to the next.

Locked.!

'Ah Hah.!' He thought, and raising his foot, he kicked the door from its frame, hurtling it across the room beyond and smashing it through the large window opposite.

"Jesus Christ" shouted a male voice from within, and he ducked his way into the room to see what he would find for all his efforts. Would this be the John he was looking for?

To the far left of the room was a large bed. Upon it lay an attractive though middle aged woman who appeared to be asleep. Unconscious was his guess as all of the noise he'd made would have most certainly woken anyone simply sleeping.

There was a metal pole by the side of the bed, holding what appeared to be water at a glance. This was then seemingly attached to her arm by a thin tube.

Then, at the foot of the bed stood a slightly balding man dressed in black outfit over a white shirt and with some kind of colourful piece of fabric hanging around his neck from his collar.

This man was standing, shakily, with his feet braced apart and he was holding out before him in both hands some kind of stubby metal thing.

"Stay away from her you monster" the man lisped at him.

From the little he'd skimmed from Sophia's mind so far he knew that the metal thing was some kind of weapon, though he couldn't see how. What was he supposed to do? Throw it at him?

It didn't even appear to have any blades on it.

Oh, what was it called again, er...oh, gun. That was it. The man Was holding a gun.

"Get back. Stay away" the man continued. "I'm not afraid to use this".

He walked forward. He wanted a closer look at this woman, and he wanted to ask this man the whereabouts of John.

There was a horrendously loud bang and something ricocheted from his forehead. This was followed by eight further bangs and eight further ricochets from the area of his head and face.

Stepping further into the room he swiped the gun from the man's hand, hurtling it across the room. He then took the man by the throat and lifted him from the floor, pushing him back against the wardrobe door.

"That, my friend, becomes tiresome very quickly" hissed Oblivion, his eyes blazing into those of the other. Then, suddenly, he released him and he dropped to the floor and fell to his arse.

"However" Oblivion continued "I must congratulate you on your accuracy. Your grouping of your shots, considering how badly you were shaking, was quite impressive".

"Now. Tell me. Where is the one called John? "

"I... I don't know" lisped the man. Nursing his gun hand that oblivion had struck. He was sure there were some broken bones there now.

"I just know that they called me and asked me to nurse Eleanor"

"This woman?" Oblivion gestured to where Eleanor lay, unmoving, on the bed."

"Yes".

"What's wrong with her?"

"Oh, not much really, she's just out".

"What?" Oblivion turned and fixed the man with an icy stare. "What do you mean she's out?"

"Well, she's one of you lot. You gifted chaps. And it happens that one of her abilities is that she can kind of step out of herself and inhabit the body of someone, or perhaps I should say something else, as she's quite fond of cats and dogs. So, it's just that her minds not there right now is all, and I'm looking after her body in its absence".

Oblivion froze. Inhabit the body of another?

Didn't they have an empty vessel on their hands since he'd taken Sophia?

But why? Unless it was to try to utilise her gift?

Could that be done?

If so, then they had a worldwalker again, and that could only mean they were coming after him.

But how could they know he even existed? He'd made no fanfare and they were a couple of thousand years from his time. They shouldn't have been able to make any kind of link.

Hmm, maybe they hadn't, and they were using a worldwalker for something else.

Suddenly he remembered that odd sensation he'd had back in the gym.

That was it. That was where they'd made their transition. If he checked that place out he might be able to track their trail. Find out where they'd gone.

He turned tail abruptly and bound out of the door, almost running back to that gym. The two in the room forgotten behind him.

They were of no consequence.

With Oblivion gone, George pulled a handkerchief from his breast pocket, and mopped at his brow.

Thank God that was over. He wasn't the hero type.

Seventeen

During all of this activity Sophia had been watching through the large living room window, which was now a representation of his eyes.

During his search through the manor Sophia had begun to feel a great sense of relief. The place appeared to be empty. No John or anyone else to cross paths with this Bastard Pancras.

But then he'd reached the second floor, and the locked door.

'Oh dear 'she thought, and suddenly the door was smashed inwards with tremendous force.

Suddenly she saw before her good old George, standing at the foot of a bed and pointing a heavy calibre gun directly at her. Also, lying there on the bed, looking dead for all she knew was Eleanor, but she assumed she was just on one of her out of body escapades.

Something passed between Pancras and George, but she couldn't hear what was said. This window wasn't equipped with audio regretfully.

Abruptly George's pistol flashed. In rapid succession there were nine flashes. All seemingly aimed directly at her, so obviously intended for Pancras's face.

She momentarily hoped George had killed the bugger, but the bullets just seemed to ricochet from his face without even rocking his head back from what she could see.

And then, in a flash George was being held up against a wardrobe by the throat, and again it seemed that they spoke.

The image within the window passed back and forth between Eleanor and the sweaty fear strained face of George.

George was then casually dropped to the floor with a quick flick of the wrist, and Pancras was on the move once more.

This time he was moving quickly and appeared to have a destination in mind.

Eventually he arrived and Sophia could see that it was the gym.

He'd been here once already but it was only now on his second visit that she noticed that the area had been cleared. All the gym equipment pushed back against the walls.

Oddly however in the middle of the room appeared to be a selection of the benches that usually sat back against the walls themselves.

They seemed to have been upended and then somehow cleanly sliced into pieces.

What was this? Were they experimenting with some new kind of weapon?

Pancras stood in the centre of the room and spread his arms wide, as though embracing the world. Then everything went black for her.

She stepped back from the window, cursing under her breath. Was the damn thing broken all of a sudden or was something more ominous occurring?

A moment passed and then the image returned flickering at first.

Ahh, she understood now. He had simply closed his eyes.

A faint line began to take form in front of her. A slight tear in the fabric of the world.

He was opening a rift, but he was doing it very gently, as though he was afraid of disturbing something.

There before her now lay an unending field of threads of light. All seemingly different colours, some she was sure unknown in the normal earthly spectrum.

Pancras gently ran his hands through these threads and she understood what he was doing now. He was searching for the thread used most recently from this location

She also now understood something else. She hadn't heard what George had said earlier, but she now felt sure he had described Eleanors ability, and he had come to the conclusion that she was inhabiting Sophias body and had managed to utilise her gift.

Sophia slapped herself on the forehead. Of course, Eleanor. Why hadn't she thought of her before? She would be able to keep her body in shape whilst she was here in confinement. But her being able to use her gift? That wouldn't have occurred to her at all.

Pancras stopped his caressing of the threads and his hands settled on one in particular.

However, he didn't pull on it. He simply froze in place a moment.

Then, suddenly, he straightened up, closed the rift, turned and left the manor.

Eighteen

The window image blinked out and the view of the manor garden with its frozen cloud returned.

"Well, well, well" came the voice.

Sophia spun on her heel. Shocked out of her wits by the sudden break in the silence.

Behind her, framed by the rooms doorway and leaning nonchalantly against its frame stood Pancras.

He looked slightly different to her, and she took a couple of steps forward to see him in a better light, as he was currently in shadow.

Then she saw it.

He'd gained two small hornlike things on his forehead and his eyes were now a deep scarlet.

She thought that perhaps his skin had become somewhat grey too, but she couldn't be sure.

Maybe his mask was slipping slightly she thought. Maybe she was finally getting to see something a bit more like the real him.

"What?" She asked, feigning innocence and ignorance of his meaning.

"Well, as you obviously know, me having allowed you to see what passed before me on my little excursion, there appear to have been developments.

It transpires that one of your crew, something that I didn't pick up from you before, has the ability to inhabit your empty body.

Now, it appears that she has also found the ability to utilise your gift. The place now being empty I have come to the conclusion that your little band are on the hunt for you my dear. Or more relevantly, on the hunt for me.

How they've learnt about me is what I'd like to know.

I've never entered your place before. When I took your mind I didn't pass through the rift at all. You know how it works. Your able to open a rift visible from one side only as long as you don't pass through it. From there you can see what's beyond and you can influence things there. So, from their prospective you simply crashed and burned, no one else was there. They saw no rift so shouldn't have linked your situation to worldwalking at all.

So, how is it they've suddenly taken that route. How is it that they suddenly seem to be aware of me. I've not even been on your damn world for thousands of years.

Well, if your lovely gorgeous John is going to hunt me down I do believe I'm going to need some sort of leverage.

Not that he could hurt me in any way of course. Oh no, he might be fairly powerful with that telekinesis of his, but my flesh is impervious to injury of any sort. There is no weapon on earth that can harm me.

However, he could become a damn nuisance.

Now, thankfully, since he's your darling John he was forefront in your mind when I took you, so I know more about him than anyone. Consequently this has given me the perfect bit of leverage I'll need.

Just a little trip to pick it up, then off to your love for a little confrontation.

Oh yes. I examined the strands from where they left. They'd made no effort at concealment or obfuscation of any kind. I'm sure your current lodger, new to your gift, wouldn't have known how, or perhaps even thought of it."

"Did you?" Blurted Sophia

"What? "

"Did you conceal your movements through the threads?"

"of course not. Having taken you I thought I was the only walker"

"There have been walkers before" Stated Sophia bluntly "and since we can use time".

"One my dear. Only one on record, and he's been very quiet

Anyway, I want him off my back. I don't want some damn child running around interfering in my activities."

Finally, his ranting ended and there was silence.

"Don't hurt him" Sophia Whispered. "Please".

He took two strides towards her then halted, his arms crossed across his chest.

"Girl" he growled under his breath "if he gets in my way I'll tear him to pieces. But I'm going to be generous. I'm going to make him an offer. An offer he cannot refuse. As long as he makes the right decision, and I'm sure he will" at this he gave a slight chuckle. "Then all will be well. We can move on contentedly and never meet again".

"What.... What's your offer? ",

"That my dear you will have to wait and see. You'll find out at the same time he does".

Then, once more chuckling to himself, he vanished.

Nineteen

Amelia, having finished her discourse gestured to one of her men who stood at attention by the entrance to the room.

He, in turn, swung the door wide and a flurry of young women attendants rushed into the room bearing trays of food and flagons of various beverages.

This was obviously the refreshments she'd requested earlier. They'd been available for some time it seemed. Just outside the room and waiting on a signal from their tribune before they were allowed to serve.

Amongst the platters were a selection of cold meats, a roast fowl of some kind, also something that resembled a roast boar. It was very similar in shape, quite difficult to tell at this post roast stage, but Lazarus thought that there was something peculiar about the bone structure.

There were also a variety of breads and a selection of fruit. Some of which were definitely unfamiliar.

All round quite an impressive selection for some light refreshment.

"Please, help yourselves." Purred Amelia "after having spent a night in our woods I'm sure you require some sustenance. Frankly, I'm very surprised to hear that you managed such a feat. Those creatures travel in large packs and they would have smelt your presence there as soon as night fell".

Amelia, Lazarus and John rose from the table together and walked slowly to a window overlooking the village, still speaking as they walked.

"Hmm, yes well" Lazarus began "You know that we have a worldwalker amongst us, yes?"

"I do" answered Amelia.

"Well, that is not the only gift within our little band. We each of us possess our own gift, and it was with the use of one of those abilities that we were able to survive a night in your lovely forest".

John flashed Lazarus an angry and surprised look. What was the man doing for God's sake? You don't go around telling virtual strangers about our powers damn it.. That's usually a given. An unwritten rule of law as it were.

Amelia froze in place, her eyebrows raised in mild shock.

"you mean to say.... You mean to say that you all have powers? Like.... gods? "

"Oh no, no, no" spluttered Lazarus around the drumstick he'd been chewing on experimentally.

"We're definitely not God's my lady. We are merely men, men who have been granted gifts beyond the normal ken".

"Laz?" Muttered John warningly

"Ahh, don't worry John" sighed Lazarus in response " I feel it necessary that we begin our negotiations with this lady in a completely open and honest way.

Our hostess here is an intelligent woman and understands that we're after 'HIM' .

She understands that a battle beckons and if by chance 'HE' reappears here before we've moved on, then that battle is going to be in her backyard.

She will have to suffer the consequences, if, by chance, we lose. "

Lazarus paused to brush crumbs of food from his chest with a begrudging tut.

"So, I feel it only fair to make her aware of what we're bringing to the fray. Also to make it clear to her that we wouldn't expect she or any of her subjects to involve themselves.

If battle comes it will be only between we and 'HE'.

Amelia gave Lazarus a gracious nod of the head and smiled.

"And I thank you for the courtesy sir.

How do you suggest we continue from this point.

Am I to assume that this is but a quick visit and that you'll be continuing your pursuit tomorrow?

Or do you plan to stay with us for any length of time? "

At this Lazarus scratched at his stubbly beard and turned to face John .

"What's your thoughts boy? We setting off first thing or you wanna give Eleanor some time to see if she can't find out where he's at first?"

John felt momentarily overwhelmed. He was furiously anxious to get to grips with this oblivion bastard, and so leaving as soon as possible was his initial impulse. However, if he gave Eleanor a little more time, she might be able to identify exactly where he was at rather than just where he'd been.

John ran his hands through his hair then down across his face and his closed eyes.

"Ok Laz" he muttered "let's give Eleanor a day. See if we can't pin this bastard down for certain. Finally get my hands on the son of a bitch".

He glanced back over his shoulder at the table and their group of antagonists. Eleanor caught his eye and gave him a wave.

"Hey, are we gonna make ourselves some kind of plan or what?" She called.

John's face cracked into a worthless grin and he turned back to Amelia.

"I'm sorry, but have you a largish area we can run through some tactics and that kind of thing. Prepare ourselves as it were for our run in with Oblivion when it comes"

Amelias's face looked mildly shocked as she drew in a slight gasp and her hands performed that strange motion he'd seen from the guard outside earlier.

He suddenly realised that he'd named Oblivion for the first time. Till now it had always been 'HIM' or 'HE'. Obviously they had something against the name.

She saw the puzzled look on his face and gave a slight sigh followed by a self conscious smile.

"You may think it foolish young John, but our people have become slightly superstitious over everything that's happened. In this case, it's the old adage of 'Speak the devil's name and he shall appear'. We try to avoid referring to Oblivion as much as possible".

As she said his name her voice dropped to a quieter tone and she seemed to surreptitiously look around the room.

"Er, with regards to a training locale for you" she began, shaking herself back to the moment. "Perhaps you'd consider outside at the gathering place. It's where we built that creatures throne and so consequently it's avoided by the populace. You'd have the whole area all to yourselves."

John looked up at Lazarus for confirmation but the old man just shrugged. "Your call boy".

Rubbing at the slight beginnings of stubble scattering his cheek and chin, John gave a decisive nod. "Ok. It sounds ideal. Let's do it".

He looked to Amelia. "Would you mind showing us the way".

"of course" she sighed in reply.

John turned to the group at the table. "Right team" he called loudly "gather up ya kit, we're heading out for a run through".

"about bloody time" called Eleanor in response, and there was staggered chuckling throughout the party.

And so, with Amelia at their lead, they headed to the door and the gathering place.

Twenty

Sophia still lay the length of the imaginary sofa, in the imaginary lounge of the imaginary manor. Still staring through the large imaginary window at the frozen imaginary world outside.

She had no idea how long it had been since that Pancras arsehole had last paid her a visit. Here, she had no idea of the passing of time at all. The clock on the mantlepiece might tick but the hands themselves always remained frozen at just past midday.

She wished she could just go to sleep. Turn this horrendous reality off and hide in dreamless darkness.

But again, since even she was imaginary here, her body felt no tiredness, and sleep would be an impossibility.

She was just a formless consciousness, tucked away somewhere in that bastards head.

She'd wracked her brains in an effort to find some way of fighting back, but to no avail.

She was powerless, and that fact was slowly driving her mad.

Suddenly, there was that damned infuriating voice again.

This time it came from somewhere behind her and she pulled herself up on the couch and looked over its back to find its source.

There he sat at the table. The usual computer hardware all pushed to one side and an enormous cloth covered box of some kind sitting in its place.

There was a slot of some kind in the centre of the material, allowing a metal carry handle to protrude from its top.

His horns had gone and he was back to his enigmatic self. Obviously his previous frustration was in retreat and he felt back in control.

"Still lounging around?" He had said. Fanning the smouldering flames she felt inside.

Sophia simply gave an irritated humph and threw herself back into lounging position.

She wasn't going to let this bastard wind her up. She wanted to hear nothing from him other than to let her know he was releasing her.

"John" he cried, loudly.

She quickly tried to blank her mind, sing a song or something, whatever it took to block him out.

But she knew she hadn't been fast enough, he'd caught her unprepared... Again. And she knew a little info had got through. Only a little, she thought, but anything was too much if he was planning on using it against her man.

"Yes, yes" he muttered "I already know he's a big whiner over all the people he's killed. But what's this?

Skulls?"

She knew then he was thinking of John's knives and their skull designed pommels.

"Skulls" he said again. "Now what the hell does that remind me of?

Something I've heard somewhere.

Hmmm. No, nothing. Oh well I'm sure it's not important. Or if it is, it'll come back to me".

"what the.hell do you want?" snapped Sophia "are you here to mock me or to threaten my boyfriend again?" .

Pancras gave an evil smile. "Well, actually, yes. The latter that is."

With a sly sounding chuckle he tapped the top of the large box beside him.

"I think I've now found the shackles for your lover. I've a surprise for him that ought to dissuade him from his continued pursuit of me.

"you want to be free of him, then just give me back" hissed Sophia.

"Oh, I could, I could" he murmured, as though to himself. "I really don't think I'm going to get much more out of you now. But I just don't like having my hand forced my dear. It angers me to be pushed. Whatever I choose to do will be at my discretion, not forced on me by trivialities like your man John."

"He'll kill you you know" growled Sophia in a fit of sudden rage at this creature.

Pancras gave a harsh laugh. "Oh yes. John the killer. Hah, and then I'm sure he'll weep over me afterwards"

"Not for you he wont" Sophia whispered.

Still chuckling to himself, Pancras tapped the top of the box on the table before him.

"Well, your John is going to be faced with a dilemma. One that I'm sure will relieve me of his harassment."

"What have you done?" Asked Sophia anxiously " what's in that box? "

"Ahh, my dear" chuckled Pancras , tapping at his nose with a finger "that you will find out soon enough. When your John and I meet. Soon."

And then, as before, he was gone.

"Damn him" cursed Sophia.

She didn't know what he had up his sleeve, but she was worried. He had claimed he was going to put John to the test. She was worried for John. Would he be up to whatever was coming at him?

Twenty one

The group had gathered in the courtyard near the throne that
Oblivion had demanded be built.

He'd told them to make it of iron, no gemstones or frills of that kind,
and they'd done a fair job.

Obviously their smithy was kind of stuck in his ways and all his
work was of a similar theme. Swords. The bulk of the throne seemed
to be made of interlaced swords, the rear of the throne a fanlike
affair of blades. At first glance John thought it looked very much
like that throne depicted on the tv series 'Game Of Thrones'.

"Nice" he said in a long drawn out breath. "I like it. I do. Doesn't
look too comfortable though to be sure".

"Good" growled Amelia who had suddenly appeared at his side, her
hand resting on his shoulder.

"Personally I hope it cuts his balls off".

"Ouch" sighed John "let's hope huh?"

He noticed a platform off to the thrones right, where stood two men
either side of a large looking bell.

He gestured to it. "What's that?"

"that's the alarm" she sighed. "We built the throne at the point he
enters our world. It seemed like he might appreciate that. The men
are there to raise the alarm at the first sign of one of his rifts in the

world appearing. Give us time to be prepared and for some, those with the greatest fear, to take to the hills."

"Damn good thinking" said John "from what I've seen of these rifts, if the alarm comes at first sign of it you should have just under a minute."

He turned back to the rest of the group who seemed to be loitering near the courts entrance.

"right guys" he called, and the group spread out somewhat. "Its time we put our heads together, work out our mode of attack yeah?

Now if anyone has any ideas, any at all, tell the rest of us. Even if you think it's a stupid idea, I want to hear every suggestion you've got".

Vladimir raised a hand in the air tremulously and John chuckled. "You don't have to put your hand up Vlad. Now, what ya got".

Vlad shrugged and shuffled his feet slightly.

"Well, I was just gonna say that if we're out here to do a kinda run through as it were, then maybe we should use that throne thing over there as our target. Use it as the enemy, ya get me?"

John looked from Vlad to the throne and back, then nodded decisively. "Yeah Vlad. Good idea. Chaps?"

Here he pointed at the throne "that's our target, yeah?"

The group all nodded and there was a mumbling sound from them all.

"I've a thought" called out Isaac.

"Yeah? What ya got man?" Replied John .

"Well, I was thinking that the ladies, no disrespect" here he tugged his forelock towards the girls " Well I was thinking we should keep them out of the main fray, keep them to the back like. It's just that if Eleanor gets taken out we don't just lose our coms but we end up stuck on this rock too".

Again John nodded "I'd had some similar thoughts myself, but with a twist. Kathryn?" He called " yeah, whatsup? " was the response.

"I'm thinking that you and Eleanor stay way back, but that you also use your gift to turn yourselves invisible. Then he won't expect anything from your location. Then, he might well be bloody bulletproof but he's still got eyes like the rest of us. So on a called keyword or something you blast his eyes with light. Blinding him, even if it's just momentarily, might make all the difference".

"uh huh" responded Kathryn "I like it. To be honest John I can focus a laser beam and take out an eye permanently. Well, hopefully permanently. You don't know the extent of his power".

Vladimir jumped in. "Yeah. How about as soon as he's actually here, stepped through or whatever, you give him one of your lightbursts, then simultaneously with that me and Isaac come at him from left and right. Hit the bastard hard. "

"Yeah, I like it" said John.

"What about me boy" said Lazarus, his tone of voice indicating he felt rather left out.

"Christ, I don't know old man. I guess you come at him from the front with me".

"and how are you gonna come at him lad? You know that your blades will probably just bounce off the bastard" Lazarus asked thoughtfully.

"Well" John began, his face screwed up in thought. "Firstly, before he's through I'll have scattered a number of blades in a semicircle behind his point of entry. Up in the air like, three or four meters or so. Sure, I might not be able to hurt him with them but I might be able to confuse him a little. Then, I guess I'll just have to come at him straight up, blades in hand. I can hit him with conclusive blasts on the approach, keep him on his toes."

A thought obviously entered his mind .

"Oh, and I can envelope his head in a shield. Cut off his oxygen, assuming he needs any".

"woo hoo" cried Vladimir, "that's the stuff man, yeah. This asshole doesn't stand a chance".,

"Right boys" called out Eleanor "everyone assume your positions n stuff and I'll link us up. Ok?"

"all good maam" cried Vladimir and made his way to the right of the throne. Isaac likewise approached the left. Studying the soil and his environment as he did so.

Lazarus and John walked back to where the girls stood at the rear. John slipped on his helmet and lowered the visor.

Eleanor briefly closed her eyes, then opening them she sent out a mental call. "Coms check boys. Vladimir? "

"Here" came the mental shout and Eleanor winced.

"Isaac?"

"loud and clear m'lady". Came Isaacs response.

"Lazarus?"

"On the spot girl".

"John?"

There was a lengthy mental silence, then " John? " Eleanor called again.

Nothing.

She stepped forward and grasped him by the shoulder "You not hearing me lad?" She asked him in a concerned voice.

"Hearing what? " he asked in puzzlement. "Have you started then?"

"Yes" she sighed "and it looks like I can't connect to you for some reason. My thinking is that it's that helmet of yours".

John slipped the helmet off.

"Try now" he said.

"John? Ya hearing me?" She sent.

"loud and clear" he sent back.

"Right, so the helmet cuts me from coms" John sighed "well, I guess I'll just go to battle without it then. It's not like I need it" .

"No John" growled Lazarus "if that helmet keeps out Eleanors gift, then it'll probably protect you from HIS mental powers too. Protect your psyche, your memories, your consciousness".

"I agree" said Eleanor with a smile "Don't worry, your forgetting we brought those walkie talkies. This is just the kind of thing they were for, right?"

John held the dark helmet in his hands, turning it over and over. "I wonder where the hell all this kit came from in the first place"

He nodded thoughtfully. "Well, I never knew the helmet was capable of that. But truthfully, if this thing can protect me from his power then that's a great advantage".

"sure is" said Lazarus "just make sure you've got the bloody thing on eh".

"Mate, from this point on, it's never coming off" John chuckled.,

"Right, hang on a mo" John continued, as he went through the contents of his pack. He finally pulled out his walkie talkie and set it's frequency, which he confirmed with Eleanor. This particular model of walkie talkie came with ear buds and a clip on mike. So, taking off his helmet momentarily, he inserted the earbuds. Then once the helmet was back in place and the mike clipped to his collar he gave the set up a trial run.

"You hear me now love?" Called John. " Yes, yes" responded Eleanor in slight irritation "no need to shout".

"Excellent" said John. "Now, it looks like I can keep the line permanently open on this thing. So, I'll do that" he fiddled with the unit "then I don't have to press any buttons or anything".

"Sorted then" said Eleanor "just don't forget, from this point on I can hear every word you say" and she gave a malicious chuckle.

The rest of the group set their own units to the same frequency to complete the circle of communication amongst them. And John made a mental note not to slag anyone off whilst he was hooked up with this gear.

"Right then" John called, though not so loud as before. "Lets get back to it guys.

Everybody assume your positions"

He paused a moment, then "done? Good. If we assume that he's coming through now, you wait till he's completely in this world, then kathryn, you flash him, nice n bright, then Vlad and Isaac attack."

Meanwhile, Vlad had checked his surroundings and found a layer of granite at his feet.

Lowering himself onto one knee, he thrust his fist hard into the granite. Where one would have expected knuckles to bruise and bleed, instead it appeared as though his fist had actually melded with the stone itself. Then, rapidly, the granite seemed to grow from his rooted hand, up around his arm, shoulders, chest and face, until, in his place stood a giant of stone.

Opposite him, in the other side of the throne, Isaac had shrugged off his concealing hooded robe, and flexing himself, long claws began to protrude, his tail seemed to reform itself into a sharp pointed blade, and fangs hung over his lower lip.

He assumed a crouched position as though about to leap forward.

"Good, good" resonated John's voice amongst the multitude of walkie talkies. "We're right on schedule guys. Now, Eleanor, he's through the rift".

Suddenly Kathryns voice was in their heads, calm and composed. "Close your eyes guys".

And then it came. A blast of white radiant light. Piercing and intense. It wasn't a short flash like that of a camera, but lasted for a couple of seconds, the better to blind it's target.

The moment the blast of light was over both Vlad and Isaac leapt forward. Isaac a whirling blur of sharp edges and Vlad a cacophony of crashing fists. Upon teaching the throne they both came to a sudden halt with a high five.

"Yay..! " screamed Isaac whilst Vladimir was only capable of giving an approving roar. Deep and resonant through his stone larynx.

"Good going boys" called John, smiling enthusiastically. However, there was the slight glimmer of disquiet in his eyes.

"And what happens next" sighed a brooding Lazarus "when our initial attack is unsuccessful" .

There was a moment's silence, and an atmosphere of malign powerlessness settled over the pair.

"Well, then I guess it's up to me and you. We take a walk up to the bastard and twat him"

He gestured to the sky above the throne and for the first time Lazarus noticed the semicircle of blades suspended in the air behind it.

He'd not seen John release these and he "humphed" with approval at the boys skills of concealment.

"Well, I've not got much to offer I'm afraid" Lazarus sighed. "There's just me and this old axe. So, I guess I'll just walk up to him and try n clobber him. But if he's already passed through these two" he gestured to Isaac and Vlad. "Then I don't think I'm gonna have much effect son".

"to be honest old man" John breathed, his voice sounding worried "I'm in much the same place. If your axe and my blades are just going to bounce off this guy, then what can we do?"

There was a lengthy silence as both men gazed at the iron throne with pained expressions.

"Well, when the time comes, I guess we'll just have to have a chat with the bugger".

175

"a chat? " asked Lazarus in a confused voice.

"Yeah. Negotiate like".

"what have we got to negotiate with? " Lazarus chuckled.

"Our perpetual, never ending pursuit and harassment of the swine".

Again, a lengthy silence.

Then "I like it" Lazarus breathed, smiling a wicked looking smile.

Twenty two

Amelia allowed them quarters in the tower for the night.

The place was deceptively large and they could well have been able to have a room of their own each. However, they chose just the one large room to share. Insistent that they all bunk up together. There was safety in numbers.

Eleanor, as before, insisted on spending some time with each of them as they attempted to go to sleep. However, now it was only for a very brief interval, and so didn't intrude on anybody's slumbers too badly.

Finally, lying on the marble floor, a rough blanket thrown over him, in a room full of snores, John stared at the ceiling.

He was definitely feeling disquieted, as Lazarus would say. His own definition would have been that he was creeped out. He had that
176

feeling that there was something terrible hiding just out of sight. Somewhere in the periphery of his vision, just waiting to spring. He felt, no, he knew, somewhere inside, that there was something terribly wrong out there somewhere, and that he was going to cross paths with it imminently.

It most definitely wasn't a pleasant sensation, but he just couldn't shake it off.

It was late. Way past midnight, he knew.

Even Eleanor had finished her strange routine at everyone's bedside a long time ago now, and was lying on her side snoring gently.

"You ok John?" came a quiet whisper from his right.

He started convulsively and momentarily. The voice had made him jump, he'd thought himself the only one awake in this still, dark, silent room.

Turning his head he saw that it was Kathryn. She lay on her side, her head raised on the palm of one hand, the elbow planted firmly on the floors cold surface.

"Can't sleep?" She asked softly.

"Er, no. Afraid not love. I seem to have too much on my mind I guess. Can't seem to switch off, ya know? "

"Uh huh" she breathed "I get ya John, really I do. We've got a lot at stake here. Sophias family, and none of us want to let her down. But John? There's only one thing you can do for her".

John pulled himself up onto his elbows and stared at her hard.

"And what's that Kat?"

177

"your best son. Just do your best. She couldn't, and wouldn't ask for more".

John threw himself back to lie once more on the cold marble floor. He got it, he did. He knew what she was trying to do for him. Unfortunately, he also knew it wouldn't work.

He rolled over, turning his back to Kathryn.

"Goodnight Kat" he whispered.

"Night John. Sleep tight huh?" .

Twenty three

Dawn came, in a tentative almost bashful fashion. As though ashamed of waking the group from their dreams or concerned for them all at what the day might promise.

Lazarus groaned and stretched and rubbed at his eyes before opening them to the grey mornings light.

Immediately he saw that John sat at the large table. Leaning back into the upholstered throne of a chair and with his feet firmly planted on the tabletop.

He was leisurely tossing one of his dark blades at a cat like creature that lay sleeping on the top of a cabinet against the far wall. Tossing

178

the blade, yet stopping its flight before it could strike the beast and recalling it to his waiting hand. Time and again.

Throw... Recall.... Throw.... Recall, it was almost hypnotic to watch.

"John" he called to the boy "are you ok lad?"

"Huh?" cried John suddenly, as though woken from a trance. The blade stopped in his hand and was quickly sheathed.

"Eh?" Gasped John " what? Er, oh, yeah, I'm good old man"

Now that, thought Lazarus, was obviously a lie.

He threw off his sleeping bag, climbed to his feet with an involuntary groan, and made his way over to the table and John.

The others around them were beginning to stir.

Sitting himself down next to John at the table he noticed how thin and pale he looked. There were dark circles under his eyes and under close examination he could see that the boys hands were trembling.

"You don't look ok kiddo . In fact, to be brutally honest, you look like crap.

What's up son?"

"Christ, I don't know Laz" groaned John, leaning his head back and staring at the ceiling. "I don't know what it is, I can't explain it, but I just have the strangest sensation of imminent approaching doom. There, that dramatic enough for you?"

"Aahhh, come on lad, it's just stress. Stress and worry. We're here to save the woman you love. We don't know how things are gonna go, if we'll be able to get her back or if we're all going to die. So, I'd say your feelings are probably quite appropriate. "

John tilted his head back down to face Lazarus, then, suddenly broke into a grin.

"Ahh Laz old man. You bring me such comforting words. Nah, your probably right, just stress. It's just it feels like so much more than that. As though I'm on the brink of something."

Lazarus slapped John on the shoulder "come on then lad. Let's see what our hosts can supply us for breakfast, then we'll get Eleanor cracking on tracking this arsehole down".

All were now up and about, packing their bedding and preparing their kit.

"we all up to speed guys? " asked John.

"Sure are" called Isaac.

"We're practically good to go boss" added Vladimir.

"Cool" sighed John, almost to himself, "Eleanor, are you up to, er, searching the web as it were for our target".

"Ahh, searching the web. I like it John. Not bad for you. You been saving that one up? "

John just shrugged and smiled.

"Well John, I'll give it a go now ok? Maybe if I have no luck you'll let a lady get herself around some breakfast before she tries again eh? "

She took one of the comfortable seats at the table, leaned back into its cushioning and closed her eyes.

John turned to ask a question of Lazarus, when suddenly he heard Eleanor cry "oh shit" under her breath.

He spun back to her to see she was already back to her feet and heading towards kathryn, snatching up a walkie talkie as she did.

He was about to ask the question, finger raised before him and a half smile on his lips, when he heard it.

The frantic ringing of a bell.

"Shit" John repeated "everyone?" He shouted "to the throne, assume your positions. The buggers here".

The whole group burst into action, until, snatching up his helmet on the run, John found himself to be the last one to exit the room.

Erupting onto the courtyard, helmet now in place and visor down, John was pleased to see Vladimir and Isaac in their positions. Vladimir's fist thrust into the ground, his body encasing itself in granite. Isaacs cape thrown to the ground and all his sharp edges in place.

He himself released eight of his blades from their sheaths and propelled them into the sky, where they spun for a moment, then settled into the semi circle in the air behind the throne.

He couldn't see Kathryn or Eleanor anywhere, but that was good, that was the plan.

Kathryn would have bent the light around them and rendered them invisible.

John saw that the glowing rift in space had now lengthened dramatically, and first one booted foot, then another appeared at its base as the huge figure stepped through. Apparently it was bearing a large box, covered by a coarse blanket and it had to duck slightly due to the inconvenience of its horns.

John was about to shout, to drop his raised arm to signal kathryn. But before he could do either, it came. That flash of intense blinding light that lasted a couple of seconds.

He assumed that Eleanor had told the boys to close their eyes and glancing round he could see that Lazarus had closed his. He wasn't in their mind loop of course, and it seemed that the walkie talkie had been forgotten. However, luckily, his visor had seemed to protect him from the blast. He'd seen that there had been a blast, but it was as though his visor had dimmed, just enough, at the right moment.

Sometimes he counted his lucky stars that he'd found all this kit when he had. Hidden in the basement as it was, it could have lain gathering dust for eternity.

Isaac hit first in a green blur. Oblivion was slashed and stabbed uncountable times in mere seconds. However, only his clothes seemed to bare the effects. A sleeve was torn from his coat, his shirt and breeches were slashed open in a multitude of places. But his flesh didn't show so much as a scratch.

Bent over and rubbing vigorously at his blinded eyes, he was still able to suddenly snatch Isaac out of the air before him with one hand, and hurl him with all his might at a wall off to the side from where Isaac had originated. He then took his staff and spun it in his hand. For the first time, John noticed that the base of the thing was one long bladed spike.

This he now hurled after Isaac, striking him in the shoulder and pinning him to the wall.

He was lucky it was just the shoulder thought John, if he'd caught it in the chest as was probably the intention, he'd have been dead for sure.

Vladimir hit next. Huge granite fists raining down upon the bowed head of oblivion as he rubbed his eyes. You could see that Oblivion was effected. He initially fell to one knee under the force of the blows, and his body rocked mightily. However, he didn't appear in any way injured, simply moved by the force of the impacts upon his person. Finally he turned and caught the falling fists in his hands. The two seemed to freeze momentarily. Vladimir stood mute and immobile, as did Oblivion. They were both immensely strong, perhaps evenly matched, and the skin of Oblivion matched the granite coating of Vladimir for toughness.

It appeared as though they were wrestling, pushing each other back and forth, until, abruptly Oblivion smiled, ducked his horned head under the arm of Vladimir and came up behind him, the two now back to back and Vladimir's arm cruelly twisted out of true. Then, with a deafening roar Oblivion leaned forward, lifting Vladimir upon his back, and hurled him. High, high into the sky, and he disappeared over the town walls and into the forest.

"Shit" muttered John.

Oblivion straightened up, then stretched his imposing muscles with an almost audible creaking sound.

"Now that" he cried "was fun. It's been a while since anybody has tried to test me. That stone man thing was a very nice touch."

He reached into an inside pocket and rummaged about looking for something.

"Now, you've obviously got a child of the light on your team." He gazed around the courtyard " I can't see them, but of course, they'll have cloaked themselves in invisibility if they have any sense.

Ah hah".

And he pulled from his pocket a pair of incredibly thick dark glasses, which he proceeded to put on his nose.

"Wouldn't want to get my eyes burnt out now would I?"

He finally came to rest, hands on hips and gazed out across the courtyard.

"So, do we finally meet at last. Our darling John. The killer. Oh yes, I know all about you and your perpetual lamenting of those you kill. So, killer, where shall we go from here? I must admit, you do look rather ominous in that all black outfit of yours".

His gaze slid from John to Lazarus then back again. Suddenly he froze and his eyes, protruding in shock, darted back to Lazarus .

"No. Surely it can't be. Balendin? "

Lazarus said nothing but stood, his grasp tightening on the shaft of his large axe as he gave John a questioning look.

"Ahh, of course" Oblivion continued "You must be the one she knows as Lazarus. I picked up the name but never delved for your features. Good God's old man, it never even occurred to me that you'd still be alive after all this time. But of course you would."

He finally noticed the perplexed look on Lazarus's face.

"Oh. Oh dear. Of course, you wouldn't remember would you. You and I had that falling out and I wiped your memories.

Well, after all this time, and in order to make this conversation a two sided one, I guess it's time I gave them back to you eh?"

At this, he seemed to take a deep breath, moved his hands together in the air as though rolling a ball of dough, then tossed this invisible ball to Lazarus.

184

Lazarus suddenly reeled, his eyes slipped flickering back into their sockets and the axe fell from his numbed fingers.

In alarm, John grasped at the man's arm and went as if to hold him up. To support his trembling frame.

"What have you done to him you bastard?" Cried John plaintively.

"What? Oh I've just reminded him of something is all".

Finally, his back sliding down the wall behind him, Lazarus slid to the floor, where he sat, looking dazed and confused.

John, grasping him by the shoulder, shook him gently. "Lazarus? You ok old man?" .

"Yeah old man. How ya feeling? Got time for a catch up?" Crowed Oblivion.

Lazarus gave his head a shake and grasping onto John for support he pulled himself back to his feet.

"You utter bastard" he growled

"Ahh Balendin old man. Surely even you can't hold a grudge 'This' long"

"You...You actually know this arsehole?" Asked John unbelievingly.

"it's a long story son" replied Lazarus, giving him a plaintive look.

"Oh, we've got plenty of time old one, why don't you go ahead and tell your tale" chuckled Oblivion

Lazarus looked perturbed and shifted his gaze from Oblivion to John and back again.

Finally he began a short tale in a husky broken voice.

"Well John, I regret to say that once, a long long time ago, I did indeed know this man.

Would you believe, we were friends"

"The very best of friends indeed" crowed Oblivion joyfully.

Lazarus hurled a violent Look of hatred at Oblivion.

"Yes John, we were close. You might say I was his mentor. I had been given the task of introducing him into the ways of the gifted. Of how we didn't interfere in the ways of normal men, but kept ourselves apart. We would only step in if we felt there was a grave injustice taking place, and even then we would try to avoid making a spectacle of ourselves. In essence we lived a rather epicurean life, keeping everything simple and living peacefully with each other in commune.

Well, it seemed my words of advice to Oblivion here" at this he gestured contemptuously at the figure before them. "It seems my words fell on deaf ears. It seemed that he fell to the breaching of our conventions almost immediately, and he very quickly became immensely wealthy by the abusing of his gift".

"Oh for God's sake man" cursed Oblivion "What else was I to do, having been given such a useless gift. The wiping of memory for the love of god. What damned use is that to anybody eh? So, I put my pathetic gift to more positive use and stole from the wealthy without their faintest idea".

"Your useless gift" sighed Lazarus. "You might have put it to the aid of the broken ones. Those that had been abused by the looting and rapine of warrior bands. Those that had been violated and that bore eternal scars upon their soul. You might have given peace to those shells of men and women who wandered our streets begging alms for survival whilst simultaneously begging for the release of death.
186

You could have been a balm for these lost souls. Wiping from their memories the torture and loss they had endured."

"Oh yes" Oblivion moaned mockingly. "Now I remember, your perpetual moaning at the ills of the world and how you felt we could make a difference. So damned self righteous, so damned " here he paused a moment, struggling to find the right word " so damned selfless, humanitarian and altruistic.

Frankly it made me sick. Fellow man you'd say. But no, these weren't my fellow men. They were an inferior model. I, I was one of the master race".

"You hid it well didn't you. You had me fooled. Right up until the end". Sighed Lazarus.

"ahh yes, the end" Oblivion purred

"I'd managed to keep from you my sudden immense increase in wealth. I wasn't being ostentatious. And yet you had your suspicions, yes?

There I am at the mercenary encampment, negotiating and perhaps exchanging some monies as a sign of good faith, when who should suddenly appear to confront me with my perfidy?

"You'd begun to change" sighed Lazarus, and to John his eyes appeared a little moist.

"It was only very subtle at that point, most men wouldn't have noticed a thing. But I'd seen it before, I knew the signs. And so, that night when you sneaked out of our encampment, I followed.

And there you led me to the mercenaries, and I tried to intervene" "Oh yes Balendin" crowed Oblivion mirthfully "one moment I'm making secret negotiations with the leader of their band, next

187

second, you appear, shouting and yelling and waving your arms around furiously. With your great age you managed to make me feel like a naughty schoolboy, caught in the act."

"Now hang on" burst in John, "Lazarus, he keeps referring to you as old. Now, obviously I was somewhat surprised to find you dated back to ancient Greece, but why does he keep referring to your age? Aren't you contemporaries?"

Oblivion burst into laughter as he walked in a circle around his iron throne. "Good God's boy. Even back in my day we knew he was ancient. No, we aren't contemporaries. Nobody knows his true age, even he I'm sure. Balendin is an unusual one, so he is. The thing is, before any of us knew anything about the artifacts. Our Balendin here was born in a dark cave somewhere, but a dark cave with its own strange kind of illumination. Oh yes, he was born beneath the naked rock bearing a fragment of the artifact. Personally I'm thinking some time during the bronze age, but I could well be wrong. "

"More like stone age I think" growled Lazarus "Now that you've returned my memories I have a vague recollection of the times. Oh yes John, when this bastard wiped my memories when I caught him, he didn't just wipe the recent ones, which would have been more than adequate I'm sure. Oh no, he wiped pretty much everything. From that point on I didn't even know my own bloody name. I was a waif and a stray upon the streets for some time before someone from our group found me and brought me back. I had a lot to relearn."

"Your welcome Balendin old chap" Oblivion chuckled.

Lazarus started forward, his hand tightening on the shaft of his axe. But stopped short of the charge he'd obviously been tempted to.

"I don't go by that name anymore" he hissed.

"Oh no, your Lazarus now aren't you? An odd choice I'd have said, but then I'm sure it makes some kind of sense to you".

"Well" barked John a growing feeling of anger and frustration rising within him.

"I'm sure that this reconciliation between you both is all very lovely. However, we are somewhat drifting from the whole point of our assembly here. Sophia... Give her back".

"Ahh, the killer speaks" chuckled Oblivion. "Straight to the point eh son. Good, good, I like it.

"are you not perpetually troubled by the thought of all those lives you've taken killer.

Isn't it amazing to think that you've killed more people than even I?

Well, I have of course anticipated your request".

"Demand" hissed John.

Oblivion continued to laugh mutedly, "well, I could give her back to you of course killer. I honestly don't feel I'm going to get much more out of her now. Obviously you have her body here somewhere with you, or you wouldn't be here. So it would be simple for me to hand her back to you.

However, I do find her company entertaining, so I thought I'd offer you an alternative transaction, on the agreement of course that you will cease to harass me."

At this he ceased his circling of the iron throne and walked purposefully towards the covered box like object.

He grasped the top of the cloth and paused menacingly. "So killer, will you consider a different transaction with me?"

"No" John growled.

"Ahh" and he pulled the cloth from what transpired to be a large metal cage. "Are you so sure of that oh murderous one?"

On the floor of the cage lay a woman, curled into the foetal position and weeping silently.

John stared at her in growing dismay. Of course, now some things fell into place. Oblivion wasn't curtailed by the usual rules of time, not with his worldwalker gift. He could have decided only yesterday to abduct her and have then done so months ago. As he had.

The woman who lay there was John's mother.

There was an audible groan from beneath the mask of the helmeted head and John fell to his knees.

He slid the visor of the mask up to reveal a tear stained face.

"Mum?" He called

The woman pulled herself up from the floor and grasped the bars of her cage. Peering out into the courtyard she saw him.

"John?" She gasped " what are you doing here, and what are you wearing? "

John's tears turned into a chuckle. A mother to the last eh.

"Yes killer" Oblivion sighed sardonically. "This is to be your choice. You can take back your beloved Sophia, in which case I shall keep this woman as my slave and torture her occasionally for my entertainment. Alternatively, you can take back this woman and I shall keep your Sophia for my company. I'm sure we could have the most entertaining of conversations.

"Mum" called John.

"Yes son" came her plaintive response.

"I love ya mum" he said, chokingly.

"And I you" she called back.

"Do me a favour huh? Please, just close your eyes and think of the good times for me"

"Oh, I've been such a bitch to your father haven't I?"

"Don't you worry about that mum. Just close ya eyes for me"

"Ok son".

John turned determinedly to face Oblivion, and slid the visor of his helmet back down into place.

"Give me Sophia" he growled menacingly.

"What? " gasped Oblivion, seeming to reel back on his heels. "You'd sacrifice your very mother to me?"

"Give me Sophia, now".

"my God's killer" Oblivion began to laugh maliciously. "This is going to be fun. Ok, right, sure, take her then".

He waved a hand lazily in John's direction as though swatting at an annoying fly.

Suddenly there was a buzzing from the walkie talkie hanging at his hip. He quickly grasped it and brought it to his lips.

" Talk" he barked

"I've got her John. She's back, and she's in good shape too" came Eleanor's joyful voice.

"Good" John breathed in response, then returned the walkie talkie to his belt.

"Right" he sighed to Oblivion. "That's our transaction over, you can piss off now".

Oblivion laughed in amused malice.

"very well John, I'll be on my way then. I'm already concocting an amusing torture for your mother. Oh the very joy of it. Whenever I think of you in the future I'll be able amuse myself with a brutal whipping or something. To have this perpetual power over you from now on is going to be a fantastic pleasure".

"There'll be no torture" sighed John "you'll not harm my mother you arsehole" .

"And what can you do to stop me" Oblivion barked angrily. "I hold the cards now boy. Your mother is mine to do with as I please".

"I need do nothing. Now, just go".

Oblivion turned to the woman in the cage, his hand falling to a whip curled at his hip.

Suddenly he stopped. Frozen in place with a look of astonishment on his face.

"What? What have you done?" Oblivion gasped.

"like you said before. Many times" John spoke in a monotone, his voice devoid of emotion. "I'm a killer".

There, lying upon the floor of the cage. Still and silent. There lay John's mother, a skull hilted blade thrust deeply into the base of her skull. Impaling the brainstem.

The death would have been instantaneous.

Oblivion roared in outrage. To have had his entertainment curtailed like this was unthinkable.

He ran to Isaac where he remained impaled by Oblivions spear against the wall.

He slapped his open palm down against his upturned face. "Forget" he growled. Then he withdrew his spear from the wall and Isaac both, and raising it aggressively he charged at John and Lazarus where they stood silently.

Lazarus moved, throwing himself between John and oblivion, his axe raised before him and an almost exultant look upon his face.

He parried the swing of Oblivions spear against the shaft of his axe, then swung it tremendously,

The blade of the axe crashing against the side of Oblivions head in a shower of sparks.

Oblivion, although unharmed in any way, was forced to stumble a few steps sideways from the force of the blow.

"Dammit man" he cried "I'd forgotten your strength. Well, I know I can't kill you, but I can certainly make you uncomfortable for a while".

He lunged again at Lazarus, attempting to drive his spearpoint through lazarus's chest. But the thrust was easily parried aside and once again the head of the axe struck Oblivion a mighty blow.

"Ahh, I've had enough of this foolishness" brawled Oblivion, and leaning back he suddenly raised his leg and gave Lazarus a tremendous kick in the chest, kicking him a great distance and no doubt breaking many ribs, if not rupturing organs in the process.

Lazarus, unlike Oblivion, could be harmed, he wasn't indestructible like his foe. Whatever his injury however, he would rapidly heal. He couldn't be killed, but he could be indisposed.

Oblivion finally turned to John. The boys mask, his helmet, irritated him. All he could see was his own reflection. There were no features, no eye slits, just a blank black mirror. It gave one the impression he was fighting himself on some level.

Also he couldn't see the expression on his face. He'd hoped to see fear or something of the sort, but the boy just stood there, immobile, inscrutable.

"Damn you boy" he cursed "Your time to die". And he charged at John with the point of his spear thrust before him.

If he had been able to see John's face he might have been surprised, if not somewhat disconcerted.

He did indeed feel somewhat fearful. He had no weapons that could touch this man, and his telekinetic blows would be just as ineffective.

However, his face showed no sign of this. It was completely impassive. A stony inexpressive mask of a face. Emotionless and cold.

As Oblivion charged at him John didn't even bother to raise a shield. He simply drew a blade in each hand and countercharged.

As they closed John suddenly dropped to his knees, sliding across the ground like a celebrating footballer.

Oblivion's spear sliced over his shoulder, biting into flesh, but not deeply.

John in turn simply stabbed downwards into Oblivions thigh as they passed each other.

Into Oblivions thigh!

Oblivion screamed in a mixture of both shock and pain. John himself was so startled at the success of his attack. His puny knives had actually penetrated Oblivions untouchable flesh.

Still sliding on his knees he pulled his right hand blade free of Oblivions body, but as startled as he was he let the left hand blade slip through his fingers and remain in his thigh.

Swiftly, Oblivion waved his spear in the air beside him and a rift rapidly opened for him. He dived through it, screaming the words "You and I aren't over killer". And he was gone.

John was busy cursing himself as the rift began to close. The airborne knives. Hovering in an arc above them. He should have rained them down on the bastard. If these blades could actually harm him, they could have ended their war there and then.

Before the rift had completely closed, he heard a strange voice resonating from the ether.. "Come seek me out boy. I've a gift for you".

And then it was gone, as was the rift.

Twenty four

John simply sat there, on his knees in the silence of the courtyard. His helmeted head tilted back as he stared up at the vacant sky. Not a cloud to be seen.

He felt strange. He knew he should be elated. He'd actually got Sophia back and he'd managed to wound the bastard in the process.

Ok, so there was the business of his mother.

He looked over to where the body lay slumped in the cage.

It had seemed like the only option at the time. He wasn't, he'd thought, in any way capable of rescuing her. And he'd learnt enough of Oblivion to know he'd hold true to his talk of torture and the like.

All he could do was save her from that. That indignity. That suffering.

The strike to the brainstem, something he'd been practicing when alone in his training room at the mansion.

There would have been absolutely no pain and the death would have been instantaneous.

Like flicking off a light switch.

But now.

Now he knew his blades could cut this son of a bitch. If he'd known that then, then his mother would still be alive. He'd have rained death down upon him and set her free.

If only he'd known.

His mother's death now hung heavy on his heart. It was just such a waste of a life. An unnecessary waste he could have avoided.

Recrimination grew and grew within him. If only he'd bloody known.

He'd have to take her back. His dad would have to learn of her death. They'd have to come up with some explanation of it. Or just leave her in a ditch somewhere for the police to find.

He tore the helmet from his head and ran his hand down his face and through his short growth of beard.

"John" came a quiet tentative voice. As though afraid he might explode or something.

A gentle hand fell upon his shoulder and he recognised the shade of nail varnish.

Without turning his head, or moving in any way, he asked "Eleanor or Sophia?"

"Sophia John. I'm back my love. Eleanor's been lent a maid for a while, so I'm all alone in here. "

He finally pulled himself uncertainly to his feet. Turned to face her, and saw the true Sophia in her eyes.

He then fell into her arms and wept.

Twenty Five

The group gathered once more in the hall where they'd spent the previous night.

Lazarus was back to perfect health and he and a recovered Vladimir, who had found himself lost in the forest, unable to find his way back. The two of them carried the drooling Isaac back and lay him, trembling and crying out incoherently, upon the large table at the rooms centre.

John sat in the darkest corner of the hall, alternately brooding angrily then slipping into bouts of morbid anguish and melancholy.

Sophia engulfed him in her arms, but was silent with him, as though in mourning.

"Christ" Lazarus growled, breaking the deathly stillness of the room. "He's taken Isaac back to babyhood or something. The lads buggered".

An unfamiliar face appeared at his shoulder. It was the maid that Amelia had allowed Eleanor to inhabit so that Sophia might have her body to herself. She'd arranged with Amelia that they would give her one of their cat like pets for when they left too.

"don't worry Lazarus you old sod. "she purred in his ear. "I've got this one".

She then pulled one of those comfy upholstered chairs over to the side of the table by Isaac's head, where she sat herself and placed her hands at his temples.

Immediately he was silent and he closed his eyes.

"shouldn't take too long I'd say" she almost sang "he's only young so there's not too much to work with".

"what the hell are you on about woman? What are you doing to the boy? " Lazarus asked in as steady a voice as he was able.

"Why do you think I've been spending my time each night by your bedsides. It's certainly not been for the company, let me tell you.

No, I've been downloading your memories old chap. Knowing that that guy could wipe your memories with his gift it seemed like a sensible precaution."

Lazarus's face suddenly took on a look of concern. "You've got my memories?"

Eleanor chuckled mischievously. "oh yes, that I have".

She continued to laugh at the look on his face, then continued. "But don't worry old chap. I haven't read them or anything. Couldn't if I wanted, as I'd have to do it in real time, so a year of your life would take me a year to review. No, I've just recorded them all as a block of memory, if that's the right way to put it.

Yeah. Just a block of memory, like a memory card. I'm just putting it back in.

He'll have memories right up till last night when I topped him off as it where."

"you know love? " asked Lazarus with a huge smile. He stepped to her side then enveloped her in a huge hug "sometimes you can be a real treasure".

Meanwhile, Vladimir strode about the room, cursing under his breath and occasionally kicking at the furniture.

Lazarus accosted him and grasped him by the shoulders. Staring steadily into his eyes he breathed "what's the matter with you son? We won for Christ's sake."

"Yeah" blurted Vladimir "and I wasn't bloody there for it. One second I thought I had the son of a bitch, pounding him in the face I was, repeatedly, with granite fists.

Next thing I know I'm flying through the bloody air and landing somewhere in the woods.

And like a bloody idiot I couldn't find my way back.

There's you lot fighting for your lives and stuff and I'm not there. I'm busy wandering around aimlessly in their God forsaken bloody woods.

It's soooo frustrating. I should have been there man".

Lazarus patted his shoulders sympathetically.

"to be honest son, I'm not sure you could have helped us. If John's evil bloody knives hadn't miraculously turned out to work on the arsehole, then we'd probably all be dead. Well, you'd all probably have turned up dead anyway".

He turned away from Vladimir and strode over to the brooding figure of John.

"Hey John. Son?"

John looked up at him with red rimmed eyes.

"What?" He asked sulkily.

200

"your knives boy. I was thinking. You remember back to our previous excursion into the world of the weird.? You remember us getting attacked over in Canada? That monster came in through the window, blazing hot and about to go bang big time yeah?

You remember how we couldn't touch the bugger. All our bullets just flamed away before they could hit him yeah? "

"Yeah, how could I forget. I almost lost Sophia that day"

"Well I've been thinking back, and I remember that one of us did hit the monster. You son. I remember that one of your blades stuck him in the shoulder or somewhere. It didn't melt, to my recollection it didn't even start glowing from the heat or anything. And then you'd have called it back to your hand without any problems. No burnt fingers or anything".

"So. What are you getting at old man? "

"I'm saying that those blades of yours are something special, obviously. I'm saying that it might pay us to look into their origin when we get back, yeah?"

John shrugged uninterestedly. "Yeah, whatever man" he sighed.

Lazarus looked closely at the boy. He was wasted. Broken. He hoped Sophia's tender touch might bring the boy back to them. He was useless like this.

The boys mother. Christ all mighty. If something like that doesn't screw you up.

He understood why he'd done it.

If he'd been in the same position he'd have done the same thing.

But then to discover the ability of those dark knives of his. With them having been hovering over Oblivions head the whole time.

Yeah. That surely would screw anybody up.

He lay a gentle hand on John's shoulder. The boy didn't look at him but just continued to stare at the marble of the floor, as if he might find some answers there.

"John" he whispered "John. You did the right thing boy. With what we knew at the time, you did the right thing. There wasn't any other way. Please, don't blame yourself for this. You saved her, that's what you did. You should be proud of that son. "

John didn't even blink. There was no response from the boy. Yet then, suddenly a change came over him. His eyes flashed up into those of Lazarus and he stood. This sudden movement threw Sophia off her feet and she fell backwards. But he caught her and grinned a grin that sent a cold shiver down Lazarus's spine.

"This isn't over. I'm going to kill him" John said in the coldest of voices that any of them had ever heard before. Each of them at that moment thanked the heavens that he wasn't an enemy of theirs.

Sophia looked at John through tear streaked eyes.

From within the mind of Oblivion she'd stood at the large window in the lounge and watched everything unfold before her.

Firstly the shock of seeing finally the contents of the cage he'd carried. John's mother for heaven's sake.

Then the offer of the deal. This time Pancras had allowed her the facility of audio. All the better to torture her with she imagined.

She'd known how torn John would be. And she'd half expected him to immediately free his mother.

But no.

And then the sight of the knife, jutting as it was from the back of her head.

Her stomach had turned at the sight, and yet she understood why he'd done it.

As far as they knew they were powerless against this monster. This was the only way he could protect his mother from Oblivions ruthless attentions.

But then the sudden discovery, the accidental realisation that they weren't defenceless after all.

And it was John's knives. The same knives with which he'd just killed his mother.

The same knives he'd had surrounding Oblivion from the moment he'd arrived.

He could have killed him instantly if he hadn't been trying to release Sophia first.

No, it was such a horrible, unbelievable irony.

Looking at the state of John now, she wouldn't be surprised if he had a complete breakdown.

suddenly, as if in answer to her thought, John spoke out to the group.

"Did you know that back in the old days, the original spelling of the word evil was yfel.

Still pronounced the same way but spelt so differently.

I just thought that was interesting is all.

I wonder why they changed it?"

Uh oh thought Sophia, her previous thought of a breakdown ringing alarm bells at the back of her mind.

"come on John " she said quietly, taking his arm and leading him away. "Lets go find something to eat eh?"

And she found that she was indeed leading him. His own feet seemed to have lost any volition of their own and just allowed themselves to be drawn wherever she led them.

None of this was a good sign.

"Something to eat, then an early night eh hun?"

"Sure, sure" he replied, looking as though he hadn't actually heard a word.

Tomorrow, they'd head home to the manor. A dead body in tow. Then they'd have to work out what to do about it.

Twenty six

Morning came and the group gathered together in the courtyard. Besides them, tilted up on a two wheeled hand cart, was an ominous looking plain wooden box that Amelia had arranged to be constructed for them.

John made sure that he always had his back to it and he averted his eyes from it constantly.

Amelia seemed sorry to see them leave. There had been observers hidden away during the previous days conflict, and when word spread that they had actually managed to hurt the hated oblivion, stabbed him no less, they had been elated.

Sophia imagined they would like them to stay in case the evil one returned.

She couldn't blame them.

Isaac was back to his old self. Laughing and joking with Vladimir, though somewhat upset that he had no memory of the battle.

He bore a bandaged wound through his shoulder, so a battle scar at least. But he had no recollection of how he came by it.

The last thing he remembered was trying to get to sleep whilst Eleanor hovered disconcertingly by his bedstead.,

Lazarus leaned nonchalantly on his axe whilst Eleanor and Kathryn were busy negotiating with Amelia over the gifting of a small pet cat like thing.

It did look remarkably catlike, however on closer examination you could see that the paws had an opposable thumb and elongated claws giving them the disconcerting look of hands. Also when you looked it in the face, it very quickly became apparent that the eyes weren't cats eyes but looked much more like human eyes. The whole creature seemed remarkably creepy to most of them. Especially Lazarus who didn't like cats anyway.

Finally, their negotiations done, Eleanor, still in the form of the maid, took the proffered animal in her arms, stroked it meditatively, then placed it at her feet.

Suddenly she seemed to reel on the spot. Her eyes blinked rapidly and then she stared about herself as though not knowing where she was.

Amelia took her gently by the arm and led her to a courtier to take care of her in her recovery.

Meanwhile the cat had strolled over to and joined the group where they were gathered together awaiting departure.

John rested a hand gently on Sophias shoulder and gave it a meaningful squeeze.

"Do your thing hun" he whispered to her.

Sophia raised her hands before her, palm to palm as if in prayer. She then parted them and before them all appeared a closed white wooden door.

It was of the old fashioned style of a large country house and it was itself large and almost imposing with its iron hinges and lockplate.

"Go ahead sophia" called kathryn, "this is your homecoming love".

Smiling at the suggestion of a homecoming and feeling that it was a very accurate suggestion, considering how she had been brutally torn from this place, she stepped forward, laid her hand on the door handle and swung the door wide.

There, as if by magic, was the familiar lounge of the manor, and each of them felt a pang of relief at finally coming home.

John quickly strode to Amelia and gave her a brief curt hug. "Thanks for everything" he breathed, then strode back to and through the door with Sophia. One by one they each marched through the neat gaping hole in the world. Lazarus trailed in last place, wheeling the trolley and coffin behind him.

" bye guys" he called, then he closed the door.

At that moment, as Amelia and her entourage looked on. The door simply popped out of existence.

"Aahhh, home again, home again, jiggedy jig" Sighed a suddenly deathly weary John.

It was an expression he'd used, well, forever as far as he could recall. And he'd always wondered to himself fruitlessly where it came from.

Yet now, suddenly, it came to him. Out of the blue.

"Bladerunner" he murmured to himself in surprise.

Really ? Bladerunner? Hell, he was going to have to dig out the film now to check.

The rest of the group were busying themselves around him. Unpacking equipment, setting up the coffee machine, and discretely hiding coffins behind curtains that were never drawn.

He, he seemed to have frozen in front of the large window in the lounge, staring out at the well cultivated garden and the mature trees that graced the place.

Sophia watched him from the doorway feeling uncomfortable. The fact that he was staring through the same window through which she'd watched his last battle sent a shiver up her spine.

She was going to have to be careful with John for a while she knew. Time for the kid gloves. He was in an extremely fragile state and she couldn't bare the thought of tipping him over the edge.

Eventually the bustle of arrival settled down and they all found themselves relaxing in the lounge.

John had chosen to monopolize one of the sofas and lay its length, supping on a hot coffee and appearing to bliss out on the experience.

"It's always the coffee I miss most" he said "when we're away on any kind of mission. Not my bed, not the usual creature comforts, just this damned coffee".

And he supped some more with an appreciative smile.

"Now, tell me guys" he continued, as he stared meditatively through the steam from his coffee cup. "Did any of you hear a voice? After he'd passed through the rift but before it had closed?"

He glanced around at the blank faces surrounding him.

"Hmm, only me then. I wonder what that means? A message for me in particular I guess."

He then fell silent. Alone with his thoughts and his coffee.

There was a kind of expectant stillness and silence throughout the party. Things felt unfinished, incomplete.

"Hey" broke in Sophia. "You know, all the time I was stuck in that buggers head, he kept calling himself Balendin. Why was that do you think?"

Lazarus broke into laughter. "ahh Sophia, he renamed himself for you. It's another of our Latin names I'm afraid. This one means fierce, or brave" he chuckled some more "Perhaps you should feel flattered".

Sophia humphed. "Stupid git" she muttered to herself.

Lazarus now stood and began to walk back and forth before the window.

"Well John, I'm guessing we're gonna be in pursuit of that son of a bitch. Certainly now we know we have the weapons to do him harm eh?

As for you boys". At this he gestured amicably towards Vladimir and Isaac. "I'd like to thank you greatly for your assistance lads. Your free now to return to your homesteads boys. Your jobs done here".

At this Vladimir rose in agitation. "Hell no it isn't" he barked. "That bastard is still out there, and I'd for one kinda like a pound of his flesh".

Lazarus huffed and crossed his arms. "But Vlad, dear boy. You can't harm the man. None of us can except our Johnnie here it seems. I'd thought we were all done for until that blade of his slid so exquisitely into his flesh. And what a pleasant surprise that was eh?"

At this he slapped John on the shoulder.

John's face momentarily slipped into a dark frown. "Oh yes indeed" he growled ominously. Then his face was once more a passive blank.

"So er," continued Lazarus " much as I appreciate the sentiment lads, I can't see as how you'd be of any help, ya understand me? "

"Well, ok" gruffed Vladimir irritatedly. "So, we can't hurt the bastard ourselves directly. But surely there's things we can do to help. To back John up somehow. I just don't like to leave a job undone ya know. Besides, what credit am I going to get from my peers when I tell them we let the swine walk away from us and didn't even follow after? Christ lazarus, I missed half the battle anyway, lost in the damned woods as I was"

Isaac was nodding at this. "Sure, I might have some scars to carry home with me, but I've no memory of the battle at all. I don't even recall seeing the guys face".

Lazarus grumbled incoherently under his breath, his fingers tugging at his long dreadlocks.

Finally "ok, ok you two. You can come along on the pursuit. Just bare in mind that you might not have much input yeah? You might find yourselves a bit of a fifth wheel yeah?"

"sure Laz, sure" cried a greatly mollified Vladimir. "As long as we're in on the hunt is all".

Abruptly, John called out. "Sophia love? Come sit on my lap eh?"

Sophia raced to oblige, and once settled in place John said to the group in a subdued voice "we're heading up for an early night lads, ok?"

At this his figure rose from the sofa and momentarily he and Sophia hung in mid air, before finally sweeping across the room and out through the open doors, heading for the stairs.

"Bloody hell" cried Isaac "Yeah man, er... Wow?" Followed Vladimir. " Ahh, of course" chuckled Lazarus "You've not really seen John use his power that much have you? It can seem quite disconcerting sometimes when he uses it at home. Even though you know it's amongst his abilities, it still manages to seem slightly out of place".

"Yeah" responded Isaac, "we all knew he could fly, from that time in the forest when he spotted out the town. But still."

"well guys" came the high voice of Kathryn where she sat at the table. "You'd better get used to it. If he's going after Oblivion and knows he can hurt him now, you might see all kinds of strange crap".

Twenty seven

John and Sophia lay side by side upon the large king sized bed of their room. Sophia was curled up at his side, her head resting upon his bare chest.

"can you do it Soph? " asked John quietly.

"What?" She asked, though she thought she knew the answer.

"can you track him down? Can you take us to him?"

"Oh yes" she answered definitely "in fact, now the fools had me in his head he's like a homing beacon to me. I can easily find both where and when he is. No trouble at all."

"when he is? "

"Oh yes" she answered.

John smiled broadly "interesting".

There was a short silence, then John rolled over to face her, and he gave her a long intense kiss, full of all the emotion fermenting within his breast.

"I love you so much" he choked "I'm so glad to have you back, I couldn't have gone on without you".

She smiled and returned his kiss, just as passionately.

"And I love you too John Cohen" she breathed "and there's nowhere I'd rather be than in your arms."

And it is at this point that a discreet veil is drawn across the two lovers to allow them the peace and privacy to prove their love for one another. With all the passion and depth of feeling they could muster.

"Oh, it's good to be home!" she breathed.

Twenty eight

Later, as the two young lovers lay spent and bathed in the sweat of their love. The bedclothes laying in a disorderly mess upon the floor. There was a lengthy silence as their entwined bodies recovered and the two of them caught their breath.

Finally, John reached, stretching, out to his bedside table. His hand returning with a bottle of champagne. "Fancy a drink love?" He asked amusedly.

"where'd that come from" gasped Sophia in surprise.

"I put it there for the day I got you back. To celebrate like.

I only just remembered it."

She smiled at him adoringly "we should have started with this surely"

"Oh hey" he chuckled "Lets just think of this as an intermission" .

At this they both laughed.

That is until his hand returned again bearing not just the two glasses she'd expected but also a thin white stick which he inserted into the corner of his mouth and lit with the sudden flick of an unnoticed Zippo.

"Hey, what's this?" She exclaimed in shock.

"I know love, I know, and I'm sorry. But whilst you were gone, God knew where, and I was desperately in search for you, I kind of found the habit. Or perhaps it found me, I don't know. Either way, it kind

214

of felt like it helped at the time, and I was grasping for anything that might ease my pain.

I'll give up, I promise. But would you mind if we waited until we've killed this arsehole."

She stared at him a moment, then her stern face broke into an exultant grin.

"Sure John, no worries. I can't say I blame you, I can't imagine what you must have been going through."

She paused, then " actually, I've never tried. Could you light one for me? "

He stared at her for a moment in a shock of his own. Then, without a word he quickly scrambled for the pack on his bedside. The flick once more of the lighter, and he handed her a cigarette.

She put it to her lips and took a short drag. There was the slightest of coughs, then she took another longer drag. No coughing this time.

"And, of course" she declared "with our gift, we don't have to worry about cancer do we? We're protected."

He looked at her in awe. "You know. That never even occurred to me."

And so the two naked youths lay entwined upon the disordered bed, smoking enthusiastically, defiantly perhaps.

Sophia was feeling so much happier now. John seemed to have broken out of his dark troubled state and seemed much more like his old self.

She was so thankful for that. He'd had her worried.

It's not every day you kill your mum.

Finally, once all the champagne was gone and John had had to open a second packet of fags, seriousness descended upon them.

He had been thinking about that voice, and of how it's presentation was always in accompaniment of a rift.

He'd mentioned the voice to Sophia before now, but she had no idea what it meant either. In all honesty it had made her slightly concerned over his sanity. He'd been through so much.

He brought the subject up again now, and Sophia listened to him seriously.

"it feels" he began "it feels as though somebody's reaching out to me. Trying to contact me. And their doing it through the rifts, so they never have much time".

Sophia nodded thoughtfully. "Perhaps" she stated "Perhaps I can just open an untargeted gateway for you and we see what happens eh?

What do you think hun? "

"My worry is of course that it could be another threat. And I can't bare the thought of putting you in any danger" John replied.

"Yeah" responded Sophia "I get that John, I really do. I mean, Jesus, just look at all the different crap we've come across already, and I'm only nineteen".

John chuckled at the mention of her age. "Yeah, me too love. I kinda get the feeling that we've been forced to do our growing up a tad too quickly".

"but seriously John " continued Sophia "I think it's something we should try".

"on our own? Or with back up? "

Sophia's face screwed up into that endearing look she wore when thinking hard and John smiled to himself.

"I... I think we can do this one on our own John" .

"Fair enough" John joked "your the boss. I guess we'd better get our kit on first eh?"

Slowly, precariously, the two disentangled their limbs from one another and disengaged.

That done, they each had a quick shower to wash away the sheen of sweat that bathed their naked bodies.

Then, finally, they slipped into their clothes. John rearranging his harness of knives with a little help from sophia. Sophia herself adorning a simple outfit of jogging bottoms, t-shirt and hoody, with two lightweight .38 revolvers tucked into the back of her trousers.

It was only whilst dressing together that John realized he was short one knife, and giving it a moment's thought came to the happy conclusion that he must have left it in Oblivions thigh.

He had difficulty suppressing the enormous smile that struggled to encompass his face.

Finally the two of them were ready. Sophia had clipped her now quite lengthy, wet blonde hair back into a ponytail. She felt pumped and ready for anything.

John however was still feeling hesitant. Worrying that he might be putting her in danger. And it took her some convincing that she was ok and wanted to do this thing.

Besides, if she were to die, she wouldn't want to be anywhere else than by John's side.

The two of them sat at the foot of the bed, facing the opposing wall and the large mirror that hung there.

"You ready hun?" Sophia asked gently, taking his hand in hers.

"Sure" he grumbled "Go for it".

At this, Sophia once more ran her hands through those motions of prayer, and when drawing her palms apart, she created a beautiful white oaken door in the wall before them . The mirror was now gone.

She then rose to her feet, and leaning forward she swung the door open, then sat once more by John's side and grasped his hand tightly.

They both stared in subdued awe at the misty void within which billions of threads of coloured light seemed strung.

"anything yet hun" asked sophia.

"No. No nothing yet". He replied.

Again, they continued to sit in silence and stare.

Suddenly came the voice. "Ahh, John. Back at last, and in no hurry this time I see".

"There" cried John "that's the voice".

"but I can't hear anything" Sophia cried apologetically.

"Oh, and you have the lovely Sophia with you this time I see. You've finally defeated that parasite Oblivion".

"Ahh, ahh" cried Sophia excitedly "I heard it that time, I did".

"yes Sophia dear" came the voice again "it's only those I speak to that can hear me. And now I know your there, I'll include you in our conversation".

"Er.... Thanks? " muttered Sophia distractedly. Unsure how to respond to the manners of a disembodied voice.

"We haven't exactly defeated Oblivion yet I'm sorry to say. But just bare with me on that one. I fully intend to kill the bastard" said John feeling slightly mollified.

"Well John, I know you will at that" the voice continued. "but you need to come seek me out. I have something of yours".

"Really? But, who are you? What can you possibly have of mine? "

"We shall speak again together soon boy. And then perhaps you'll pay me a visit. Until then, please just carry this thought with you. Everything you've ever done has been for the best of intentions, and no man can ever ask for more than that. Oh" and here there was a thoughtful pause "as for my identity, I think you should call me Masamune".

"Ok. Masamune, what is it you want from me? "

But there was no response.

"I think we've been cut off" said Sophia .

"What? Already? Jesus, we'd barely even started talking".

"maybe he's a busy man John. But look, he said we'd speak together again soon. Now I've heard him too and can testify your not crazy.

We'll give it another try tomorrow eh? Maybe we'll have more joy. "

Twenty nine

Come breakfast time they were all to be found around the dining table, waiting expectantly for Kathryns famed full English. In fact, as an added treat this time she was including the fabled black pudding, which she actually made herself to a family recipe she concealed from all.

Lazarus was greatly pleased to see the improvement in John's mood. The boy had had him worried.

He didn't know what Sophia had done to bring him back from that brink.

Well, to be honest that was a lie. He had a very good idea what she'd done, and he found he had to smile at his own prudishness.

As he was pouring himself a coffee he heard Sophia call to him.

"Hey Laz. You know that business about the voices John was hearing".

Lazarus frowned to himself. Yes, those voices. It was rarely a good sign when one of your crew, one who's gone through as much as he had too, started hearing disembodied voices that no-one else could hear.

"yes sophia" he said carefully "What of them?"

"Well, I just thought you'd like to know that I've heard them too now. So you needn't continue to worry over John's sanity. It's real. Calls himself Masamune."

"Really ?" cried Lazarus in surprise. "Masamune... Really?"

"Yes Laz, Masamune. Mean something?"

"Well, yes and no I guess. Believe it or not, I actually knew a Masamune back in the day. It's not a common name, but I can say that the Masamune I knew back then wasn't someone that could go around talking to people through rifts.

I'm thinking your voice is using an alias. Maybe one he finds amusing or meaningful in some way."

Lazarus hmm'd to himself, lost in thought.

"Well, who was this guy and when did you know him?" Sophia continued. " it might be important. Apparently we're due to meet him sometime soon."

"Really?" Asked Lazarus feeling a slight twinge of alarm. Yet another card face down on the table, waiting to be turned.

"Well" he sighed and scratched at his deadlocked head. "It would have been, what? Oh, back in the thirteenth century I think it was. Yeah, Japan, Masamuni was the greatest ever living swordsmith. No-one could come close to his work, and his swords were greatly prized. I once owned one myself, I wonder whatever happened to that? Anyway, there you go. Greatest ever swordsmith. And he truly was. Nobody ever managed to equal his work. Perhaps your voice thinks he's pretty handy in the same field eh?"

"Maybe" muttered Sophia. "He says he has something of John's that he wants to give him".

"Hmm" Lazarus hmm'd. "We'll have to keep an eye on that one I think. Perhaps, next time you talk to the guy you could include me? If that's OK John?"

John looked up from his heavily loaded plate.

"What? Oh, yeah, sure Laz. We'll let you know next time we try and give him a call."

The talk at the table moved on to the pressing matter of Oblivion.

"So, what's the plan then boss" Isaac asked Lazarus as he chewed on some bacon. Nice and crispy, just how he liked it, and he gave Kathryn a thankful wink, at which she blushed.

"Well, it all seems rather simple now" replied Lazarus. "Now that we know of the ace up our sleeve, Sophia can track him and open a portal, we go through, our ace taking the lead of course. Then we kill him and come home".

Vladimir was nodding decisively at this. "Yeah, we finally kick his arse. But hang on. What if, at the mere sight of us, he just opens another gateway and does a runner. Like last time."

"Then we pursue" answered John

"Sophias got this guy's number now and can home in on him like a guided missile. He opens a gate, we'll be right behind him. He'll have to turn and fight eventually."

"So" blurted Vladimir, feeling somehow that he might be overstepping some invisible line he wasn't aware of. "So, er, when are we planning to do this thing then?"

Lazarus looked up questioningly at John.

"Your call boy" he said.

John looked from face to face, back and forth. But he wasn't undecided.

"How about this afternoon? That suit everyone?"

There was the muted rumble of assent around the table as they all agreed to the proposed schedule.

"And just think" cried Sophia, grasping at Johns arm and hugging him tightly. "You'll finally be able to avenge me for his awful abduction of me. Pay him back for stealing me from you".

She was worried that she might be laying it on a bit thick. She was trying desperately to draw John's thoughts away from his mother. Going in that direction would only lead him to pain. She knew he still blamed himself regardless of everyone's insistence he'd done the best he could given the knowledge he'd had. No, it would be so much safer to make it all about her.

"so what are you going to say to him love. You know, your departing words when you've the knife at his throat but before you go in for the coup de grace".

John seemed to think for a moment, but only a moment.

"I'll tell him that what's mine is mine, and that anyone who takes or harms what is mine. Be it girlfriend ... Or mother. " and here he gave her that look. That look that told her he knew what she'd been trying to do. But that it was OK. He understood her reasons. "Dies."

"Good stuff my man" cried Vladimir. And he raised his coffee mug in toast. "This guy deserves what's coming at him. And coming we are".

Vlad and Isaac clunked their mugs together and laughed.

After breakfast, John took Lazarus to one side and asked the question he'd been dreading to ask.

"so Laz. What are we doing with my mother's body? What's the plan?"

Lazarus sighed, obviously not relishing the topic.

"Well, firstly John, she's obviously going to have to be found. I'd suggest somewhere remote, like an abandoned warehouse or something."

"how about an old graveyard " suggested John.. "One that's pretty much shut off to the public, like where we first met old man".

"Er, yeah, that'd probably be ok.

Well, another thing is the nature of her wound. Because of its location and the immediacy of her death, there's pretty much no blood and that tiny entry point would be hidden by her hair.

What I'm getting at is that the police won't be able to come up with a cause of death, that'll be left to the coroner yes? "

"Er, yeah, I guess so. But how does that help us?"

"well son" Lazarus continued "it just so happens that we've a few coroner's on our books as it where. We just ensure shc's handed over to one of them, and next thing you know it's announced as a heart attack".

"Really?" breathed John "You can do that?"

"certainly boy" chuckled Lazarus "You don't think this is the first body we've had to explain away do you? Oh no, we've things in place for this".

John nodded thoughtfully "ok. Make it that graveyard then. Nobody goes there since they shut it off. they'll think she was visiting the family graves when she was struck down".

"Good thinking lad" murmured Lazarus as John turned to leave.

"You might want to get your blade back first before we can do anything son" Lazarus's words seemed heavy laden, and he feared momentarily that he might have pushed the boy a little too far.

"Oh, yeah, of course" replied John quietly "I'll get on that, don't worry".

And he walked away.

Somewhat later, in passing, Sophia noticed John at the kitchen sink. He was wearing his weapon harness, but not properly strapped and buckled into place. It seemed to just have been casually slung over his head.

She approached him slowly, not wanting to make him jump, when she saw what he was doing at the sink.

He would call a blade from his harness to his hand, then hold it under the running water from the tap and scrub it with the kitchen brush.

The water would flow red from beneath it.

Slowly still she backed away. This wasn't something she wanted to interrupt. Just having seen it at all felt vaguely heretical.

She backed out of the kitchen and hurried away, pausing only briefly as she passed his mother's coffin to notice that the lid had been lifted and was leaning against its side.

226

Of course, she realised, he'd had to reclaim the blade.

She felt a pang of heartbreak for the poor boy. But then she shrugged it off as best she could. There was no point dwelling on this. She'd just be sure to be extra loving to him later.

As lunchtime approached, John put out word that they wouldn't be pursuing Oblivion that afternoon after all.

He'd had a rethink he said and had decided that they'd head off tomorrow morning instead.

He wasn't himself seen by anybody that lunchtime nor at dinnertime later, and they each of them exchanged worried glances. But nothing was said.

Thirty

Night fell and they each of them headed off to their respective bedrooms. Isaac and Vladimir currently being housed in the guest rooms on the first floor.

Neither of them could quite believe the opulence of the place. The stately grandeur of the furnishings alone left them feeling as though they'd been transported back in time to an age of royalty and their entourage.

Needless to say, they were both very pleased with their accommodation, and both of them looked forward with some regret to their return to their respective homes and the banality of normalcy.

That night, a short while after everyone had retired, there came a subdued knocking at Lazarus's door.

He rose from his desk where he had been attempting to catch some of his returned memory and the various exploits he'd long forgotten.

Gods, it was all such a long time ago.

Now, the gifted naturally lived longer than normal mortals, but only by about a hundred years of so.

He, now he had the memories of millennia.

He walked to the door where the knocking had begun again and opened it, expecting for some indefinable reason to see the face of John, who had been so reclusive throughout the day.

It wasn't John however, instead, there on his doorstep stood Sophia. A look of quiet expectant excitement on her face.

"Hello Sophia" he said quietly " and to what do I owe the pleasure?"

"Its John" she replied" he's decided he wants to have another go at finding that voice, and from what you'd said, he expected you might want to join us".

Lazarus nodded thoughtfully. "Sure, I'm very interested in all this voice business. Lead the way hun".

At this Sophia spun on her heel and lead the way back to their quarters on the top floor where they lay. Lazarus following closely behind in silence.

Finally, Lazarus stepped through into the bedroom of John and Sophia. John was laying at the foot of the bed, his legs dangling over the edge as he stared up at the ceiling, an expression of earnest puzzlement on his face. As Lazarus stepped into the room, John, on seeing him, immediately sat up straight and gave a wide smile.

"Hi Laz" he said croakily , then he coughed to clear his throat. He chuckled briefly. "Sorry old man" he said, his voice now much clearer "it's been a weird day for me. I'm kinda feeling a bit fagged out ya know".

Stepping forward, Lazarus lay a hand upon his shoulder and gave it a comforting squeeze. "No need to apologise boy, you've been through a tough bloody patch."

Sophia stepped around Lazarus and took her place, seated at the foot of the bed besides John.

Then, looking up at Lazarus where he still stood, his hand upon John's shoulder,she tapped the bedclothes besides her.

"Come sit?" she asked, smilingly. And Lazarus, smiling in return took his place besides her.

"Right" continued Sophia "What I'm going to do here Laz, is open a rift, untargeted. No destination in mind. Simply open to the ether as it where. It seems to be the way he communicates with us".

Lazarus nodded thoughtfully "so it appears he can communicate through the void, but maybe can't traverse it like you can love."

Sophia nodded. "Those were my thoughts, but I don't understand how he could do that. I mean only communicate. If he's access to the rift world then he should be able to travel, surely?"

John simply shrugged. "Maybe now's where we find out my love".

Sophia went through her prayer like motions as before, parting her hands to create the white oaken doorway that took shape before them in the opposing wall, obliterating the mirror. She reached out and took Johns hand in hers. With her other hand she reached forward to turn the handle of the door and swing it wide.

There, before them were the millions, billions perhaps. Perhaps even infinite coloured threads of light.

Just hanging there in space, a multitude of spectral coloured threads, some of which she would swear were of no spectrum she'd ever seen before.

Then, suddenly, the voice. "Ahh, children. It's good of you to return for a chat". Both John and Sophia jumped at the voices abrupt presence, even though they'd been expecting it. They exchanged glances but looking at Lazarus they could see he'd heard nothing.

"Er" stuttered Sophia "it's not just me and John this time. We've a friend with us, called....".

"Lazarus" interrupted the voice, in a tone of faint amusement.

Now, Lazarus heard that time, heard his name mentioned and stared deeply into the rift in astonishment.

"Greetings Lazarus old man. Ahh, it almost feels like some kind of reunion, although we two have never met. How strange is that? Purely because you and I share an origin story." .

Lazarus exchanged glances with John and Sophia both, and shrugged. He had no idea what the guy on the other end of the line was talking about either.

"What is it you want with us?" asked Lazarus, his serious voice turned on to the max.

There was a chuckling from the void. "Now, now Lazarus, please, don't try to intimidate me. I know you too well. I've been following your exploits since the day you were born. Oh yes old man. I'm even older than you".

Now the face of Lazarus was one of both shock and awe. He tried to speak, but couldn't find any words with which to respond.

"Well, like Lazarus said" spoke up John. "What is it you want with us?"

"my son. I want nothing with any of you. As I said before, I've a gift for you John. Something that will lend you the much desired sense of completeness. Just a gift boy. "

"And what will this gift cost us?" Continued John . He knew the game well enough now to know there was no such thing as a free lunch. There were always conditions hidden somewhere.

"This might shock you son, but the answer to that question is 'Nothing'. All I'll want you to do in exchange for my gift is to continue living. Don't get yourself killed boy. I happen to know that there's a great future ahead of you. One that would shock you all. And you will have the fate of millions in your hands" .

"What the hell?" Blurted John .

"Look folks. Why don't you come and pay me a visit. Sophia can easily bring you here. I can send you a targeting signal my love to make your task a touch easier. Incidentally, you too have a famous future. Standing at the side of John".

At this, one particular thread, one amongst the millions, increased in brightness and began to run through a series of colour changes. Not a single stable colour like all the others.

Sophia looked to John, and he nodded his head. "Do it hun."

Consequently, Sophia took the oddly acting thread in her hand, and after another look into the eyes of John, she pulled upon it.

Suddenly they saw through the doorway a vast luscious green field, ending at what appeared to be a precipice beyond which waves crashed upon a sandy shoreline.

"Ready guys?" Asked John , and at their nods he stepped through the rift and the others followed.

On the other side of the oaken doorway they found that they'd appeared at the edge of a deep dark forest. A lush green field ahead of them and dark rustling boughs of tall leafy trees behind.

Looking all about himself John said "I like it. This looks like a really nice place. A bit of everything. Forest, field and sea. Yeah, I could see us setting up a nice little place here."

"it is nice isn't it" came a deep familiar voice.

Their eyes swung to the forests edge, and there stood a tall black man, his hair heavily deadlocked and a soul patch on his chin.

He could have been Lazarus's twin, and their eyes darted involuntarily between the two.

He walked to where Lazarus stood, frozen in place as though spellbound, and he held out his hand.

"Well met brother" he grunted as they shook hands together. "Its probably about time the two of us met I think."

Meanwhile, John had been having a good look around and had noticed that in numerous places at the treeline were large heavy duty ballista and in some places even cannon. All were firmly mounted in place and so could not be moved. Also they were all pointing directly at him.

"Hey, er... Masamuni man" and he pointed to the barely concealed heavy artillery. "How comes that's all pointed at us here? I mean, it all looks like it's been there a while, so I'd be surprised if it's there for us exactly. But how likely was it we'd turn up right in your line of fire? We could have come through anywhere".

"Ahh boy. Well spotted. Well actually I'd say it's one of my favourite creations. I like my little world here and the thought of some dimensional traveller or worldwalker turning up and throwing his weight around bothered me.

"So" at this he pointed to the ground at their feet.

Looking down they discovered that they were standing in the middle of what looked like an ornate golden pattern laid into the ground.. It had to be about four yards across and it's decorations included what looked like runes around the circles border and Latin script scattered elsewhere throughout the many Celtic knot looking designs.

"Yes" continued Masamuni "that there is like a magnet for dimension walkers. If they choose to visit my world uninvited they have no option but to appear at this spot. In which case, if I discover them to be hostile, I have some initial distracting defences.""nice touch" nodded John. "However, I'd just like to stress that we're not hostile, and we were invited, yes? "

Masamuni chuckled again and turned towards the forest. "Follow me" he said, and he began to walk towards the treeline, taking long decisive strides, much like another of their party, much to John's interest. He just couldn't believe how similar this guy and Lazarus were. It was spooky. And he could see from her face and the way her eyes darted between them that Sophia felt the same.

They followed Masamuni into the woods, and they hadn't travelled far before they came to a large clearing. It was obvious from the symmetry of the place that it was man made, and there were patches of ground dedicated to a large varied selection of beautiful flowers.

Ahead of them and opening on to this clearing come garden, was an enormous opening or cave in the side of a rolling tree topped hill.

The closer they came to it the more features began to become discernible. There appeared to be a large chimney jutting from the top of the hill, and smoke billowed from it in streams.

There were multiple, what looked like tools of some sort, hanging from the ceiling near the caves entrance and somewhere deep within could be seen a white hot glow.

"So, Masamuni" piped up Sophia. "Is this home sweet home for you then?"

He in turn gave her a look as though he thought her an idiot. "No no girl. I don't live here, God's no. This is my place of work. This is where I create and experiment. I'm going to take you to my office out back".

And he continued his forward strides.

They entered the cave and traversed their way through its confines. John was pleased to see what he had expected to see. A large forge, the source of the bright illumination he'd seen, with a small boy sitting on a stool to its side and working the bellows. This was obviously the reason for the chimney.

They continued inwards passing numerous workbenches strewn with numerous tools of different kinds. John was in fact just beginning to wonder how far back this place might go when they suddenly reached a dead end. Dead that is except for the single door at its centre, over which a pattern of silver had been inlaid into the wall.

Masamunu opened the door with a large key from his waistband, but before he entered he reached up to the silver pattern and tapped it three times with his hand.

He then stepped inside and waved for them to follow.

As they entered the room the first thing that struck them was that the place looked like it had undergone a tornado or some similar catastrophe. The.place was surrounded by work surfaces and shelving covered the majority of the walls. Everywhere on all of the visible worktops lay scattered various unidentifiable brick a brack. It wasn't at first glance possible to tell what might be a tool or what might be the project. Obviously, organisation wasn't this guy's forte.

He waved them to a large desk that day in a corner of the room and he slid himself behind it to his seat which he took shortly after having swept the desktop clear of debris with a swipe of an arm.

"Take a seat, please" he said to them as he himself settled down comfortably into his own.

There were however only two seats so Lazarus elected to remain standing whilst the two youths made themselves comfortable.

"Well well" sighed Masamuni "it's a pleasure to finally meet you John. After all these years and all the work I put into you. Ahh, the many decades of work."

John raised a hand In uncertainty at this. "Many decades?" He asked querulously "I'm only nineteen".

"ah yes" Masamuni continued "we'll come to that eventually my son. Don't concern yourself with that just yet.

Well, I guess the best place to start is at the beginning. In this instance, my beginning. So, please accept my apologies for the short biography I'm about to relate to you. I know you have many questions, and I will answer them all for you at the relevant point in my tale.

Anyway, I was born in a dark cave in the mountains. Now, I say dark, yet it actually had a strange luminescence that emanated from some of the rock in the ceiling. Obviously, because of this nobody would enter the place for fear of demons or some such nonsense.

My mother however had found herself in a predicament. She had been busily climbing the mountain in search of some of the berries that grew in certain scrub bushes that littered the side of the cliff. Suddenly she found herself in labour, and she had to find somewhere level and secure to go through the birthing process.

So, pushing her fears aside, she took to the cave, and that's where I was born. In the illumination of what you'd call an artifact.

Now, as I'm sure Lazarus has informed you, since he actually knew the chap back in the day. Thirteenth century or so wasn't it Laz? Well my name isn't truly Masamuni, I just took it for ease of use and because I so admired the man. He was a swordsmith. But he was the best swordsmith the world has ever known. The quality of his work, for a mortal, was exceptional.

The only name I've truly ever had was when they all called me The Maker. So, if you agree, let's just say that my name is Maker.

It has a certain ring to it I think.

Anyway, I digress.

My mother, regrettably, died when I was far too young to have yet learnt my name, though I'm sure she would have given me one. Also, with her protection of me gone, the tribe, superstitious fools that they were, decided to eject the demon child of the cave. They therefore left me out on the barren wastes to be either taken by the beasts that roamed that place or to perish from the cold.

Don't look so shocked child" he whispered to sophia, leaning over his desk to tap her on the hand. "I regret to say that in those times infanticide was a most common affair. Whether it be that you don't want yet another girl to be of little use in the field and to burden you with a pricey dowry. Or perhaps your family is simply too poor to raise another child. Or maybe your husband has been away at war a long time and would be rather shocked to find he'd fathered a child whilst far in the east. Oh, my dear, there were reasons without number for such a thing. Most commonly it was the wealthy who's rampant licentiousness surely couldn't be interrupted by such a nuisance as a child.

Anyway, they were all most shocked and probably frightened to find that several days later, I still lay there, healthy and uneaten.

Eventually I was discovered by a farming family and raised with them a while. I assume the husband was thinking of how to have a useful farmhand to have on call in the future.

Well, I guess I wore out my welcome. Perhaps they found me too much of a handful. So, eventually they sold me to slavers.

I went to market with the rest, a good looking young boy, things could have taken a frightful turn in hindsight. However, in my case I was bought by a wealthy landowner to be put to work somewhere within his interests.

Now, please don't look too shocked when I tell you that my time as a slave was one of the happiest times of my life.

I had peers of a sort. Other slaves with whom we could whine and complain together about our conditions or treatment. Though in truth, for slaves, we were for the times very well treated.

Eventually, I discovered my niche you might say. My talent and eventual employment within my masters holdings.

I was given some basic training and a trial with the man's blacksmith. Eventually it became apparent that I was born to the art, finally surpassing my master with my creations.

The Lord therefore pensioned off my master and left the running of the forge to me.

I rose to the challenge admirably, and it soon became known that my lords Smithy made the best swords, or for that matter, the best of anything you wanted.

Some years passed this way. But I'd reached a point where I was creating things that many of that time would have called magic, had I shown them.

Obviously they weren't magic and today's current technologies would consider them quite antiquated. But considering what I had to work with I don't believe anyone could have done better, or for that matter have matched me.

My mind kept slipping back to that legendary glowing cave, and so one day I sequestered a horse and cart and I rode off for that far place where I'd been born.

When I finally found the place I discovered that what was glowing in the ceiling of this cave was a single huge rock. Quite different from the surrounding materials that formed the place. Looking at it it occurred to me that it must be one of those meteorites I'd heard about in certain circles.

A rock fallen from the heavens and crashed into the side of this cliff. Eventually becoming buried by the forever moving surface.

So, I selected my tools from the cart and began to chip away at the surrounding stone. I was obsessed at this point, I would excavate this vast lump of glowing rock.

And excavate it I did. Eventually manhandling it down the cliff side to my cart and thanking my exceptional strength to help me to load the thing.

Yes Lazarus, I'm sorry but I've neglected to mention, that as a child of that cave I was blessed with both exceptional strength and that regenerative ability of ours. An inability to die. The ability to regrow limbs and the like.

I did actually discover that there'd been another child born to that cave, and I sought you out.

However, when I found you you were living with a successful looking farmer and you appeared happy.

I didn't want to intrude on your happiness old boy, and so I let you be, with only a hired watcher to keep me informed of your situation.

Anyway, I finally got myself back to the forge and stowed my find away, before submitting, quite justly, to a whipping from my master for my running away and my stealing of a cart into the bargain.

Incidentally, my masters whipping was always a half hearted affair and never hurt me. It was only really done as an example to the other slaves. He had a fondness for me and hated it when he had to be seen to punish me.

Now, I took my time to closely examine my find.

In that close examination I identified that the glow emanated from thin threads that riddled the stone. Examining the threads in their turn I identified that they were some sort of metal.

Well, the next step was obvious. I would smelt it and withdraw this exceptional metal.

I quickly built the necessary equipment and during the night I began my work. I managed to extract an exceptional amount of metal. Although they were only thin threads, they were so numerous and so tightly packed. I honestly think that that artefact as you would call it was more metal than rock.

I rendered it all into bars of metal, for ease of use and hid it all away from unwanted eyes.

I then spent rather a lengthy period of time trying to decide what I would attempt to make first with this wondrous stuff I'd found.

I knew that nothing was beyond my skill. You see, that was my gift. The art of making, of creating things. That was the gift the artefact had imbued me with. The strength and regenerative ability came simply from having been born in its presence. A side effect of sorts."

He rose from his seat and he lay a hand on the shoulder of Lazarus. "Yes. I'm sorry son, but like I said, the strength and regeneration aren't your gift, they're just an accident of birth as it were. Even after all these lifetimes, you still haven't found your gift yet. Most strange. I'd always just thought you'd come across it some day by accident, but no. It's still to be discovered. Oh well, don't fret too much eh. You've got plenty of time still ahead of you. It'll turn up eventually I'm sure."

He returned to his seat and ran his hands through his deadlocked hair and tugged at his soul patch.

John glanced at Lazarus and saw that he appeared suddenly unsteady on his feet and was grasping at a nearby pillar to support himself.

Obviously the shock of those words had got to him. "Here Laz, old man. Take my seat" John said, standing and coaxing Lazarus to sit down.

"Where was I? Oh yes. What was I to make first? "

Maker continued.

"Well, after a great deal of thought, I came to the conclusion that I needed to find a safe place. I needed somewhere where I could be alone with my workings, somewhere where I wouldn't have to worry about unwanted eyes, nosey people or the risk of interference.

So, I came to the decision that I would build something that would allow me to look at other places without being there. So that I could look for a place and take its coordinates if I found the place for me.

It didn't take very long at all before I had a working model. One of the amazing things about that strange metal is that you don't need to use much of it at all. You can build the bulk of your project out of ordinary materials. It only takes the merest touch of this metal to be included within the work for it to take on incredible capabilities.

Anyway, there I was with this new gadget of mine, and I took a long time searching through the various locations that I found through its optical aperture. Finally, eureka, there it was. The place looked beautiful. Lush fertile land and woodland. A cliff with caves that looked ideal for my purposes. There was also a coastline with beautiful white fine sands and gorgeous blue waves.

The place seemed to have plenty of wildlife but very few predators. And the one important thing, there were no people. Not a soul to be seen anywhere and on fertile ground like this that was very odd.

Eventually I came to the conclusion that no living people existed in this place.

The thing is, I'd created this device to look 'Elsewhere' as it were, and it had never occurred to me that I was looking interdimensionally. Yes, I had created a device that gave me a gift of the worldwalkers.

I could see the other worlds.

Well, I took the coordinates of the location and left the device tuned to it to keep myself incentivized.

step number two was to build a way there.

So, I created a door.

It was a lovely piece of work if I do say so myself. It was predominantly fashioned of oak, but smoothed and stained into utter gorgeousness.

The fittings were of the magic metal and I inlaid a pattern of sorts including certain runic symbols and Latin text into the face of the door with the metal also.

The very door itself glowed.

Taking that final step, seeing that it had worked was an almost terrifying moment.

I kept putting it off.

Then finally, my heart filled with great trepidation, I reached for the handle and swung the door wide.

There on the other side, lay the large cave. The very place I'd targeted with my calculations.

I jumped straight through it in joy and ran out into the long lush grass of the field outside.

I ran to the edge of the woodland and stared up at the tall tall trees. I ran to the edge of the bluff and looked down at the sea and the sapphire waves that crashed upon the shore.

I was home.

Eventually of course I had to return, and reluctantly I closed that door behind me at my arrival there.

The door currently stood in the middle of the floor at the rear of the forge, held up with an improvised wooden framework I'd hastily and roughly knocked together.

Now, what was my next step to be.

I wanted to live in my newly discovered land, but I couldn't just leave this door lying around behind me. If found by anyone, they could follow me through. They could bring others with them. No it was unthinkable.

So, what was I to do.

Firstly, I once more opened the door and transferred through it all of my tools and personal effects. This was followed by the many bars of lustrous glowing metal.

That all done, I closed the door once more and affixed around its frame some lead weights. At the corners and down the sides.

Then, once more I stole away the horse and cart.

The door went into the back of the cart, and for a moment I just stood there and looked around the place I was leaving for good. I had many memories here, but I couldn't go seeking people out to say goodbye. It would be far too suspicious and would be assured to halt my departure.

So, finally, feeling slightly sad, I whipped the horses into action and headed the long distance to the sea. It took about four days to reach the place, but reach it I did, and I dragged the heavy door down to the beach with me, where I sat for a night and a day. My reason was to monitor the tide and identify the furthest point it withdrew down the sands.

That done I marked the point with a little flag.

I then waited for the next recession of the waves.

As they reached my marked point I hefted the door to my shoulders and strode decisively towards the waters.

I reached the flagged point and the waters wet my feet, but I didn't stop but continued to walk forwards. First the waters were at my knees, then shortly after at my waist. The water slowly rose up my chest as I continued my advance forward, until finally the waters were lapping at my neck.

This was it.

I positioned the door before me, and swung it wide open.

There was an enormous torrent of water that gushed through the door and I was swept with it.

Initially, having hit the ground quite hard I was briefly stunned. But then I saw my door leaning up against the wall at the back of the cave and dispelling enormous volumes of water.

I finally pulled myself together and grabbing the door I pushed it shut, struggling all the while against the force of the waters that tried to engulf me.

That finally done, I sat myself down into the deep puddles of water flooding the cave, and exulted at my success.

Back there, that door would have fallen to the sand beneath it. Weighed down by the lead weights it would stay in place, out of the sight of man, and eventually become buried beneath the sand and silt.

And so there you have it. That is, in encapsulated form, my history and my reason for living here on this unpopulated world. Seriously, there isn't anything resembling a human being on this planet. And you know the marvellous thing about that? It's untouched, undefiled, untainted. The nature of this world is how ours used to be before we all turned up and buggered it up.

There are forests here you could truly get permanently lost in they're so immense.

There are deer, rabbits, buffalo even, or something much like them. Parallel evolution or something, isn't that what they call it? I may be wrong.

Well, I've been here a long time now, and I must say I really don't miss having other people about me. My own company is something I'm very happy with.

So, anyway, I've been here busily making this and that as the urge took me.

When one day I decided to try to create a device that would allow me to see all the important events of the future. You know, Armageddon events or mass plagues or alien attacks and that sort of thing.

Incidentally John, the angels need the light, ok? "

"What? What do you mean? I don't understand." Spluttered a very confused John.

"Oh, don't worry about it for now boy. It's just something for you to remember in the future is all. Might be useful for you.

So, anyway. Create this device I did. And let me tell you. Worlds are such fragile things. There's one that's dying due to the actions of the inhabitants. Too much carbon dioxide and that sort of thing being pumped into the atmosphere. The planet is rapidly heading to a tipping point where it'll become uninhabitable for them.

And you know what they're doing about it?

Nothing. Not a damn thing. They're just ignoring it hoping it'll go away. Or they're just thinking, 'well, I'll be dead by the time it happens, so so what?'.

Ridiculous huh?

Otherwise there's attacks from beyond as it were, or there's evil gifted buggers out there that cause chaos and destruction. Oh, there's so much that can threaten a world, hell, threaten the entire multiverse.

Now, all this is future stuff yeah. What I see is stuff that's going to happen in the future. And there are certain points that the image becomes fuzzy. No that's not the right way of putting it. There are times that become kind of contradictory. Like two different things could happen at those points.

Looking closer into this, I discovered that these were axis points in history. Points were the actions of people could change the outcome. Places where a hero could save the day.

Then, looking closer still, I identified the same face turning up at a number of these incidents. An incredible coincidence I'm sure you'd agree.

Anyway, this face was armed in various ways. It had a certain power of its own and some of its weapons were perfectly suited to that power.

He was, in his way, very impressive. He would arrive on different worlds, he didn't just stick to his own. No, he would turn up on other worlds and help to save them. He didn't travel alone either, he would have others with him that would support him. But he was the dangerous one.

I became fascinated with this individual and spent some time watching his battles. Suddenly I was struck by the realisation that his weaponry had all the hallmarks on it of my work.

The conclusion was obvious.

This device showed me the future, and in that future, this individual, this guy was fighting with weapons that I had made.

So, my next step was to make the weapons, and obviously they couldn't just be ordinary weapons, they would need the touch of my magical metal. They would be weapons of excellence.

Now boy" and he raised a quizzical eyebrow at John. "Who do you think this mysterious warrior was, hmmm?"

John just sat there looking dazed. He wasn't bloody stupid. He could see where this was going. But seriously?

"Your going to tell me it's me aren't you?"

"Ahh hah" cried the man calling himself Maker. "Lazarus my boy, you picked one with brains to match didn't you? "
247

"I would say that you lay the path rather clearly for him there Maker" responded Lazarus.

"Really?" Asked Maker, looking somewhat crestfallen " I was trying to build it up for you all. The big reveal, you know? Ahh well, I guess I've been away from people too long, I'm missing the art of subtlety.

Well boy. What it all boils down to is that I created all your weaponry besides some other aspects of your kit.

Somehow, how I don't understand, you've already found some of your equipment. I'm referring obviously to your knives and helmet.

But what you don't realise is that there's more to your weaponry than just that.

I've made the effort to track it all down and I've gathered it all together".

"But" interrupted John. "What I don't understand is why you didn't have it all already. I mean, I found my knives and helmet buried at the back of an old basement. Where have all the other bits been and why?"

"Ahh, yes, good question boy. Now, looking back I really don't know what I was thinking, but it occurred to me that they needed breaking in as it were, before you inherited them.

And so, I transported the bits and pieces to people I thought deserving, back in time. Now the things themselves are indestructable, so I had no worries on that score. Meanwhile, other people, normal people, mostly anyway, could use these tools to their advantage and for the good of the people around them. "

"So what your saying" asked John "is that you kind of armed various heroes throughout history, to help them battle their foes or fulfill their quest or whatever yeah?"

"Yes John " replied Maker "obviously I was able to monitor their careers through my device and there were tipping points where my creations helped that hero to win the day and thus avoid catastrophe. "

John leaned back against the pillar Lazarus had been grasping at so recently and took his stubbly chin in his hand. The very epitome of thoughtfulness.

"Well John" maker continued " there's a whole bunch of world risking events coming up lad. Not just our world but others too. Yet here you are, betrothed to a worldwalker, so your influence could save other worlds where their tipping points lay and yet they have no powerful hero of their own to intervene for them. You have to admit boy, with your gift your quite formidable to begin with. Just think of my equipment as an accessory eh? I'm fairly sure they've been of use to you already . Especially those knives eh?"

An image of his blade buried in the back of his mother's skull flashed through John's mind. But he gave his head a violent shake. No, he wouldn't think of that. He refused to.

"Yeah, sure" he responded "the helmet too. Especially the ability to see in the dark".

"ahh yes, the mirror mask. One of my favourite creations that one. It'll serve you well in the future son. Trust me.

However, back to the actual point of your visit I guess. There is some equipment you've yet to add to your arsenal. And with the things you will be facing in your future boy, I believe you should

249

have the full set. You'll use some more than others surely, but all will be useful to you at some point or other".

He rose from his seat and squeezed out from behind his desk. He then walked over to one of the work surfaces scattered about the room.

At a glance, all John could see there was a large bundle of dark cloth.

This bundle Maker picked up and gesturing for everyone else to follow him he moved to a clear work top in the centre of the room.

They all followed in kind until they all found themselves standing in a rough circle about the work surface as Maker laid the bundle down upon it.

He then jumped up, as though just struck by an afterthought, and jogging over to yet another worktop he returned with a separate bundle which he placed on the table besides the other.

"I haven't forgotten you Sophia my dear" he said in hushed tones "I have a couple of gifts for you too."

He then stepped back and rolled up his sleeves, like an illusionist proving he had no card hidden there.

"Right John" he breathed " are you ready? "

"Er, yeah, sure" replied John, feeling a little nonplussed at all the drama. So, this guy was going to give him some more kit. He couldn't see the reason for all the theatrics.

"Right then" Maker said in almost awed tones, "Here goes then".

He reached into the large bundle and pulled forth something black that he placed before John on the tabletop. Two things in fact he now saw.

Looking at them, it took him a second to identify them, but then realised that they were dark metal forearm guards, or vambrace he thought they were called back in the day.

"Yes" blurted Maker excitedly "with these on your arm you can block any blow, however severe. Also it absorbs all the kinetic energy, so you'd barely feel any impact. And one more thing, if you cross them before yourself you'll created an immense impenetrable shield in front of you".

"But" said John, worried that he might offend this man "I can already create shields with my telekinesis".

"oh I know John, I know. But nothing like this. Besides, with these in use you won t have to concentrate your mind raising shields, you'll have one permanently strapped to your arm. Trust me boy, you'll find it most useful".

"Er, OK" was all John could think of saying in response. Though in reality he couldn't see the point of these things.

Next from the bundle appeared a pair of black leather boots. The toes capped in a black metal as were the heels.

"And what do these do?" Asked John, becoming a touch more interested. He liked the boots. He thought they looked cool.

"Ahh yes" Maker blurted " well, the most obvious ability of these boots is that if you kick anything or anyone you will create a great blast of force"

John nodded thoughtfully.

"Secondly, and much more importantly I think, these boots allow you to walk or run on any surface".

John raised an eyebrow at this "And What does that mean exactly?" He asked amiably. He liked the boots very much.

"Well, you can walk on water for example".

"Really?". Asked John ."That's kind of cool."

"Well, that's the least of it" continued Maker "when I say any surface I mean it. For example you could walk on a lake of lava and the boots would protect your entire body from the heat. You could walk on walls or even the ceiling, and from your perspective, whatever your boots stand on will be 'Down'. So, you won't feel like your hanging anywhere. Your entire perspective will change".

"Hmm" breathed John "I'm impressed" he said

Makers hand groped within the bundle once more.

Whilst Maker was busy groping, John was busy kicking off his trainers and slipping on the boots. They went on with ease, a perfect fit, and were fastened with a simple leather strap and buckle arrangement across their face. He had them on in no time at all, and taking a few steps backwards and forwards he mockingly asked Sophia "What do ya think love?"

She smiled and nodded "they look good John, how do they feel?"

"they feel kind of strange. It almost feels as though my feet were bare, as though the boots weren't there at all. Really comfy".

His attention returned to the table top and Maker.

"Sorry old man. I guess I got a bit carried away."

"no problem John. I'm glad you like them".

His hand next produced from the diminishing bundle a large bright silver star like thing.

It was made of an extraordinarily shiny silver metal, about the size of a man's hand, and gorgeously engraved with runic symbols and knotwork. It was a thing of beauty.

"And what's that?" Asked John .

"Ahh" sighed Maker "well, firstly, it's a form of armour as it where. It's to be worn over your heart, and with its contrasting colour, the silver against all your black, it will tend to make itself a target.

If you find yourself grievously injured and your heart failing, this thing will kick in and support your heart for you. And lastly, it's a form of communication device, though we'll come back to that later".

John couldn't think of a response, though looking at the thing, he did think it looked rather attractive, almost beautiful to his jaundiced eye.

"And finally, you have these" Maker said, lifting from the now empty bundle two large dagger like things. John thought dagger rather than sword due to its short size. But for daggers they seemed exceptionally long. The handle was strange John thought until he realised it was actually a grip. There were two metal sides to the grip and halfway down their length there were two subtly curved crossbars. These were some sort of punching dagger They were sheathed at present and seemed connected together by some sort of harness arrangement. Maker freed one of the blades from its sheath and John marvelled at the workmanship. The blades were double edged to a razor sharpness and engraved their full length with a complicated though subtle pattern.

They were gorgeous he thought.

"Yes, I based the design on the old Indian katar punching dagger. They would pretty much penetrate any armour"

"And what do these do?" He asked.

"Well" replied Maker "fundamentally, they kill people boy. They're much like your daggers, the blade will always remain razor sharp and it will cut through anything. That's pretty much the lot son".

"Well" said John "I love them regardless of whether they have any fantastic powers or not. How does this harness thing work?"

"Ahh" Maker breathed "that's just how you wear them boy. Here, let me help."

 And Maker took up the blades and harness which it transpired linked to the harness of blades he was already wearing. This positioned the long lethal blades, crossed across each other at the small of his back. Easy to access and out of the way at the same time.

The silver starlike thing was gathered up and placed over John's heart, where it remained in place without any form of fastening.

Finally it was time for the vambrace, and these could be simply slipped up his arm, like a sleeve, yet once in position they held their place indisputably without any other fastening needed.

The end of them ran up his upper arm and came to a distinct point. John couldn't see the point of this other than perhaps for the look of the thing, but when he bent his arm he realised that what it meant was that he had a fairly long spike like point jutting from his elbow. Now that might surely be useful in a tussle.

"Here" cried Maker, and he pulled a cloth from the wall, revealing a full length mirror.

John stepped before it in admiration. He pulled down his visor to see himself as his enemy's would.

He looked badass he thought.

"Er, thank you" he stuttered, feeling somewhat lost for words.

"I haven't quite finished yet" said maker, pulling the smaller bundle in front of himself.

"Its your turn now my dear" he said to Sophia.

Firstly he produced a necklace bearing a small star upon it, much like the one worn on John's chest.

"Essentially, this does exactly the same as that star there" he pointed at John "now, the communication I mentioned before is between these two devices. You will be able to speak to each other however far apart you are. You could be in different dimensions and it would make no difference. Now obviously neither device contains a speaker. No, the voice you hear from it will be in your head. All you need to do is think of speaking to the other and the connection will be made. In fact, you can actually think your message to the other, you don't have to speak out loud, though You can if you wish obviously."

"Oh, thank you" said Sophia as she allowed Maker to fasten it around her neck, the star now hanging between her breasts.

"Oh" he said "and the chain is unbreakable too. That's probably irrelevant to you but you never know if it might turn out useful in the future".

He rummaged once more in the bundle, finally producing a silver ring bearing a large square ruby stone.

"My last gift to you" Maker sighed, as though disappointed he didn't have more to show off.

He handed it to Sophia "Right index finger my dear" he said.

She slipped the ring onto her hand expecting such a large stone to look quite vulgar. However, once there she thought it looked quite beautiful, as though meant to be there.

"Now" continued Maker "you see it now in its square position yes?"

"Sure" answered Sophia.

"Well, if you now carefully turn the gem until it's in a diamond position.

This Sophia did, as instructed.

Immediately a bright red light leapt from the stone. However, this light wasn't cast anywhere. No, the light projected about six or so inches from the stone, then just stopped in mid air.

John couldn't get the thought of light sabers out of his mind, and he briefly attempted to make the sound of one under his breath, with a chuckle.

"Oh" whispered Sophia.

"Yes" Maker said smiling "that will cut through absolutely any material. It will most definitely be useful for you in the future my dear.

"Oh, thank you so much" said Sophia in hushed tones.

Maker now looked up at Lazarus and frowned.I

"I'm sorry Lazarus old man, I don't really have anything for you. I'm still really surprised you've yet to find your gift. I tell you what, I'll look into that for you. Maybe I can create something that'll bring it out of you. Hmm" he pulled at his dreadlocks a moment, then "ah hah" he cried, and he darted to a drawer, where he had a quick rummage before producing two smallish box like things that fit nearly into the palm of his hand. Maker handed one to him, then made a kind of flicking motion of the hand holding the other. A flap of some kind flipped open at the top and a strange chirping sound came from the thing. As it did, his own made a similar noise and a red light appeared at its top. "Now you go" said maker, a joyous grin on his face. "Me go?" Asked lazarus.

"flip the thing like I did"

"Oh" breathed Lazarus in sudden comprehension, and he flicked his wrist as he'd seen Maker do.

Again, a flap of some sort appeared and it made that chirping noise again.

"Now we can talk to each other" said maker, his voice both coming obviously from his mouth and the device in Lazarus's hand simultaneously.

"Oh, so it's a walkie talkie" he said, suddenly understanding.

"Well, sort of I guess" said Maker looking somewhat crestfallen "it was something I saw on one of your old tv programs. Star Trek I think it was called. Yes, that's it. Well, they used this kind of thing in the show and it just tickled me, ya know? So, I knocked up a working model, just as a bit of diversion.

Now, if you take that with you, if I come up with anything regarding your gift, I can give you a call, ok?"

"Er, yeah, ok. Er, thanks man". Said Lazarus.

Lazarus slipped the device into his pocket and rejoined Sophia and John, where they were busy admiring each other's gifts.

"Right chaps" He said

"What next?"

"I'm afraid I haven't got any refreshments to offer you " said Maker "so you might as well sod off now. I've done the important thing and got you properly kitted out for your most interesting futures.

So, er, bye folks" he said and began to wave at them.

John looked to Sophia and she gave a shrug. Went through the motions and created a door, John opened it and stepped through into their bedroom, followed shortly afterwards by Lazarus. The two stood there a moment and looked at the door. Where the hell was Sophia? But then, suddenly she appeared. "You alright boys?" She asked, closing the door behind her and winking it out of existence .

"Well" breathed a rather perplexed looking Lazarus. "That was all rather interesting wasn't it eh?"

"I'd say" cried John, busy admiring himself in the freshly revealed mirror.

Sophia, being the more empathic of the couple, lay a hand upon Lazarus's arm. "Are you ok Laz? " she asked softly.

"Er, I think so love. It's just, I always thought I knew my gift. Turns out that that's just a side effect of my birth, and I've yet to discover what my gift is. I've been around a long bloody time love. It's kind of a shock to the system if you get me? "

"I understand Laz. You know where I am if you ever feel like a chat".

"sure love, thanks."

They parted, Lazarus heading off back to his room to cries of "get down from there you fool" from Sophia behind him, as John tried out his newly acquired walking on walls and ceilings ability.

Thirty one

Everyone appeared the following morning at their usual places around the dining table to devour their full English breakfasts.

Vladimir and Isaac both had acquired the taste for the old British favourite, though Isaac had decided to forego the black pudding once it was explained to him what it was exactly.

They both now claimed that their diets would change when they went home.

John, when he had had enough breakfast, took a stand for a moment at the head of the table.

"Right guys. It's my proposal that we go back on the offensive tomorrow. Tomorrow we finally go and finish that bastard oblivion off. We'll take today as a day of rest to get our acts together yeah? Feet up, relax, whatever does it for you.

Everybody happy with that? "

There was the murmur of assent throughout the whole gathering, and with the quick flash of a thumbs up from John, he was off.

He found himself in the lounge, his head leaning against the wall and his hand hovering over the telephone.

He'd had word that his mother's body had been found in the old abandoned graveyard he'd suggested.

Word was circulating that she'd had some kind of unexpected heart attack. Most unexpected by her doctor, most out of the blue.

But then again, these things happened didn't they.

He guessed that by now his dad would have been informed. Hell, he'd probably been dragged in to identify the body, poor sod.

His mum might well have thrown him to the wolves. Deserted him for no identifiable reason.

But he'd still loved her. So the news of her death, even though she was his ex now, was going to hurt him bad.

John was steeling himself up to the phonecall. The trouble was, as cut up as he was himself over his mother's death, especially since he'd been the one to actually kill her, he was going to have to go through the whole pantomime.

He in theory would know nothing of her death.

This phone call was to give his dad the opportunity to tell him of it. To weep with him down the line and go through all the motions of sudden grief.

He just really wasn't sure he was up to it.

He'd spent the last few days working through his grief and his immense feeling of guilt, and he'd come to a point where he thought he had a handle on it now. To have to imitate it, to have to pretend to go through it again. He just wasn't sure he could handle that.

He took a loud deep sigh and suddenly there was a tender hand upon his shoulder.

"Calling dad?" Asked Sophia's concerned voice.

"Trying to" replied John, his head still pressed against the wall and his eyes tightly closed, as though to dam back the tears that he knew would come.

If his father knew. If his father knew he was responsible for his mother's death. Could he ever forgive him.

"Please John" whispered Sophia as she squeezed his upper arm. " Please, don't blame yourself so much. You were trying to save her from untold suffering. I spent enough time in that swines head to know that he wasn't joking about torturing her. She'd have become a slave to his whims and she'd have suffered greatly. You did the right thing."

"But I could have killed 'Him' Soph. I had a bunch of blades just hanging over his head. I could have put any number of them straight through his skull".

"Yes John, but you didn't know that. Up to that point he'd been immune to every form of attack we could muster. When you did wound him, even that was accidental in its way. You just lashed out, instinctively, and the blade sunk home. You had no idea that would happen, none of us knew the origin of your blades at that point. Please John, you have to try to accept that you did the best you could with the knowledge you had. No body could have asked more of you".

He opened his eyes and looked at Sophia.

His Sophia.

She was worth any sacrifice.

He straightened up and took her in his arms. "I love you sweetheart, you know that don't you".

She leaned back and kissed him passionately. "Yes John, I know. And I love you too. More than you could ever imagine."

They both smiled and embraced once more, before finally John broke away.

Guess I've a call to make eh?

"Yes" she said very simply, and tapping him on the arm she spun on her heel and left him to it.

A moment passed, then he suddenly called out after her " ere love. Ya couldn't make us a coffee could ya?"

Faintly he heard her reply. "Make your call John" .

He glanced back down at the phone, his dark mood returning.

"Ahh shit" he growled, and he snatched up the handset.

It was a cordless phone so he was able to take a wander with it. He eventually found himself on the sofa, lying it's length and with a cushion covering his face as though he was hiding from the world.

He hesitatingly dialed the number, and waited.

The phone rang and rang, and he finally began to think, no, to hope, that his dad was out. But suddenly the ringtone stopped and an angry voice came on the line.

"Who's this? What do you want?" Growled the voice down the line at him. It was so rare for his father to show any sign of anger that John was momentarily taken aback, and the thought 'He Knows' briefly flickered through his mind, to be quickly buried as fast as it had appeared.

"Oh, hi dad. Sorry, have I called at a bad time?"

There was an uncomfortable period of silence, in which John could imagine the thoughts going through the man's head at the other end.

'Oh god. It's my son. I'm gonna have to tell him his mums dead. What do I do? What should I say first? How's he going to react?'.

Yeah, he thought he had a rough idea of the man's thoughts. But he couldn't think of any way he could make things any easier for him.

He guessed that this had been a call they'd both been dreading for their own reasons.

Finally his father's voice returned, though he thought it sounded a little shaky.

"Er, no son, no. Not a bad time at all. I've just got a few things on my plate right now is all.

It's good to hear from you boy. You must be psychic or something as I was going to give your mobile a tinkle soon myself for a catchup".

He was handling himself well, John thought. How was he going to steer this to the fact that his mother was dead? he wondered.

"oh right" said John, his mind a whirl "so, is there anything going on your end then?"

"why do you ask" came his father's croaky voice.

"Oh, it's just unusual for you to call me is all" John stuttered. He was hoping he was setting his father up for the big reveal.

"Ahh, well, yes son. I guess it is at that. My fault I know. I should keep in contact with you more often I think. Maybe from now on eh?"

"what's so special about now" John asked carefully.

"Well son" his father began, and John thought, 'This is it'.

"Well, you know your mum's been missing a while now ? Months in fact."

"Yeah, sure. Out on a bender or something right".

"well son." And again there was that lengthy pause "she's been found".

John squeezed his eyes tight.

"Oh, right. Where's she been then eh?" He asked

"She's, ... She's dead son. I'm so sorry".

"What?" Cried John in mock astonishment. "How, what happened?"

"Well, nobody really knows to be honest son. The coroner says she had a heart attack. But, when they found her, she'd only been dead about a day or so. So where she's been all this time is still a mystery.

But, no mysterious circumstances apparently, just a simple heart attack."

"But where? " Asked John, "where did they find her?"

"that's the strange thing" replied his father "she was found in the old graveyard. You know, that abandoned old church around the corner."

"What? " John blustered "why there for God's sake. Was she looking up grandma and grandpa's graves or something?"

That had been John's reasoning when he'd picked the location. He'd thought that might seem plausible.I

"Well it's possible son" his dad sighed "but even that doesn't really make any sense. It's my parents buried there, not hers. Why would she go to the graves of my parents. She's made it quite clear she wanted nothing to do with me".

Oh what a sodding idiot. Bugger it all to hell. He'd got the grandparents confused. Sure, it made no bloody sense for her to be visiting his dad's dead parents. Shit.

"Oh" he breathed, at a complete loss. "Well, maybe she wasn't visiting any single persons grave or anything. Maybe she just fancied a graveyard walk, ya know? Maybe she was having a maudlin moment or something. You have to admit it's a beautiful place. I've walked there myself a few times "

"Really?" asked his father, sounding unconvinced.

"Yeah, sure" John answered, his pulse beginning to lower now. This wasn't a bad excuse to be honest. It might put his dad's mind to rest on the subject.

"Oh, oh well. Maybe your right son. Still, I'd love to know where she's been all this time.

"We'll probably never find out" sighed John.

"Yeah, your probably right. Anyway, so, there you have it son. Your mum's passed on. I'm really sorry boy".

"No, I'm really sorry dad" John's voice had feeling in it "even after all the shit she put you through, I know you still loved her".

"Yeah son, I did" and John could hear that he was beginning to cry.

"I tell you what boy, I'll give you a buzz when I've sorted out the date for the funeral yeah? I'd better crack on, I've a lot to be doing as you can imagine".

266

"Sure dad, sure. You take care of yourself ok?" And that was it. The call was over.

John tossed the disconnected phone across the room to land on a nearby armchair.

He remained for a while, reclined the sofas length and with the cushion over his face.

Then the cushion went the way of the phone and swinging his legs around he sat himself up.

He noticed that there on the coffee table before him was a steaming mug of coffee.

Bless her, he thought to himself. I don't deserve to be so lucky.

He reached forward and picked up the coffee. Then slouched back into the upholstery of the sofa as he sipped at his brew.

He felt an enormous sense of relief at having got that call out of the way.

It had been unavoidable he knew, but he'd been dreading it so much. In the end, although very uncomfortable it hadn't been anywhere near as bad as he'd feared.

Well, it was done now.

Tomorrow they'd head off and end that bastard that was responsible for it all.

Evening came and Kathryn treated them all to her speciality of stew and dumplings for dinner.

Yet another resplendent feast as far as Vladimir and Isaac were concerned. They'd always been led to believe that British food was just tasteless stodge. Well, ok, with the dumplings there was a touch of stodge, but it certainly wasn't tasteless, and they intended to take a few notes and prove to their fellows back home that the tales of English food were a myth.

After dinner, and after Vladimir and Isaac had harassed Kathryn for some recipes they all reached for the beers. There was a strange celebratory atmosphere, even though they had yet to complete their task. The villain was still out there, Alive and kicking. What was there to celebrate. Besides which, surely going on the piss the very night before a mission was a bad idea.

But for some reason they just couldn't seem to stop themselves.

They knew, they truly knew, that John would have no trouble dispatching the evil lunatic, and consequently it almost felt like a done deal already.

They drank from bottles of beer. John, strangely, felt that drinking from cans was a kind of low class, delinquent kind of activity. He knew it made him some kind of snob, but it was just there, seemingly written into his bones. Bottles were ok, but cans were for the plebs.

Needless to say, the ladies, even Eleanor, much to everyone's surprise, chose to drink from glasses. Much to the lads amusement.

They were all scattered around the lounge. Some lounging on the sofas, like John, again laying it's length with Sophia on his lap.

Others, like Vladimir and Isaac predominantly, we're examining the bits and pieces they found on the shelves and on top of sideboards and the like.

Meanwhile, Lazarus, lounging comfortably in an armchair, leaning back into the upholstery and resting his feet up on the coffee table before him. Was busy expostulating the concept that even after the thousands of years he'd passed on this world, he was still yet to find his gift. A gift that during all that time he hadn't known was missing.

He'd thought that his amazing regenerative ability and hence immortality, combined with his extraordinary strength, were his gift. But no, he'd recently been informed that these fantastic abilities or powers were in fact simply an accident of his having been born under the glare of an artefact. An artefact that incidentally didn't exist any more but that had been rendered down to It's metal constituents and was busy being used to create magical powerful weapons and the like.

So, where was his damn gift. Granted he'd not been looking for it until now, but surely during thousands of years of life he'd have stumbled across it wouldn't he?

Lazarus was in a rather grumpy mood and the beer wasn't helping in that regard.

"Well maybe" said John consolingly "maybe you should consider putting yourself through the same kind of method you'd use on a new recruit"

He sipped some more of his beer as he frowned in thought. Alcohol didn't really improve John's cognitive ability, and whilst under its influence he often found it difficult to think at all.

The funny thing about all of the gifted was that they could drink and get drunk, they could take drugs and get high, yet due to their gift, the moment anything dangerous occurred, say they were attacked, they would immediately find themselves sober. It wasn't unknown for gifted individuals to arrange with a colleague in advance for him or her to suddenly surprise them, to make them jump in shock. It always worked and they'd find themselves suddenly completely sober and perhaps now able to drive home.

"Yeah" John continued, "take yourself to the gym and stand there in the middle of the room like any newbie, and kind of flex, or reach out with your mind or soul or whatever, and see what happens. Surely it can't hurt."

"Hmm" murmured Lazarus thoughtfully. "Maybe boy, maybe I'll give it a try soon. Like you say. It surely can't hurt. "

"Hey Lazarus" called Isaac across the room, interrupting John and Lazarus's ruminations on his missing gift.

"What's this old chap" and he waved what appeared to be a palm sized brown thing, like some kind of slab of something, encased in a protective layer of lucite.

"Ahh" purred lazarus "that my boy is my beginnings".

"Eh?" Queried Isaac " I can see it's covered in some kind of small symbols. I don't know if their just decoration or something, but the way their laid out they look more like writing".

"That they are boy" Lazarus said, his voice sounding strangely introspective.

"Really?" Continued Isaac " it doesn't look like any kind of language I recognise. "

"Its very old boy. The closest language to it I can think of is Sumerian, though that writing you hold there pre dates them slightly, though there's an obvious resemblance".

"Jesus" sighed Isaac "this has got to be one of the oldest things on the planet. And it's in such good nick too. This should be in a museum Lazarus. How come you have it?" He asked.

"because I wrote it boy" said Lazarus in a surprisingly sober voice.

"You what" cried Isaac, now supported by Vladimir who stood by his side peering at the object.

"But we're talking about eight thousand years ago or something like that. How old are you exactly Lazarus" .

"Pretty damn old lad" Lazarus began to chuckle. "I've seen civilizations rise and fall. I've been killed, superficially if you get my meaning, countless times. I've seen the rise of humanity, from barbarism, through various attempts at civilization. Right up to our current day. I'm just waiting for the barbarism to return, that'll be the next step".

"What? But why would we slip back into barbarism Lazarus" asked Vladimir . "Surely, right now,we're so advanced, nothing like that could ever happen".

"Boy" Lazarus sighed, sounding as though he was a teacher pointing out some basic errors in a student's work. "No civilization lasts forever. Every One of them, every one, collapsed at some point. I used to think we had a good chance with the Romans. Then the barbarism rules for a while until the next civilization rises in it's place. I grant you, this one has lasted much longer than usual, but still, there's signs out there, if you know where to look, that it's crumbling in places."

"Jesus Laz" piped up John "aren't you a bundle of joy?"

"Do you want to know what it actually says boy? Hand it to me, and I'll read it to you. There's not much to it really. As I said, it's kind of my genesis. I found An iron box, put the tablet in it to dry, then hid the thing. I hid it damn well too. Came back a century or so later, and found it still where I'd hid it. Because of what it was, I decided to preserve the thing, so I found the most perfect long term hiding

271

place, and I only recovered it a few decades ago. Then, to protect the thing, it was very fragile, I covered it in the lucite, as you can see".

Isaac approached Lazarus with a strangely anxious expression on his face. John got the impression that he regretted having asked about the thing in the first place. As though he was somehow intruding where he wasn't meant to be.

He handed the tablet over, and then seemed to retreat further back into the room as though he expected it all to explode.

Lazarus took the lucite block in his hands and peered thoughtfully at the markings embossed into the once wet clay.

"I remember the day I wrote this. Even after all this time, it's as clear as day. It hasn't faded at all.

Right. You ready boys?"

"Yeah" "Right on" "go for it" came the multiple cries in response from the room before him.

"Ok chaps, here goes"

At this, he paused, closed his eyes, and ran a hand down his face. Then opening his eyes once more, he began.

"Today I died.

Our encampment was attacked during the night, catching the watchmen and killing them silently.

The whole camp was herded to the edge of the river and put under guard till morning whilst they rifled through our possessions.

It became clear come dawn why they had waited till daytime.

It was so they could examine the women more clearly.

They took many of the women, leaving only the old or the scarred.

Then they proceeded to kill us, and cast our bodies into the river.

Man, woman and child. All were killed.

We were five thousand in number, yet all were put to the sword.

I received a spear through my chest. Then another man slashed me across the belly and my entrails slid out onto my lap.

Finally a third man buried his axe in my head.

I died. I knew nothing but blackness.

But then I awoke.

I had washed up on a mud bank somewhere down the river.

I looked down but my stomach was whole. Not even a scar. The chest wound from the spear was gone too.

And the touch of my hands proved my skull to be intact.

I lay back in awe.

What did this mean?

I had just died.

And yet here I lay whole.

I do not understand this world, but I hope one day it might make sense to me.

I put this story to the clay in the hope you will believe me dear reader.

I died today, yet now am whole.

What does this mean?"

Lazarus finished his narration and put the lucite block on the coffee table.

"There you go boys. Like I said before, that block of clay essentially marked my genesis. The first moment of my life in which I discovered I wasn't normal.

With a tremble to his voice, Isaac said "I'm sorry Lazarus. If I've upset you in any way, maybe brought back bad memories. Then please forgive me. I was only curious as to what it was."

Lazarus just smiled at him warmly. "no worries lad. You've not upset me. Sometimes we need reminding where we came from".

There was an uncomfortable length of silence, then Lazarus said "actually I'm pretty tired. We've a job on tomorrow. I'm going to bed. Goodnight folks" and he left the lounge and headed to the stairs.

"Well" slurred John around his beer. "That was all a bit heavy wasn't it?"

"Yeah" answered a contrite Isaac. "I wish I hadn't brought it up now. It obviously affected Lazarus quite a bit didn't it?"

"Yep" answered John "but Lazarus is a tough old bird. He'll get over it. Hell he's probably forgotten all about it already. And he doesn't hold grudges, so don't worry about that.

However". He continued "I think he was right on one score. I too am tired, so it's time for bed".

He tapped Sophia on the rear and she slipped off his lap to the floor.

"You still ok to do that thing for me?" He asked her as he rose himself .

"Oh, I surely am John, as long as you keep up your end of the bargain" and she giggled like a mischievous child.

They headed up the stairs to bed, leaving Isaac and Vladimir alone with Kathryn and Eleanor.

"You two staying up" asked Eleanor with a smile.

"Not for long" replied Isaac "think I'll get myself around some coffee first though".

"Now that's a good idea" spoke up Kathryn. "I'll go get the brew sorted" and she headed to the kitchen.

Suddenly there was a loud cry and a thud from upstairs. Isaac and Vladimir leapt to their feet about to rush upstairs, when Eleanor, chuckling, stopped them in their tracks.

"No, no, boys. Don't worry about a little noise. I happen to know that John made arrangements with Sophia for their bedtime tonight. He didn't want to go to bed pissed. He wanted all his, er... Wits with him as it were when sharing his bed with Sophia tonight, so he asked her to surprise the hell out of him somehow. She wasn't to tell him her plans, as that would have ruined the surprise.

She told me though" and she smirked an evil looking smirk.

"What, what did she do to him" cried both Isaac and Vladimir in unison.

"Well, you know her power obviously"

"Well, yeah, sure" answered Vladimir

"Well" continued Eleanor "she arranged for a rift to open beneath his feet. Needless to say he fell through it. Now what she'd arranged was for him to fall into an awful world. A world with all the appearance

275

of Dantes hell, with John plummeting towards the bottom of the pit. Then, just before he was to crash to the bottom of this fiery pit, she opened another rift for him to fall through, back into their bedroom. Now, I'm sure that'll have sobered the boy up. And I'm sure he'll be er... Most grateful tonight".

Both Vladimir and Isaac chuckled to themselves as Kathryn reappeared bearing a tray laden with cups of steaming coffee.

"Well, I think I'll sober up the old fashioned way" said Isaac. "Me too" echoed Vladimir.

And the four stayed up another hour or two. Chatting and drinking only coffee. The beers would now be saved for their next celebration.

Thirty two

The next day dawned.

This was to be the day of judgement.

This the day that scores were to be settled.

Lazarus, the girls, Kathryn and Eleanor, and the boys Vladimir and Isaac. Stood waiting in the gym as previously arranged.

Everybody had breakfasted early today, and the dining table had remained mostly silent throughout, a symptom of the tension within the group.

There was none of the usual banter or joking about. Everybody had their serious head on. There were deeds to be done today, and each of them were too engulfed in their own thoughts, their own premonitions of what lay ahead of them and their own overwhelming desire to pull off a good job today.

Vladimir just couldn't get the thought of being lost in the forest out of his head. That had been an incident it would take him a long time to forget, it was so humiliating. He had to make up for that today, he had to balance the books.

Isaac felt somewhat perturbed about the whole mission. He couldn't remember a single moment of their last contact with this man. All he knew was that he'd escaped the battle with a damn great hole through his shoulder. So, he really didn't know what they would be facing at all, and that lack of knowledge bothered him mightily.

Both the girls, Eleanor and Kathryn both, were unsure what they could contribute. Sure, Eleanor could link all their minds. Well, all except Johns, she'd have to remember to grab up those walkie talkies. But what else was she good for?

Kathryn felt much the same. She could make them invisible, but if he was wearing those dark glasses then she couldn't blind him, and nothing else she could do would harm his flesh.

The only consolation she could think of was that she could protect Sophia. She'd keep all them girls together and keep them invisible, thus out of any fight.

Actually, the way she understood it, now that John knew he could knife the bastard the fight would be a rather short and one sided one.

What was she worrying about?

Finally, first Sophia, wearing a beautiful diaphanous dress, with a charming star like necklace to set it off. She was also wearing a rather gaudy large ruby ring on her right hand, which Eleanor found unusual as Sophia never wore Jewellery as a rule. The necklace was one thing, it kind of set off the dress, but the ring?

First Sophia entered the gym, giving everyone a smile and a wave. "You ready folks?" She asked them all heartily.

There was the general muffled murmur of assent from everyone.

Kathryn thought Sophia looked absolutely beautiful. It was as though she had a glow to her. You could almost think.....But no. That wasn't possible.

Finally John entered. This was the first time everyone had seen him completely kitted out with his new equipment. And it must be said that they all thought he looked formidable. Almost frightening.

"Ready guys?" He asked, and there was a slightly more enthusiastic murmur of assent from the group.

He turned to Sophia.

"Can you find him love?

She closed her eyes for a mere moment then smiled triumphantly.

"I've got him John"

"Excellent" breathed John "anything we need to know about the environment love?"

"Er, no John no, it's a normal planet earth style environment. Normal atmosphere, normal gravity, the works.

Now, he has managed to throw up some kind of shield around himself. It's a rather pathetic construct and won't keep us away from him, but it will mean that I won't be able to bring you out any closer than about two hundred yards. Oh, and he's based indoors".

"Ok my love" John said firmly, placing his helmet on his head.

Isaac and Vladimir both looked at John with new eyes. He was dressed in black cargo pants and a black tshirt. But over that simplicity, there were the black leather boots, that Isaac thought looked so cool and he wondered where he might buy a pair. There was the standard harness covering his body with an array of skull hilted blades, but now he had these black metal forearm guards that ended with an elbow spike. And sheathed, crossing each other at the small of his back were two black short swords, or long knives. The overall effect was very imposing, and both lads couldn't help but feel rather under dressed for this outing.

"Right hun" growled John, obviously getting himself in the mood for a fight. "Do your thing".

279

Sophia went through her usual motions of prayer, then parting her hands to reveal a large oaken door hanging there in thin air.

This was a large double door, not her usual cultivated normal single panel door.

It had occurred to her and John both that the normal door only allowed people through it pretty much one at a time, this presenting the perfect target to any enemy. This way with the double door they would be able to burst forth as a group. Surely much more effective under the circumstances.

"Right, We all ready? Asked John, flexing his shoulders and stretching his legs as though he was warming up for a race.

"Hang on John" came the high piping voice of Eleanor . And she pushed herself forward past the boys and with an outstretched hand passed John a walkie talkie.

"Oh, yeah, right. Good thinking Ells" said John, seeming somewhat annoyed at himself for not having thought of this aspect of their mission himself.

"You want to confirm coms with everyone before we go through hun?"

"Sure John" she confirmed.

She touched at her temple and broadcast "All online?" Then one by one she looked into the faces of each of them for confirmation. They each either nodded or gave her a "yes maam" and eventually she was satisfied.

"The coms is pretty much my only contribution to this enterprise. I want to make sure to get it right lads"

"Understood Ells" said John in a thankful tone of voice. "I'm kind of annoyed at myself for not having thought of it myself earlier. We very nearly ran in there with no coms at all".

He paused a moment and looked around at his group. He noticed that Lazarus had forgone his usual double headed axe, though it was slung on his back. Instead, with the aid of his enormous strength he was carrying a rotary cannon, as usually hung from an attack helicopter or the like

The enormous ammunition box was slung from one shoulder, his left hand laying on its top.

"A bit contemporary for you isn't it Laz?" He asked in good humour.

"Yeah, well I was watching an old Arnie movie the other day, and one of his battle mates as it were had something like this. Now, it was a bit ridiculous really, as as muscle bound as the character was, normal human strength couldn't have really managed it. But it occurred to me. I don't have normal human strength. So, I thought I'd give it a try. At the rate of fire of this thing I'll be out of ammo in a mere moment, so I've still got the old axe to fall back on".

John chuckled. "Well, it's going to be a surprise to whoever we face anyway".

He turned to Kathryn "You want to do your light burst thing as we go through yeah, then turn yourself, Eleanor and Sophia invisible right? Leave the battle to us boys eh?"

Kathryn nodded "does that mean I'm going through first?" She asked meekly.

"Well, let's say, in the lead. We don't have to go through one at a time here, so you'll have somebody to either side of you. Though of course, they might have to have their eyes closed due to your flash.

Actually, I'll be one of those by your side. With my visor down I can keep my eyes open and keep you protected. OK? "

"OK John" she answered, and she moved herself to the front with John on her right side and Lazarus to her left.

"OK sweetheart" said John to Sophia. "What's on the other side?"

Sophia closed her eyes, and a finger slowly massaged her temple. "Well, it looks like it's an old castle or mansion or something. The floor looks to be simple concrete but the walls seem to be made of flint.

"Flint eh?" Muttered Vladamir from his place behind John . "Cool".

"There appears to be about five large groups of men there, waiting in ambush. Left right and centre. Then there's a large door near the back of the room behind which I assume lurks our old friend Oblivion."

"Good going hun" he said to Sophia and he gave her a wink.

"Right guys? " he called out "all ready?" .

"There was a cry of assent from the group and John opened the door and they all surged forward.

Immediate upon their appearance there was a brilliant powerful burst of light.

Then Kathryn fell back to the side with Eleanor and Sophia and they disappeared from sight.

"Freefire boys" yelled John as he ran out of the rift into the large what appeared to be subterranean hall.

Immediately ahead of him stood a large group of men armed with a varied array of weapons.

There were guns, swords, axes, baseball bats and in one man's arms a flamethrower.

John laughed uproariously as he ran at them. This was what he was born for. Battle.

With a broad grin he made his first target the flamethrower. At this moment it was dormant with the small flame sparkling at the top of its barrel.

He took a knife and with a single throw severed the connecting hoses at the top of the backpack of fuel he wore.

This caused a spray of fuel to rain down upon him and also upon a few of his companions which, touching the small flame at the nozzles tip, created an explosion of fire in the midst of their attack group. The wearer of the flamethrower was instantly blown to pieces and a few of the men surrounding him were forced to drop and roll to try to extinguish the flames. Although in one instance a man consumed by the flames ran screaming across the hall, crossing the paths of his fellow attack groups, much to their irritation and creating the occasional incident amongst them.

John then drew the two katars from their sheaths at his back. Two fists of steel like death. And he ran forward to meet the enemy.

On the left as they emerged, Lazarus turned to face his foes. In this instance he thought Oblivion might have tapped into his local yakuza groups or something. The majority of them were armed with Samurai swords, and similar, although there was the occasional gun.

He, much like John, stepped forward with a grin and unleashed the concentrated spray of death that was the rotary cannon.

283

The men before him literally disintegrated in the hail of fire, as he swung the weapon left and right.

There was initially the occasional shot from the group, one of which actually struck him in the shoulder. But a wound like that was like a gnat bite to him, and in mere seconds was healed.

He continued his storm of fire as he walked towards them, and some attempted to turn and run. But they too were caught in the fury of bullets and died as fragments of men.

Suddenly there was an audible click, and although the massive barrel of his weapon continued to spin, there was no more gunfire. His weapon was obviously out of ammo.

Yet, firing at that rate of speed he was kind of amazed it had lasted as long as it had. He shrugged the ammunition box from his shoulder and dropped both it and the cannon itself to the floor.

Then, silently and still grinning he slipped the faithful old axe from his shoulder, took it in his hands, and looked for someone to kill.

The Japanese group that had initially stood before him now lay in pieces without a single survivor. The gun had done it's job well. He would have to remember that for the future.

Over on the right there were yet another hoard of variously armed men. Amongst these were the occasional sub machine gun. Otherwise it was the usual collection of clubs, swords, axes and the like.

The first thing that Vladimir had done was to sprint over to the far wall as the enemy closed on him.

He had punched his fist into the wall, and quickly a thick coating of flint rock had grown up his arm, enveloped his torso then spread to his other extremities and his head. Finally a huge golem like creature stood before them. A man made of stone, gleaming red eyes gazing out at them from beneath a heavy brow of rock.

There were a few streams of gunfire from those armed with automatic weapons but this just raised a few sparks from points of him where their bullets struck. Their forward charge at Vladimir had slowed when they'd seen him turn to this mountain of rock. Slowed but not stopped, they still came on.

Vladimir gave a loud strangely booming laugh and smashed his two fists against each other.

This created a veritable cloud of fragments of stone, but when that had cleared it could be seen that the broken flint was now a surface of razor sharp edges and points.

Still laughing, Vladimir charged into them, fists swinging and leaving clouds of gore and death in their wake.

Kind of mid left, between the group that Lazarus fought on the far left and John's group at the centre, lay yet another mob of armed adversaries. Their target as they charged forward was a relaxed looking Isaac. He simply strode forward towards them slowly shrugging off his dark hooded robe that concealed his unusual look.

There came a few shouted obscenities and insults aimed at his strange colour and general monkey like look. But these simply slipped from him like water off of a ducks back.

He'd heard it all before in his time.

But now. Now he was free to react to it, in the way he'd always wanted to but that civilised behaviour had always forbidden.

This was going to be extremely cathartic.

As they closed upon each other, he flexed.

His tail became a prehensile razor sharp blade and spike. His fingertips extended into long blade like claws. His teeth had extended over his lower lip into the form of fangs and his elbows and knees now projected blades of their own at their ends.

He was a damned human blender.

As the combatants closed, Isaac suddenly leapt into the air a good seven feet, then came down, rotating in place and slashing out with his tail and claws, his elbows and knees, and occasionally his fangs, though he didn't like the taste of human blood so kept this to a minimum.

The group of charging men suddenly became a confused rain of limbs and severed heads. Some tried to retreat or escape, but a long prehensile bladed tail would dart out of the melee and wrap itself around a retreating neck or leg.

There would be no survivors.

There was yet another group of armed protectors of oblivion on the mid right. Between the bloodbath of Isaacs conflict and the central one of John. However, these had no immediate enemy before them and so, after briefly looking around at the mayhem surrounding them, they decided to support the group facing John, as they were the ones immediately guarding the doorway through to their master.

Consequently they headed that way.

But suddenly they found themselves being attacked from somewhere out there they couldn't see.

It appeared as though someone out there had some kind of laser gun.

One moment they were heading towards John's group of adversaries, when suddenly a beam of red light shot out of the darkness and speared the head of their leader. It had transfixed his head completely and oozing bubbling boiled brains could be seen emanating from the small hole it had caused.

Other beams of light, not always red, darted out from beyond their sight and each found a target in a man's body. Cooking a heart here, broiling a liver there. A small burning hole would appear in a man's hand or in his leg and he would fall.

The beams that shot at them from the darkness never seemed to come from the same place twice

Whoever was doing this was moving about, so they were unable to take a shot at them, not having any kind of target.

In fact, in one case a beam was held on one of the men's automatic rifles, and it first caused the metal of the barrel to melt and bend out of shape, then setting off all of the ammunition in the magazine, blowing off the man's arm and blinding him in one eye. They fell back in retreat, but the laser shots pursued them.

Back at John's battle, he thought he'd never had so much fun in his life.

With the vambrace on his forearms he was able to easily block any blows that the enemy struck. He had never realised before how the mental effort of raising a shield around himself slowed his reaction time in conflict. Now, unburdened with that task, he found all his movements so much more fluid, his reaction times so much faster. He found he could almost predict his opponents moves in advance simply from their current actions. He was just so much more alert not having to sacrifice that part of his brain, that fragment of his consciousness to shielding.

Yes, he found himself surprised at how grateful he felt to Maker for these forearm guards that he'd thought initially would be an unnecessary burden.

As for the blades, the punching daggers, katar he thought Maker had called them. Well, they were amazing. The blades were double edged and long so made perfectly for slashing and cutting. They weren't simply stabbing weapons, oh no.

And so, John would block a downward blow with his left forearm whilst simultaneously slash or stab at his opponent with the blade in his right hand. Each conflict, each opponent he faced, seemed to fall mere moments after first contact. He felt like a damned killing machine, and he worked his way through the large group of men before him with graceful ease.

Suddenly, he found himself alone in the field of battle. He looked around himself in momentary confusion, before it finally struck him.

He was the victor. All his foes were dead.

He looked further afield and saw he wasn't alone.

Lazarus was kicking at a prone figure on the floor, his reddened axe slung insolently over his shoulder. He looked up, saw John, and gave him a wave. "You all done too son?"

"sure am" he called back.

Then he saw Isaac between them as he pulled himself to his feet from the crouching position he'd been in.

He had been picking up his robe as he withdrew his sharp edges.

"And you Isaac?" Called John

"Yep. All done here boss"

John turned around. Firstly he saw the tumbled bodies immediately to his right. It looked as though they had been heading his way. But here they all lay, dead as doornails. And on closer inspection he noticed the red rimmed holes through these bodies, some of them, where clothed, we're still burning.

Kathryn, he thought.

Death at a distance. She'd remained back with the other girls, but she'd used her power of light to create laser beams and she'd slaughtered these buggers. He could imagine her blowing her fingertip after each shot.

Then, finally, beyond this slaughter he saw on the far right the sight of Vladimir.

He was swinging one body around over his head as he looked around himself for someone more to fight. His huge stone frame was silhouetted against the far wall and he looked like a complete monster. But like the rest of them, he was done. All his foes had fallen, there was only him left.

"Right guys" John called out to them all. "Group meeting" and he waved his hands for everyone to join him.

Eleanor, Kathryn and Sophia all reappeared and headed towards John's position in the centre of the hall, before the large ornate gilded door.

Lazarus, Isaac and Vladimir all walked over to him until they were all together once more.

"Right chaps" John began. "Now, we're assuming that behind that there door lies our enemy.

He might be there alone lying on the couch.

He might have a small army between us much like we just defeated.

He might have anything you can think of set up to trap or kill us.

So, how do you want to do this?

I'm his enemy number one. I'm more than happy to go in there alone and kill the bugger.

But obviously, your all involved in this too, especially you Soph.

So, how do you think we should play this? "

He paused and seemed to lean back, awaiting their answer.

"Well" came the voice of Lazarus "I agree, sophia's got an interest in this, he took her mind from her.

But don't forget. I've an interest too.

It turned out we used to be friends, until I caught him out in the middle of his evil acts and so got my memory wiped. I spent some time barely knowing who I was, so I think I deserve to be in on how this ends".

"Your right Lazarus" said John "forgive me, I'd forgotten how he'd screwed you up all those many years ago".

"Well" said Eleanor "since I had to devote my mind to keep Sophia on her feet when the arsehole took her. I'd say I've an interest too."

"I can't match all your reasons" said Kathryn "but doesn't the fact that I'm your friend have any weight here? I suffered with you all during Sophia's loss. I think I deserve inclusion".

"Well as for us two" said Vladimir, placing a hand on Isaacs shoulder in comradeship. "We were just called in to assist. However, we did assist. I got lost in the bloody woods and he got speared through the shoulder and had his mind wiped. I think we deserve something for those sufferings don't you? "

John smiled beamingly. "So I guess what's being said here is your all coming with me eh?"

"damn bloody right" said Lazarus with a chuckle.

"Ok then folks." John laughed "let's do it".

Thirty three

They approached the luxurious looking door carefully. John stretched out his mind, firstly across the floor approaching the door then upon the door and it's framework itself.

Firstly, John pointed at a large stone set into the floor in the middle way of the doors approach.

"nobody is to step on that one ok? "

"Er, ok" came a multitude of responses.

Using the blade of his tail, Isaac slit two long strips of dark material from his hooded gown. These he now lay in a cross formation over the stone that John had indicated, so everybody could see at a glance the place of danger.

"Good thinking man" said John, giving him a thumbs up and a wink.

Now he stood before the door analysing it carefully. It was a double door with lever like handles. Either gold or gold plated.

"Ahh, I see" breathed a very poised John. It almost looked as though he was standing on tip toe, he was so tense and ready to react. Now however he appeared to relax.I

"Don't worry, I've got it now guys". He said, though if he thought he was instilling them all with confidence, he was mistaken.

He reached out his hands to the two handles, but when he turned them he lifted them, turning them in the opposite direction to that which such handles would usually be used.

There was a muffled clunking noise from above them, but the doors swung wide open on well oiled hinges and nobody died..

Ahead of them was a large long hall, at the end of which lay a couch, which much to everyone's surprise following what John had said earlier, supported the lounging figure of oblivion.

He had one leg, obviously paining him, laying the length of the couch, and much to everyone's amazement John's knife protruded still from the thigh.

Also, lining the length of the hall to either side stood an array of gargoyle like statues.

"Well" said John to the rest of them and indicating the statues "I'll give you two guesses what's going to happen to them."

He called out "hey, Oblivion ya old bastard. Are we really going to have to go through all the hassle of smashing up your lovely statuary before we can have a chat?"

Oblivion, with a face of thunder, gave John a languid wave of the hand.

"This statuary as you call it was created by an old friend of mine long ago. God rest his soul. I must admit I had to, er, impress upon him the importance of the task. Set a couple of ingenious traps for me too, but I see you've evaded those. No matter

You won't find these as easy to defeat as those useless bodyguards I set outside. Five damned troops of them, and they assured me they were top class.

Well, at least I haven't paid them yet."

At this he gave an evil chuckle.

293

Vladimir shouldered himself to the front of the group. Not a difficult task for a walking wall of flint.

Standing besides John he asked "so, are these things his evil defenders are they?"

"Yes" said John with a smile "You want them?"

"Oh, most definitely" Vladimir answered.

He strode his great big grinding stone strides towards the nearest of the gargoyles and raised both his huge fists above his head.

John could have sworn he saw the gargoyle cower and wince in anticipation.

Then, with a loud grunt Vladimir brought those fists crashing down upon the creature and shattering it into pieces.

He turned and strode once more to the other gargoyle on the opposite side.

Having seen the fate of its companion, this one leered forward with a spear in its hand to attack Vladimir, but he was too fast for it and it was in small pieces before it could take a further step.

Vladimir passed, alternating sides of the hall, from one gargoyle to the other, working his way down the length of the hall towards oblivion.

John and the others followed behind him with slow steps. John struggling to keep the mirth from being too obvious on his face.

By the time Vladimir was closing on the end of the hall the gargoyles had become far more active. They were actively running to attack. However, Vladimir in his current form was invincible. As they attempted to strike at him he would simply smash them with such concussive blows that they would instantly be in pieces.

There was no escape for any of them, and by the time Vladimir was swinging one captured gargoyle to smash the other, John felt it had become faintly ridiculous. He was beginning to feel sympathetic for these damned creatures.

At last it was done.

None of the gargoyles survived, all were reduced to rubble and the group of them stood directly before Oblivion where he lounged on his couch. His injured leg elevated.

John could finally see the fear in the man's eyes, and he looked within himself for any sign of mercy. But no, there was none. This man had cost him his mother.

"Well well it's the killer" said Oblivion with a snarl. "It appears my faith in my old friends work was overrated doesn't it?"

John said nothing but just stood there, still as stone but with a look of rage in his eyes.

"When it was first pointed out to me that your blades had those skull pommels, I knew I'd heard some word or other about them on the grapevine. Yes, word had it that these skull blades had been used in the past during a revolution against those in power. They won by the way and the heads of state were all executed. Anyway, it transpired that if the wielder of the knife left it in the wound, then it couldn't be withdrawn. It would remain there no matter what energies were applied to remove it. All their actions would achieve would be pain for the wounded one.

Now, so far, all of that legend has proven to be true, much to my dismay I must say.

The word also had it that some property of the blade prevented putrefaction. The wound wouldn't fester, but neither would it heal. As long as the blade remained, there would be a wound as fresh and new as of the moment it was inflicted. And, the only one that is able to remove the blade is he who placed it there originally.

So, you'd just have to hope he'd survived, otherwise you would be, er, in the shit. "

At this he chuckled to himself.

"Well, now that your here killer, would you be so kind as to take back your weapon. I must admit it's causing me a lot of pain. Though I'm sure that certainly doesn't bother you in the least and you believe I deserve to suffer".

"That I do, most certainly" said John in a very calm controlled voice that his eyes belied.

"But it's been missing from my arsenal for too long. Would you believe I've missed it. It's felt as though a part of me had been cut away. Leaving a scar you can't help but constantly pick at".

At this he made a vague reaching gesture with his hand and with a cry of pain followed by a hissing through Oblivions teeth the blade flew from the wound to land in John's palm.

"Thank you John" hissed a relieved sounding Oblivion.

"my pleasure" answered John. "But you realise of course that it still won't heal".

"Really?" Queried a puzzled looking man " and whys that John, you've removed the blade now.",

"Because I'm going to kill you you fool".

"Ahh" sighed Oblivion "your still harping over that brief theft I made of your beloveds consciousness, yes?

Well, I gave her back to you didn't I? So why do you still have this unnatural antipathy towards me? "

John chuckled now. "You sir are quite mad aren't you? Do you honestly think I could forgive such a heinous act as that? Besides, it's not just for me. You abducted hundreds of people with your fake Apollo temple and transported them to some God forsaken world, telling them to build you a throne for heaven's sake. You turned some of them into beasts. The path of your life you have left strewn with the dead, the defiled, the abused and tortured, and many other crimes some of which I probably don't even have words for.

No, you need to be executed, and your reign of horror ended."

"well boy" said Oblivion, now pulling himself to his feet. "Thankfully, now that damned blade has been taken from my leg, I heal very quickly don't you know, a side effect of one of my many gifts, though I forget which. Anyway, I now believe myself able to fight for my life. Do you accept my challenge killer? "

John laughed long and loud. "Your only making things more difficult for yourself. If you allow me to execute you I can assure you I'll make it painless and instant. If you choose to fight me, you will suffer".

"then so be it boy" Oblivion growled, spinning his staff impressively in his hand. "Lets to it"

At this he leapt forward and brought his staff crashing down, aiming for Johns head. John simply raised an arm and caught the blow against his forearm, his arm not moving in reaction to the blow, the vambrace having absorbed all the kinetic energy. Whilst his arm blocked the blow his other hand or fist bearing the katar stabbed rapidly forward three or four times into Oblivions stomach.

He howled in pain, forgetting that he had been invulnerable for so many years that pain was still a novelty to him.

John hadn't stabbed deep. If he had he would have ended it all there and then.

Oblivion looked down at the blood streaming from his stomach. "Damn you killer, I'll die of blood loss now".

"No, you wont" said John very seriously.

"Give up to your fate now man. You'll save yourself a lot of pain. This is just the beginning."

"damn you" Oblivion cried, and this time he swept his staff across Johns chest.

John simply raised his katar as if to block the blow, but instead severed about three feet of its length.

"What the? Cried Oblivion "that staff is indestructible".

"obviously not" replied John.

Oblivion finally spun the remaining length of staff in his hand, bringing to the front the long bladed spike.

"Now you die boy" he hissed through his teeth.

He came in low, blocking John's left arm from movement with his own and thrust the spiked blade upwards towards John's stomach.

John however simply put his right forearm in the way of the strike and when it was blocked he slashed upwards with his own blade.

Oblivion shrieked and fell to his knees. There on the ground before him, still twitching, lay his right forearm, the hand still bearing the severed length of staff.

"Do you yield?" Asked John , his voice sounding almost sympathetic.

Oblivion bowed his horned head and began to weep.

"I was a God" he said in halting gulps of air.

"I was a god. How can I have come to this. How can I have fallen so far? "

"Because you were an evil god" John said without irony. "And evil never triumphs, not in the end. In the end, it always has to face justice".

"And your justice are you killer?"

"In this instance, yes, I'm afraid I am. It's not a job I relish, trust me. But you have to be taken out of the game.

Now, will you submit to execution?

Like I said, it will be painless, unlike this futile resistance of yours".

"But I was a god" whispered Oblivion once more.

"Yes" whispered John in response "but you were an evil one.

Now. Do you submit or would you rather lose more bits of yourself first?"

 Oblivion stared at the bleeding stump that had once been his arm, then at his disembodied arm where it lay in the dust before him.

"I" .... "I submit" he sighed, his voice almost inaudible.

"Very well" answered a very serious and sad sounding John.

"Please, just bow your head forward. I promise you, there will be no pain".

In silence, words seeming meaningless to him now, Oblivion bowed forward.

John took a deep shaky breath. This wasn't how he'd envisioned this. He felt no triumph. He felt no joy at the subjugation of his enemy. He simply felt cold and a great feeling of indescribable inscrutable sadness.

"Ok" he breathed "goodbye old man. No hard feelings eh".

At this he swept the blade down, severing Oblivions head through the base of his skull, aiming to cut through the brainstem.

As he'd promised, death would have been instant and there would have been no pain.

"Ok Soph, do you think you can take us home now love?"

Sophia was startled. It all just seemed so abrupt. So rushed. "Are we bringing him with us" she asked, jerking a thumb at the corpse.

"No love" said John decisively, his eyes drifting around the vast hall, the ornate ceiling and chandeliers. "I think this place will make the perfect memorial for him".

Sophia nodded thoughtfully "Ok hun".

She went through the motions of prayer as before with the parting of her hands a single white oaken door appeared, which when opened could be seen to open out into the lounge back at the manor.

"Come on guys" cried an ecstatic Vladimir, his stone body now discarded "it's hometime" and he vanished through the door. One by one they all followed suit, until only Sophia and John remained.

Sophia stared at John, that feeling of worry now resurfaced in her.

John meanwhile just stared at the headless corpse that lay upon the ground. Suddenly she saw him give himself a vigorous shake, he looked up and took her arm.

"Come on my love" he said in that sad tone, and he led her through the rift, closing the door behind him.

Thirty four

That evening the beers were back out and everyone was celebrating a successful mission.

Most especially Vladimir, who felt that his actions that day had recompensed him for his humiliating loss in the woods at their earlier conflict.

In this instance he now felt that he had a true tale of adventure and personal supremacy against a powerful foe. His position within the midst of his hierarchical Russian brotherhood would finally be elevated and his usefulness and strength of character would reach the ears of the elevated.

Consequently he became rather pissed rather quickly, and the evening was still early when John and Isaac carried him to his bed to sleep fully dressed and recover from his excesses.

Eleanor also got herself rather tipsy after their magnificent success and much like Vladimir, Sophia and Kathryn led her off quite early in the evening.

However, a touch later they noticed the appearance of a cat that lapped at spilled drinks and attempted to stick it's head into glasses big enough to accept it. The feline seemed to have a slightly staggering gait to it, and both Sophia and Kathryn found it incredibly amusing to think that Eleanor would be continuing her debauchery using a poor hijacked cat.

John drank, but only in moderation and in fact it seemed to Isaac that he was only drinking at all so as to be a part of the party.

He seemed distracted, as though he had the weight of the world on his shoulders.,

Isaac assumed that it was his execution of Oblivion that was causing him distress and he moved to his side to see if he could help.

"You know, it had to be done man".

"What?" asked John looking confused

Oh, thought Isaac, perhaps he'd been wrong.

"Oh, er, I was just saying that you had to execute Oblivion. You couldn't have let him carry on".

"Oh, yeah your right of course, I couldn't let him carry on. But you see, up till now I've been able to blame him for my mother's death. Sure, I cast the blade, but he was responsible for that, I was trying to save her from a fate worse than death. Or so I thought."

"and you did" cried Isaac.

"Did I? Besides it turned out I could have killed him rather than her. Ok, so I didn't know that at the time, but finding out later was a blow.

And now, now he's gone, I've got nobody available to cast the blame on. There's just me. Me and my knives."

He put his beer down on the table before him.

"Think I might turn in myself. Kinda tired. Give my apologies to whoever's left for me won't you?"

At this he stood and left the room.

Isaac immediately went to Sophia and let her know the score. That now familiar look of worry cast it's shadow over her face, and she quickly left, heading after John.

Now the numbers were down so much the remaining party people didn't hang around much longer themselves, and before long all had retired to their rooms.

The light in the lounge remained on, the last to leave having forgotten to turn it off.

This highlighted the cat which went from glass to glass, sticking it's head into it if it would fit, otherwise knocking it over and lapping up the spillage. Same with the beer bottles.

This cat was going to feel rather unwell come morning.

Thirty five

Finally it came.

That dreaded phone Call that he had been expecting at any time now, yet had also been dreading intensely, knowing what it would entail and the subterfuge and lies he would have to play out. He hated the very thought of the play acting he would have to endure if he didn't want to be banged up in either a prison or a lunatic asylum. That and endure the hatred of his father. His only surviving relative.

Yes, his father finally phoned him.

His voice sounded vaguely upset but also in control with that hard nosed edge to it that he remembered so rarely occurring in his father.

"Hi dad" sighed John "how are you getting on?"

"Oh, not too bad son, not too bad. You know how it is. Well, actually you don't thank heaven, but things are all in hand now. That's why I'm calling to be honest son. The funerals all arranged, it'll be this Thursday, so a couple of days time.

Obviously you'll be there yeah? "

Christ thought John, not attending his mother's funeral was something that had never occurred to him.

"Jesus dad of course I'll be there"

"Oh, sorry son, I know you will. But would you believe, when I was phoning around to let everyone know, her sister, her own bloody sister, said she couldn't make it. Apparently she's going on holiday that day or some such crap. Can you believe it. Her own bloody sister."

He gave a shaken sigh.

"Oh, and I've managed to get father Pierce to do the service for us. Great guy, you remember he did your grandparents for us. But no, you probably wouldn't remember, you were too young back then.

Believe it or not I've managed to find your mothers will too. It took me three bloody days. She obviously disparaged any kind of filing system, Christ, She simply had piles of papers scattered throughout the house. I would sit on the living room floor, a circle of papers around me in their own growing piles. Sorting each and every paper from each pile as found. Took me absolutely ages. But found it in the end. Obviously she's left you the house."

"I don't want it dad" interrupted John in a sudden reflexive blurt.

"Don't be daft son. It's yours, also a bit of money after the funeral costs. Quite a lot actually".

Again John interrupted. "Dad, I don't want her money, I don't need it".

"and again son, don't be so bloody daft. Your young, just finding your feet. And you've a love life now too. What if you decide to walk her down the aisle. How are you going to do that eh. Marriage costs a bloody fortune these days, oh and of course you'll need to get her a ring".

"Yeah dad, but, I, it's just, er".

"Look , don't worry son, you mother has left me something".

"I should bloody hope so, after, what, thirty years of marriage?" Blustered John " what do you get? "Asked

306

"Well, you know that enormous picture your mother used to have hung over the fireplace?"

"What" John asked in horror "You mean that one with the trees in it?"

"yes son, that's the bugger".

"but, but you always hated that picture dad. You loathed it so much. You once tried to create a pretend break in so You could ditch it, but it was spotted in a skip and returned.".

"Yeah son that's what she's left me" chuckled his father. Then he broke into loud gales of laughter and besides himself he found himself joining in.

"Oh Christ dad, she was a bitch wasn't she"

"Well, she seems to have turned into one. But she never used to be. Thirty years son, and most of those were good times. Even after all the time we'd been broken up, I still didn't understand why. I don't to this day know why she left me, nor do I know why she changed personalities so much. It's a mystery my lad, and obviously it'll always remain one now".

"Yeah" sighed John "I guess it will at that".

"So, anyway my lad. Thursday, midday. At St Mathews church. Got it? "

"Yeah dad, I've got it".

"OK son. See ya then. " and he hung up.

John almost staggered away from the phone.

He'd been terrified of that call coming, but now it had he just felt mildly distressed.

That mother of his had been a prize bitch.

Her leaving his father, that damned picture, it was like rubbing salt into an open wound.

She, much like everyone else, knew how much he'd hated the damn thing. Christ, it was all he could do to stop himself burning the house down just to be rid of it..

And yet he, he'd apparently been left an undisclosed though apparently sizeable sum of money, along with the house. It was a nice house too..

He made a decision there and then. His father wouldn't let him give it away for free or anything like that.. But he thought he might be able to get his father to live in it. He'd try to get him to accept free board but if he couldn't do that he'd ask for the minimum rent he could get away with.

Yeah, that's that sorted. He didn't need a house, not whilst he had the manor.

As for the money. He guessed he'd accept it. He didn't need any money, again, whilst in the manor. They had a huge pool of funds that was available for any member of the family to use, carte blanch .

He could always give his windfall to charity, that or just add it to the manors fund pool.

Sorted, again.

Relaxed at last he headed up to the bedroom where he'd left Sophia..

Entering the room he saw her sitting on the bed holding something dark in her hand.

"Hi hun" he said, suddenly feeling strangely elated at the sight of her.

"Hi John" she replied, but there certainly wasn't any joy in her face. In fact she looked strangely worried perturbed.

He sat himself down beside her on the bed and put an arm around her waist.

"What's the matter love?" He asked " and don't tell me 'Nothing' ok. "

"Oh, I'm sorry John, but when we were at Makers place, he gave me another gift for you, just as we were leaving.. For some reason he didn't want Lazarus to know about it, I don't know why. that's why he went through me.

I'd forgotten all about it till now. It's a necklace for you. "

She held it out for John and he looked at it closely.

"He told me" continued Sophia "that if we were to save worlds or lives or prevent catastrophes, that sort of thing anywhere in the multiverse where there might be a tipping point, then we would need to know where to go. That necklace is supposed to be a device to steer us to one of these tipping points where our involvement might tip the scales to the good.Though he did say that we wouldn't always succeed. Just the majority of the time".

John turned the necklace over and over in his hands, trying to see where the magic metal might have been used. Perhaps in that shining symbol on the face of it.

Fundamentally it was a black leather necklace holding a circular onyx disk. Upon the face of the disk was a strange though beautiful brightly shining silver symbol.

"Hey, I like it" he said "that symbol there's quite beautiful don't you think".

Sophia fastened the necklace around his neck, as she did so she told him "when Maker gave it to me John, it was just a plain black disk".

"What?" asked John, his eyebrows raised in curiosity. "Then what's this symbol Soph, where'd it come from?"

"well John" answered Sophia "as to where it came from, that I can't tell you, it's just doing what its been made to do I guess. But with regards to what it is, that I can say.

It's coordinates John. It's rift coordinates, telling us where to go.

End

Printed in Great Britain
by Amazon

72231884R00180